THE
SUMMER
OF
ELLEN

Also by the author

What My Body Remembers

THE NINA BORG SERIES,

WRITTEN WITH LENE KAABERBØL

The Boy in the Suitcase
Invisible Murder
Death of a Nightingale
The Considerate Killer

THE
SUMMER
OF
ELLEN

Agnete Friis

Translated from the Danish by Sinéad Quirke Køngerskov

First published in Danish under the title *Sommeren med Ellen*
copyright © 2015 by Agnete Friis

English translation copyright © 2019 by Sinéad Quirke Køngerskov

Published by Soho Press, Inc.
853 Broadway
New York, NY 10003

Library of Congress Cataloging-in-Publication Data
Friis, Agnete, author. | Køngerskov, Sinéad Quirke, translator.
The summer of Ellen/Agnete Friis; translated from the Danish by
Sinéad Quirke Køngerskov.

ISBN 978-1-61695-995-1
eISBN 978-1-61695-996-8

1. Memory—Fiction. I. Title

PT8177.16.R55 S6613 2019 839.813'8—dc23 2018057065

Interior design by Janine Agro, Soho Press, Inc.

Printed in the United States of America

10 9 8 7 6 5 4 3 2 1

THE
SUMMER
OF
ELLEN

The Summer of Ellen stems largely from the environment in which I grew up in Djursland, in the 1970s and '80s. But the story itself is pure fiction and, thus, any similarities to living or deceased persons or real events are coincidental and unintentional.

I would like to thank all those who were involved in the book during its creation. My excellent first readers, Lene Kaaberbøl and Trisse Gejl. My fact-checkers, Henrik Friis, Gustav Friis, Henrik Laier and Henrik Boje. And, not least, my hardworking and lifesaving editor, Lisbeth Møller-Madsen.

Agnete Friis

There was no light.

The windows on the fifth floor of the soulless new building reflected only the blinking red beacon at the top of the crane on the other side of the canal. Style: dystopian modernism. Exterior: windswept green trash cans and an intercom, its text in yellow scrolling across the display like a news ticker in the main square. The rust from the balconies' iron skeletons had already dripped down the newly plastered walls. Their concrete plateaus and cornices were just like the red-assed baboons' enclosure at the Copenhagen Zoo. I knew every single imaginative architectural detail. An old college buddy had once worn black jeans and smoked hash with squatters there in the youth center—later to become a totalitarian asshole who built houses that belonged in the old Soviet Union. I hated that structure, and I hated the fact that I was standing here again. Hands buried deep in my pockets, I stared at her bedroom window, whose open blinds revealed a painfully ordinary weeping fig in the daytime. She was probably already lying in bed, breathing sweetly, comforter thrown aside because of the heat.

I took out my phone and listened to my messages. There were a couple from the bank. An officious and possibly hyperactive young man whom Kirsten had asked to look at our finances and who wanted to meet us. All the time. The next message was only a muted whisper, then the sound of a man clearing his throat and muttering something incomprehensible before hanging up.

I could call her, of course. Or write. But there wasn't much

more to say. I settled for going over to the front door and study-
ing the names listed on the intercom for now. Stig and Janne
Nielsen. Her surname was so ordinary compared to her, but it
had its own charm, too. Something unusual, hidden from everyone other than me.

I shouldn't have come here, but my brain ignored those kind of
rational conclusions as it conspired with my gut. This had resulted
in a bottle of wine before leaving, drunk directly from the bottle
while I waited for darkness to fall and the noise in the street to
become cheering shouts and breaking glass. Then two beers, followed by a careful descent to street level, Nørrebro Station, an
S-train and the Metro through the city's twinkling lights. Young
people were making their way into the city, enveloped in eau de
cologne and alcohol, but nobody took any notice of me as I sat
there, leaning against the window with the world flickering pleasantly by in my skull. I alighted at the Bella Center, just as I was used
to, and walked the rest of the way along the water.

I swayed slightly as I leaned into the yellow display. Rang and
regretted it, even before I'd done it. Could hear the routine beep
ringing through the system and stood there like an idiot, frozen in
place, waiting for the inevitable.

"Yes?"

Her voice in the loudspeaker was dark and distorted, and I
knew she was standing up there in the semidarkness, naked or
wearing only a T-shirt, her short hair tousled after sex or sleep
or something in between.

"Jacob? Is that you?"

I didn't answer. Struggled to tear myself away and finally got
my not-quite-stable legs started. I was horribly visible in the yellow light of the street lamps, and a window opened up there and
a man leaned out of the window.

"Get away from here! I mean it. Next time, I'll call the police."

Something hit the asphalt with a hollow thud, splintering into a thousand pieces, and I increased my pace to a half run and tripped, my hands landing in something soft that smelled like shit. I wiped my hands on my new too-tight jeans. Vanity is truly a sin that brings its own punishment.

I WOKE UP sweating booze, glued to the plastic-wrapped box mattress from IKEA that I'd thrown onto the floor of my new bedroom. I'd apparently been clever enough to fling my clothes elsewhere in the apartment during the night, and the window was open a crack to let in the blinding sunshine.

I walked out to the kitchen and opened the empty fridge while I tried to decide if there was anything I actually needed. Food, sleep, sex. It was alarmingly quiet in my needs center. No requests besides the hair of the dog, a beer I pulled from a six-pack with trembling hands. Back in the living room, I flicked through some of the LPs in one of my cardboard moving boxes. I could buy a new record player and a pair of half-decent speakers, drink beer and listen to the Police. After all, I wasn't a student anymore, but a middle-aged man with money and a pension.

I took a sip of my beer, glaring at a dusty cobweb hanging down from the ceiling. From dust you came, and as dust you will forget your time in a three-bedroom house in Nørrebro.

I'd lived here before, in Nørrebro. First alone, then with Kirsten. Not in this apartment, but in one that resembled it with all its big-city shabbiness. A bunch of students had moved out of this apartment just a few days ago, leaving the finish on the bright parquet flooring chipped in places. Burns from discarded cigarettes stained the floor where the sofa had stood, and in the corner was a square, sticky discoloration, probably the impression of an unread textbook left marinating in dark rum. It was scorching hot in the apartment, which had been constructed in a time before the oil crisis and mineral wool insulation, with a massive south-facing window. I could hear kids shouting down in the courtyard. Arabic, Kurdish and Danish street slang. "Fuck you, n---," and "I'll fuck you in the ass."

Down by the dumpsters, the very same youngsters had stamped the intestines out of a rat and left it lying in the sun. The flesh was already black and curling at the edges. A litter of grayish fetuses the size of my little fingernail had been pulled out of its womb and lay across the asphalt like shiny beads on a string.

The physical move had been manageable: two boxes of LPs from the '80s—Bowie, Depeche Mode, the Police, U2—the four kitchen chairs, a few boxes of clothes and shoes and toiletries and the living room bookshelf. I'd chosen to leave almost everything with Kirsten. Not because I thought I owed her anything, but because I liked the idea of keeping the house intact. To preserve the memories, if nothing else. The kids' childhood home and all that. Kirsten had laughed aloud when I'd said it.

"I'm not the custodian of your relationship mausoleum," she said. "And I won't be embalming the dining room or marriage bed, either."

"Not even the cat?" I asked, and she shook her head. Was suddenly serious.

"I'm not Madame fucking Butterfly, Jacob. Nothing's going to stay the same. Not the house, and certainly not me. Just so you know."

Her smile faded. Stupid of me, of course. Insensitive. But I knew so little about the rules of divorce. How were you supposed to do it? And hadn't there always been something off between us? A grating sensation, like sand in your shoe. The first time I met her was on a sparkling, frosty cold morning at the lakes, where she was sitting on a bench blowing white clouds of steam into her red hands. I sat next to her and said something like "beautiful morning," after which she looked me directly in the eye and smiled weakly.

"And what about me?" she asked.

I could see she'd been crying and assumed it was heartbreak weighing heavily on her. When you're in your early twenties, you don't know many other kinds of sorrow.

"Very beautiful," I said, realizing how easy it was to lie to her. That it might actually be what she preferred. There was so much that surprised me back then.

"So no tragic arias in my absence?"

"I'll try to minimize them for the cat's sake—and the neighbors'," she said. And although she was smiling again, there was a bone-shattering coldness to her voice. "Don't worry. I'll be fine."

THE PHONE RANG and I let it ring. Then it started again. I rolled onto my back, holding it up in front of me, my arm outstretched. I'd become farsighted, on top of my usual nearsightedness. Everything was either too close or too far away. An eternal imprecision and a problem that, according to my optician, couldn't be fixed. I squinted, looking at the screen. Didn't recognize the number, even though it felt like I did. The phone rang out again with renewed effort, and I suddenly knew why the number seemed familiar. A landline number from Djursland, the middle four digits the same as our own from decades ago.

I answered the phone and heard a short-of-breath wheeze.

"Hello?" I spoke louder than I'd meant to, having involuntarily thought of aging and death.

Then something happened. A sense of calm on the other end. The rattling noise disappeared. The breathing was still heavy, but more regular now.

"Is that you, Jacob?"

"Yes?"

"It's . . . it's Anton Svenningsen. I'm . . . Do you remember me, Jacob?"

I nodded, cleared my throat as a piece of the past resurfaced with unexpected clarity. The sky, first orange and deep rose pink and afterward black, a black August night. The fermented sweet smell of straw, wet clover and earth from freshly harvested fields. Myself and Anton sweating over the coupling of the tractor and trailer, with the sky above us threatening to burst. Followed immediately by the sensation of sinking into a darkness I couldn't fight my way out of.

"Of course I remember you, Anton."

A long pause, tired breathing. A vacuum cleaner switched on somewhere in the background.

"Jacob. I want to ask you . . . I need your help."

I hesitated. It had been almost forty years since I'd last seen Anton, so he must be quite old. His needs would be best attended to by a nurse.

"What is it?"

There was a deep, trembling sigh at the other end, followed by a series of wet, violent gasps.

"Anton . . ." I dared not have the thought.

He didn't answer. The vacuum cleaner behind him was turned off, and the only thing I could hear through the receiver was soft sobbing.

"Anton, I—is anyone there with you? Are you sick?"

A deep breath. I could hear him collecting himself, or at least trying to.

"I'm not sick, Jacob," he said. "I'm sorry to call you . . . but I have to."

I knew what he wanted. Maybe I'd already known it the second I'd heard his voice.

"What is it?"

"I have to find her. Anders is asking for her." A glimpse of dark hair, fluttering in the summer wind, and an almost deranged yearning to touch it.

Ellen.

PART I

1978

"Shut up!"

Sten fired the ball into the back of my knee so hard that I involuntarily placed my hands on the burning skin there and breathed through clenched teeth.

"What the hell, Sten?"

He looked at me briefly, his lips tight, and gave the ball another kick out over the field.

"Go get it yourself!"

"You're an ass!"

Sten didn't make a move to get it. Not an inch. His mouth was half-open now, offering a clear view of the rabbit teeth he'd always been teased so much about. They made him look dumber than he was. He turned his back to me and walked, narrow shoulders pulled back and chin lifted. He would have resembled a soldier on the march, had it not been for one hand pulling restlessly on the short, sweaty hair of his bangs. Lost in his own fury.

There'd been that thing with Toad.

I knew about it, of course. Flemming and Jørgen had laughed about it all week, tormenting him mercilessly. Jørgen's mom had talked to Sten's mom, and had heard the whole story about what had happened at the chicken farm. That Toad, whose name was really Lise and who was Sten's sister, had become wild and started drinking, and the latest was that she'd run away from home, if you could say such a thing about someone who was already an adult and moved as slowly as Sten's sister. I imagined an escape in slow motion, with her liver pâté–colored Prince Valiant hair flowing and jumping around her head like a soccer player's when they've scored and their run is shown in slow motion. Toad herself bent double, running with a sloppily packed suitcase in one hand, powerful calves thundering down the gravel road. Fee fi fo fum. Like the troll in a fairy tale.

Toad was almost as wide as she was tall, and her face bore a constant scowl. One of the many reasons Sten called her Toad—not a compliment she'd ever appreciated. But she had beautiful eyes tinged with gold. Despite being twenty-one years old, she still lived at home, and therefore Sten and I had the pleasure of seeing her unfriendly mug every afternoon once she was finished sorting pens and putting paper in stacks, or whatever it was she did in the office in Auning. She got off the bus at the end of the dirt road, and we then followed her furious, targeted march directly to the farm and her room on the first floor. If we happened to fall into her line of sight or even stood on the side of the road, she would immediately acknowledge us with hatred in her eyes.

The war between Sten and Toad was legendary.

When she'd still been strong enough to hit him, he'd always had black-and-blue bruises on his arms and collarbones from her hard knuckles. Later, the power balance shifted a little, becoming scuffles and more cunning cruelties. Toad cut up Sten's new leather ball with a pair of rose shears. He barricaded himself in her room and stuck her oldest Cliff Richard poster under the door in little pieces while she yelled and called him a perverse little creep. Sometimes Sten's mom shouted at them from the kitchen, in which case the fight would go on quietly and fiercely for a moment. Neither of them was interested in interference, both so sure of their own victory.

But maybe the battle was finally over.

Toad had been exceptionally quiet for a few days, had had a furious quarrel with her mother and had walked out without any explanation. That was what Jørgen had been able to get out of his mother, at least, and then all hell had broken loose.

"She's screwing some hippie. Guaranteed. And when he's done with her, a new one will come along. Oh, oh, oooh . . . Lise."

Flemming played with his tongue and rocked his hips. The affront to Sten was especially spiteful because Lise wasn't really a girl anyone wanted to screw. No one wanted to stick it up in Toad. That was common agreement among the boys in the class. And if you did, it wouldn't be because you liked her, but out of a kind of pity and triumph. Like you'd defeated a dragon or a wild animal.

I retrieved the ball, wedged it onto the baggage carrier and cycled through the main street, bathing in sun. Past the bakery and cafeteria and further on up Skolevej. Crossed onto the sidewalk and out onto the road again, both arms spread out wide as though I were flying. That's why I only saw her when I had to put my hands back on the handlebars for the rumble over the pearly gravel.

Mom.

She was standing slightly bent over, as if she'd stopped mid-motion while locking or unlocking the door. Her light-blue travel bag was at her feet, and when I put the bike away and she finally straightened up, I noticed the heavy fragrance of perfume. Her already straight hair was combed tight in the way she wore it when inconvenienced by a parents' evening or receiving guests.

"Well . . ." she said, lifting up the bag. "I didn't think you'd make it home in time."

"You're leaving? Now?"

"Stop, Jacob. You know how it is," she said, fiddling with the handles of the bag. Her mouth pulled tight as though I'd said something ugly. "I'll be home in a couple of days. You two can easily get by for that long. Where have you been? With Sten?"

I nodded, and she smiled wanly. Stroked my hair, even though I was a head taller than her.

"His mother rang asking for him. She's out of her mind."

I thought of Sten's gaunt, heavy-smoking mom and how she'd been clutching the handset with her skeletal hand when I'd dropped by last week. The curtains in the living room were drawn, and it was as though she didn't really see us as we passed her and went on up to Sten's room. "Out of her mind" was pretty accurate.

"You should hope you don't have girls," said Mom. "It's a bit more difficult."

"Why?"

She gave me a cryptic look, stuck her hand in her coat pocket and took out a cigarette, which she lit with a single click of her lighter.

"You can figure that out for yourself," she said.

I shook my head, and she laughed so I could see her straight but yellowed teeth. Coffee, tea and smoking will do that to you. She was forty years old, and attractive except for her teeth. A knee-length skirt and a loose white blouse. Her coat draped over her arm on account of the sudden arrival of summer.

"You remember what happened to Irene Poulsen last winter, right?"

What had happened to Irene P. was widely known, but as far as I could tell, it hadn't much to do with Toad's trip to Randers, or wherever she was. They didn't look like each other. Irene P. was hot. Hot, hot, hot. Big breasts, a pout and eyes lined in black. Glam rock and tight pants. Officially, she'd moved to the boarding high school in Grenå because she needed a "change of scenery," as the adults called it. Unofficially, everyone knew that she'd been raped by some bastard who'd offered to drive her home from the disco in Hornslet sometime after Christmas last year.

But Irene was Irene, and Toad was Toad.

"Toad isn't . . . It's not the same."

"Don't say that," said Mom. "All girls are in danger of that kind of thing. It might be hard for you to understand because you're such a good boy, but there are men out there who are . . . would do it to anyone. Not just the pretty girls. And they can't control it."

I trampled past her and put my own key in the lock, hoping strongly she wouldn't say anything more. My mother could be very direct when she wanted to be. Even vulgar. Back then, with Irene, she'd tried to tell me how to know if a girl "wanted to," which was painfully embarrassing to hear from your own mother.

I kicked off my shoes in the hallway, still not looking at her. Her perfume was everywhere.

"Will you tell your father that I'm with my sister?"

I could hear the tension in her voice. The attempt to sound happy and carefree.

"Can't you tell him yourself?"

"It might be better coming from you," she said. "Then I don't have to talk to him. Please?"

"Okay."

"Oh"—she blew me a kiss—"that's great, honey. Thank you."

Her footsteps on the stairs were followed by heels in the pearly gravel. Quick, in the direction of the bus stop.

"**DID SHE SAY** when she'd be back?"

Dad leaned back into the sofa so his shirt crept upward, revealing his hairy white stomach.

"No, not really."

He had poured his first beer into a glass and took a hefty gulp.

"And what about you, Jacob? Are you coming with me tomorrow?"

I shrugged.

"You can earn twenty-five kroner an hour over the summer," he said. His breath reeked of alcohol. "I need the four regulars on the floor. We're behind with everything."

He got up, went out into the kitchen, rummaged for a moment before returning with two plates, a knife, liver pâté and a bag of rye bread, which he set on the coffee table.

There was always extra work at Feed Stuffs when they were clearing out the storehouse. The big silos had to be emptied and prepared for new truckloads of grain. And orders for the winter feeding crops were already coming in. I'd helped out before when it was needed. Driven the forklift and moved around the heavy paper bags without breaking them. Compound feed, powdered milk, calcium nitrate and pink-stained corn seed. It was a good job, and I liked the men in the storehouse, slow and dawdling with heavy stomachs and broad, fleshy shoulders. Their T-shirts and button-downs were shields of sweat, and when they took a sack or gunned a forklift's transmission, their sinews and muscles rippled in wide wrists and upper arms. They often gave me a soda when we sat breathless on the loading ramp.

It was Dad who was the problem. In the mornings, he sat in his glass cage at the end of the storehouse. Jovial and drunk enough that anyone with eyes could figure out he was an alcoholic. Told bad jokes to the haulers who stuck their heads in to arrange receipts and bills. Pasty and friendly on the constantly chiming phone, and with his beer standing freely on his desk in between curled order notes, dried-up pens and a stapler that never had staples.

If I went to work with him while Mom wasn't home, he'd end up sending me out for beer at least twice before closing time, and although I could alternate buying them at the grocer and Hansen's

Drugstore, I couldn't stand being a laughingstock for holding a bag of rattling bottle deposits and a new six-pack of cold Carlsberg.

"I promised to help Anton," I said.

He pushed his plate farther in on the coffee table and threw his feet up. Wriggled his toes in his holey socks and glared angrily at the news on TV. Soldiers marching in some dusty place in the world.

"Anton? While Mom is away?"

"Yeah, it's a bit different. Their stable has to be whitewashed."

"Oh, okay." He pouted angrily. "Just don't come complaining to me when there's nothing else to do down there."

I went up the stairs, leaving the light in the hallway on so he could find his way to bed. Lay down and stared up at the sloping wall while I conjured up the girl from the baker's in my mind's eye. Her breasts were big, and you could see her nipples through her Vagn's Bakery T-shirt. For once, I couldn't really do anything with it. Just lay there, sweating in the summer night until I finally heard my dad stumble up the stairs to the second floor and piss noisily into the little toilet.

I shaped the comforter into the little baker maid, put my arm around her and fell asleep.

I WAS HUNGRY and maybe still a bit drunk when I stepped into my sandals and walked out into the afternoon sun.

Children were screaming in the municipal wading pool a little farther down the street. The leaves on the slender, newly planted roadside trees were tired and yellow, moving unwillingly in the wind and casting flickers of sunlight across the sidewalk.

I'd forgotten what summer was like in the city, but through the physical shock of the smell and the noise, I felt an old joy in the meeting of the brutal heat and all the ugliness greeting my eyes. The fluttering remnants of plastic bags and paper. A lost pacifier whose rubber was black and stained with age. The graffiti on the concrete walls. ERADICATE HUNGER—EAT THE RICH illustrated with a grinning skull and SUCK MY DICK accompanied by an unpleasant depiction of ejaculated semen in all the colors of the rainbow.

Kirsten had hated it when we'd rented a one-bedroom apartment on Jagtvej. If it had been up to her, we would have lived in a garden chalet community in Amager. It was me who insisted on Nørrebro, and me who spent my afternoons driving from one closed-down factory in the northwest to the other, photographing marred surfaces and broken windows, rusty iron and crumbling concrete. If Kirsten put lipstick on, I smeared it over her chin and down her neck. Moistened my fingers and spread her black mascara down over her cheeks, or colored her eyelids skull-deep.

Black was the new black.

I listened to the Sex Pistols and got a crew cut, while Kirsten held on to the passions of her early youth. Acoustic guitar and candles, and even an active membership to some environmentalist movement. They used to hold hour-long meetings on our sofa, where they made a list of impending doomsday scenarios and despaired together.

Kirsten was blonde—I preferred blondes with long hair—and she was good for me. Agreeable. Unproblematic. Subdued. It was a relief for me when I realized that her body odor wasn't particularly arousing and far from my natural preference. She was also the first girl who said she loved me, and miraculously didn't come to meet my parents for the first three years of our shared life. She found it easy to live with what she called my "pangs of morbidity." All the black, my apocalyptic drawings of towers, like huge space stations looming in a dead moon landscape.

I kicked an empty beer can—it was the kind bought in

Germany and sold under the counter in kiosks. No bottle deposit, so it'd been allowed to lie there long enough to rust. The can rattled out onto the road, where the asphalt bubbled in the heat, stinking of tar and gasoline. When I rounded the corner to Nørrebrogade, the reek mixed with the smell of kebab and pizza from the many small eateries.

I fished out my cell phone and dialed.

"Jacob? How are you?"

My father sounded awake. Up and walking around. So far so good.

"Fine, fine."

"And Kirsten?"

"Fine, I think. Kirsten is Kirsten."

He hesitated. He'd remained quiet and level when I'd called and told him I was moving out of the house. It was a long way from Randers to Copenhagen, and it had been a couple of years since we'd seen each other. I preferred the phone, because I couldn't smell or see if he was drunk.

"Anton called me."

"Anton?"

"Uncle Anton."

He sniffed, fumbled with something, and for a brief moment it was deathly silent on the phone. Then he was back.

"I see. And how is he?"

I pulled a fifty-kroner bill from my pocket, threw it on the counter in Halif's Pizzahut and pointed to a piece with ham. Halif or one of his assistants gave me twenty kroner in change and a smoking-hot slice of pizza, abundant in melted cheese. I balanced the cardboard box on a greasy table for one and sat down.

"He'd like me to find somebody for him. A woman he once knew."

"Well, now." He coughed dryly and began to fumble with

something. "You'd think he'd be too old for that kind of thing, but those two are indestructible."

"Are you going over?"

"I don't think so."

My father grumbled quietly.

"You live closer to them," I said. "You probably have more time, too. It's a bit far away for me, and there's so much going on right now."

The silence at the other end was long enough that I already knew the answer. My father always had to get a running start when saying no to someone.

Get a running start or be very, very drunk.

"Me and Anton, we've always had a bit of a strained relationship. You know that very well. If he needs help with something, you'll have to deal with it yourself. It'll probably be good for you to have something to keep you busy over the summer."

"He's your uncle, not mine."

I took a bite of my pizza, burning the roof of my mouth. Cursed.

"Jacob. I don't want to get involved in all that. Not with Anton."

He clattered with something, and I involuntarily braced for the clink of bottles or the weak wheeze of a can being opened. Old habits died hard.

"Okay."

"But if you want to drop by—"

"Thanks."

My father was gone without any further formalities. He got snappy when he felt pressured, and he felt pressured as soon as he was asked about anything other than sporadic company and small talk. Before the call dropped, I heard the whistling of the wind and the rustling of leaves on the other end. The chaotic cheeping of birds. Sparrows or maybe some invasive species from rugged Spanish mountain ranges. And his image appeared before me, as he was probably standing in his little town house, the phone in his hand. Gaunt and sunburned and alone, completely alone, like he preferred. He'd cut back on his drinking after my mother left him but had the occasional relapse.

I ate the last of my pizza and walked back out onto the street, oil and garlic running down my fingers. A bit farther down was a hi-fi shop, selling both new and secondhand. The record player they had for sale was okay, and the speakers nothing less than impressive. I paid and got one of the young men to help me drag it all home—a stocky black-haired lad who was no more than eighteen years old, but already equipped with distinctive muttonchops and the kind of well-developed self-esteem that came from having been useful in his father's or uncle's shop since the age of twelve. His student cap sat firmly on his head, bearing the marks of the sun, bright nights and an undoubtedly intense partying program.

He set the boxes in the hallway and wiped the sweat off his forehead. "Are you going to listen to loud music?" He laughed. "You won't be a popular man in the ghetto."

I sighed and thought about how loud it was in the building. The crying children of the neighbor above me were clearly heard. My player would end up collecting dust until I found a more permanent place.

"Yet further proof that man isn't free," I said, opening a can of beer. "Can't find peace from each other anywhere."

The lad sent me a long look and shrugged his shoulders.

"And it would be pretty boring if we could," he said. "Mind your neighbors and friends, old man. They're the ones who'll be bringing you soup when you get sick."

I sent him a half smile.

"Turkish proverb?"

"Nope." He laughed. "Universal truth. What goes around comes around."

I THREW MYSELF onto the mattress and browsed *Ekstra Bladet*'s web videos on my phone. An attempt to distract myself with things that had nothing to do with reality. In the first clip, a beautiful woman in her midthirties was demonstrating how to give a blow job on a rubber dildo attached to the table in front of her. She lowered her open mouth down over the phallic object until you could see her throat bulging, straightened up and explained the technique, saliva and gag reflex she'd been practicing to get control of it all. She was naturally beautiful, with blonde hair put up in a slightly messy bun. A sexologist named Signe. Resembled to the point of confusion one of the slightly boring but 100 percent healthy women of Østerbro. Academics with husbands and children and creatively messy apartments with stucco features.

I zapped out. Found the homepage with pictures of refugees in a camp somewhere in Europe. A secret lotto millionaire in Vojens, in southern Denmark, images of Michael Jackson's corpse at his funeral and Donald Trump, red-faced and furious about something or other.

The Østerbro woman's exercises on the enlarged rubber dildo had struck a very weak tone in my central nervous system, and no more. I considered finding a porn clip, but gave up again. Too much work for a predictable, short-term pleasure. I wasn't in the mood, maybe because of the pain in the pleasure center of my brain.

A text from a number I didn't know.

Stay away. I mean it. Next time, I'll rip your fucking wrinkly balls off.

I knew exactly what he looked like. And that he was stronger than me. Younger and angrier, and besides, I was a grown, civilized man. This shouldn't be happening. I still needed to call Janne and apologize, but she'd stopped taking my calls a long time ago.

I felt sick now, so I found Ravel's *Boléro* on YouTube and closed my eyes, listening. The cellos and bass were without depth, and the fine vibrating notes of the violin were impossible to distinguish from the rest on the phone. A small, compacted version of great sound. Something that reminded you of something, but wasn't quite it. Just like me and Kirsten the last few years.

Something big, locked away in little boxes.

I didn't want to go to Jutland—I couldn't. But maybe I had to.

1 9 7 8

I cycled uphill in third gear. Standing up on the pedals. I'd oiled the chain only last week, the gears quietly gripping the clean, shining links.

My Raleigh Grand Prix was decorated with dark-red sparks and ragged goat-horn handlebars and had so many gears that my father blessed himself when I brought it home. I'd bought it in Auning, four years old and well used, for all my confirmation money and a bit more. The seat post and screws were rusty, there were two long, deep scratches on the former, and the paint was chipped in several places, revealing the frame, but I didn't give a shit. I was the only one in class who had a racer. Next time I was going to get a Bianchi Strada, the bike of Fausto Coppi on winding Italian mountain roads. The champion's champion. Ole Ritter had ridden a Cinelli last year, but I'd never seen one. Not even in Aarhus in one of the big bike stores.

I reached the top of the hill and bent down over the handlebars for the descent, my T-shirt and new Adidas sweater fluttering madly, the air cold against my skin. The rhythmic, insect-like clicks of the gears, getting faster and faster until it all blurred together, becoming a loud whir in the wind. I had my backpack with me, stuffed with T-shirts and underpants and my library books. My drawing things. A sketch pad of the slightly thicker paper from the office store on the main street, and pencils with nibs so soft that the lines flowed like brushstrokes across the pages.

I was in my drawing-naked-ladies phase.

Pinups from Dad's brittle and yellowed men's magazines in the garage. Posing in bikinis on beaches and across the hoods of broad 1950s cars, but in my artistic interpretation they were all naked, and with a very direct view of the dark cracks between their legs. I'd looked in a few of the art books in the library, staring at she-dogs, cows and sows, and the last uncertainties I camouflaged with dark pubic hair. And despite my having to stretch my imagination for the final details, my drawings were popular collectibles among the boys in my class. They might not be anatomically correct, but as there were already numerous confusing and contradictory bits of information about the ins and outs of pussies, my take on it was just as good as anyone else's, and it was something to look at during physics class and to appall the girls with during recess so that they curled up and fled, their faces red.

I took five kroner for the most successful ones, and ten for those where I'd drawn the same couple screwing on two pieces of paper. When you rolled them over each other with a pencil, the asses moved up and down, or you could get the dick sticking up.

I also drew trees and leaves, but mainly houses.

From all sides and angles. Sketches and hard lines. The church. The school, which was the only three-story building in the town, with finely carved cornices and drinking fountains of gray granite with troll heads, and eagles and edges of finely painted grapevines under the eaves. The butcher's yard and the furniture factory with its almost one-hundred-foot-high brick chimney.

The bike wobbled through a pile of lost gravel on the path where the road divided itself at the cluster of small farms. I was going too fast, but the brakes didn't grip like they should have. The blocks were so worn that it was metal being pressed against the tires, and I had to stick the toe caps of my shoes into the asphalt and steer the bike into the ditch, where it bumped over rocks and knolls, finally coming to a sharp stop in the knee-high grass.

"Who the hell are you . . . a little asshole?"

Anders was standing in the wide driveway on the other side of the road, glancing at a point a little to my left, grinning quietly from ear to ear. Happy. He had dropped the wheelbarrow loaded with bags of feed and stuck his large, restless hands into his pockets. He was almost bald, and a disease had made the skin on his forehead and under the long stump of beard red and scaly. When he scratched hard under the cap, white flakes sprinkled down around him like a microcosmic snow shower.

I got off the bike, wincing slightly. I'd received a few unwelcome knocks to my balls and scratched my shin on the pedal. Unfortunately, the rear derailleur also seemed to have taken a hit.

"So come on, then, you."

The dog appeared behind him, on stiff legs. Soffi. A medium-sized, black-eyed bitch with a short, greasy coat that barked angrily at everyone, but was always ready to reconcile quickly if you rubbed her behind the ears. Her teats were naked and swollen, so there were puppies somewhere. Or there had been recently. Anton usually put down the entire litter by whacking them in the neck with the back of an axe. It was difficult to get puppies off your hands, and the dog ended up skinny and exhausted.

"I'm here."

"For a lot of days . . ."

I smiled.

"Yes, Anders. For a lot of days."

He put his hand in his pocket and pulled out a shard of glass that he held up to the light. Red.

"Beautiful. Did you find it today?"

He nodded eagerly, closing his hand around the clear red glass and letting it slide back into his pocket.

"Where's Anton?"

Anders smiled broadly at his wooden clog shoes, rubbed his neck. When he, on the odd occasion, met your gaze, his water-blue eyes were filled with a happy astonishment that reminded me of Jørgen's four-year-old sister when we snuck her a wine gum or half a raspberry jelly pastry.

"He's inside." He bent over the dog, kissed her muddy snout and blew into her nostrils as the animal wagged her tail with delight.

He'd forgotten me again, but that was how it was. Anders had the uncanny ability to disappear in the middle of a conversation. Not physically, but more of a kind of gliding in and out of focus, like a defective piece of photography equipment. His huge hands moving restlessly over everything in reach in the meantime. Animals and tools, belt buckles and the knees of his pants. He grabbed the worn handles of the wheelbarrow again and straightened up. Pushed it across the yard to the pig house. I leaned my bike against the gable wall, sat on my haunches beside the dog and shook her lightly on her greasy neck.

"And what have you done with your puppies?" I said. "Have you been a good dog?"

The fur on her stomach was stiff and tangled with dried milk, the teats tender, so the puppies were probably lying atop the dung heap with crushed skulls. I bit back the disappointment in me and went over to the back door.

"Anton!"

I remained standing on the flat staircase where the brothers and everyone else banged the dirt off their shoes and rubber boots before carefully placing them in a row in the hallway. It smelled of cow and pig, and grease fumes from meatballs and boiled potatoes. The kitchen table was wiped with a not-very-clean cloth that hung over the kitchen sink, and although it was tidy, almost barren, dirt was still plastered along the floorboards and tiles and behind the stove. When Mom occasionally stuck her head into the house of her uncles-in-law, she inspected the kitchen with an index finger, running it over the range hood, on the lamp, and in one of the pots to conclude dryly that the place lacked a woman. The last one had been my great-grandmother, but I didn't know anything about her. She'd died many years before we moved to town. All that remained was the oilcloth with coffee stains on the table in the dining nook and the steady, stammering clock over the door to the living room. Time at the brothers' passed slowly, flowing thickly like the honey or resin or tar pits that had once trapped saber-toothed tigers and dinosaurs, preserving their bones for posterity.

Both Anton and Anders were born in Great-Grandmother's room, which backed onto the living room, and according to my father, it was a true miracle that the boys had managed to escape from their mother's womb, because she was a woman who held on to her sons. Since then, they'd been left hopelessly on the farm of their birth, where they'd grown up with four older brothers, a living mother, and a dead father.

"There you are, Jacob."

Anton waved at me with a palette knife in hand. He was so tall that he had to dip so as not to hit his head on the door frame. The house wasn't built for men like him and Anders, and it had apparently never occurred to them to add to the height. As they grew so much taller than their mother, they must have hunched more and more as they went from the living room to the kitchen and back to the living room again. In contrast to his brother, Anton had a lot of hair on his head, carefully combed with water in the early morning and maintained during the day with a comb that he walked around with in his back pocket. Once upon a time, he had resembled Marlon Brando, said my mother. Not anymore, not completely at least. But he was still handsome in a John Wayne kind of way. Broad shoulders and a stocky upper body.

"You can stay with us for a while, can't you? You're not too busy for a pair of old codgers like us?"

"No, of course not."

He smiled, grabbed my hair, tousling it roughly. He believed it was too long and said so to me often enough. When I was younger, he used to shake my hand in his until my eyes welled up and I had to wrestle myself from his grip.

"Do you want something to eat before we get started? There's a fried egg left."

I shook my head.

"I ate at home."

"Well, then." He nodded and walked back into the kitchen. Let the egg, fried potatoes, and onions slide from the pan onto his own plate before sitting down and tucking in.

"You can put your things in the bedroom."

He was the uncle my father resembled the most. Actually, much more than he looked like his own father. A little genetic hop, especially evident when you saw them from the side. The same wide nose, heavy jawline, brown eyes and dark brown hair. Even when taking into consideration my father's unhealthy swollen and chronically reddened cheeks, the physical resemblance was hard to escape, despite him doing what he could.

My father didn't like Anton.

He'd whisper, "Momma's boy," when Anton passed by Feed Stuffs. "That's what happens when you grow up under your mom's apron strings."

I went in, put my backpack on the floor of Great-Grandmother's room, and skimmed the short bed of dark polished mahogany. She had given birth to six children in it, and it was here that she'd taken her last breath. The mattress had been changed since then, and was now light blue and crackled electrically under a yellowed flannel blanket.

"Jacob."

Anton was standing in the doorway.

"You can start by digging up the potatoes. And put a couple of bags out by the curb now. Svendsen's wife came by twice yesterday asking for them, and she's . . ."

Anton stopped midsentence, settling for waving his hand in an irritated manner. I'd discovered that wives could have that effect on him. Especially the ones who liked to talk.

I retrieved the pitchfork and a few buckets from the stable, knocked a little sticky clump of soil off the bottom of one and headed for the kitchen garden on the other side of the middle stable. The long, winding rows of potatoes and asparagus, blue-green silver beets and little red cabbages with smooth, cool leaves were mainly the work and responsibility of Anders. As were the dense raspberry bushes and fruit trees in the chicken yard. I set the pitchfork into the earth and stepped on it, pushing the shaft toward the ground and loosening the potato plant so the earth-scented tubers could be glimpsed in white-yellow flashes along with fat, pale-blue and red rain worms and threadlike strings of fungus. I coaxed and tilted a little more with the fork, then began to pick up the potatoes from the sandy soil. It was a good yield this year. The potatoes were large and smooth, and there were a lot of them. The bucket was already more than half-full after plant number two.

"That looks good."

I straightened up and turned toward the narrow, trampled garden path to where a woman had stationed herself, arms crossed. I hadn't heard her coming. Hadn't even registered the movement outside of my field of vision. But she was standing there for what had apparently been a while.

She was darker than most people I knew. Blue eyes that seemed lined with black, but probably weren't. No makeup on the rest of her face. Her dark brown hair hung loosely, falling almost to her waist. Long, floppy trousers and an old man's button-down. Her suntanned feet were stuck into a pair of open-backed wooden clogs. Her feet were dirty, as if she usually walked barefoot. On her fine collarbones hung a white mother-of-pearl mussel shell on a leather cord.

She had to be from the commune. One of the hippies.

I'd been there once with Jørgen, who went to buy a guitar but didn't dare cycle out there on his own. So I was there when he reluctantly handed over his eight crumpled ten-kroner notes and in return received a beaten-up Spanish guitar covered in stickers of peace signs and communist slogans: BROTHER, THE TIME HAS COME! POWER TO THE PEOPLE. It was winter, and the living room we were standing in was cold and dark, smelling of wood fires, cigarettes and bitter tea. Lying directly on the glazed tile surface of the coffee table were crumbled slices of white bread beside a ceramic mug and a few dirty glasses with the dregs of juice at their bottoms. A curled pack of butter and a few greasy knives. The floor was raw concrete, like in a stable, scattered with frayed, colorful and filthy little rugs lying crookedly and on top of each other in several places. The sofa was covered with a huge crocheted blanket. My mother would have blessed herself.

The woman nodded at the potatoes. "Can I take some?"

"Sure . . ."

I stepped aside slightly so she could walk past me and to the bucket, where she bent down and lifted some of the thin-skinned large tubers into a braided shopping net. She was wearing loads of bracelets. Some were braided black leather strips, but most were delicate and thin, shining silvery in the sun. Her scent was unperfumed, strong and frightfully exciting, despite my having no idea why.

"I don't think I've seen you before," she said. "Are you just here for the summer vacation?"

She worked fast with her hands, the bracelets jingling and jangling on her slim wrists with every movement. And when she stooped, I could see half of one of her breasts under the loosely buttoned shirt. There was neither undershirt nor bra, and the little pert breast jumped animatedly every time she moved.

"Kind of," I said, tilting another potato top. It was a relief to have something else to look at. "I'm helping out here for the summer. Just until I start high school."

She sent me a sideways smile, took a potato and rubbed a piece of the fragile peel off with her thumb. "We have a vegetable garden, but it's . . ." She sighed dramatically. "We don't understand how to do it. The salad is rotting, and Karsten, my boyfriend, tries to scare away the grubs with old urine. But now everywhere stinks like a men's toilet, and we've no potatoes at all."

"Mmm." I didn't know what else I was supposed to say. I knew absolutely nothing about vegetables—or boyfriends and girl-friends, for that matter. It was a strange word to use at her age. Boyfriend. It sounded like a boy who stuck his hand up under a girl's shirt in the back row of the movie theater. Or like having sex on a creaking single bed under posters of ABBA.

"He's over there."

She nodded toward the fence, where a guy was walking over to the cows with Anders. Ragged denim shorts and a bare, tanned upper body. His shoulder-length hair reminded me of the men on the covers of those books about the last Mohicans. He strad-dled the fence and headed for the cows, who flocked curiously around him.

"He thinks we should get one," she said, nodding in his direction. "A bull calf that we ourselves can fatten up. Or a cow with a calf. He's started to build a brick box out in the stable."

"Okay."

Karsten, grinning widely, waved in our direction, bent down, and stroked one of the cows on its chest. He said something to Anders, but the woman had turned toward me again, smiling.

"And what are you going to do, then? After high school?" she asked. "Do you know already?"

"I'd like to be an architect," I said, and she nodded, her brow furrowed in concentration.

"The new Utzon?"

A cloud moved in front of the sun, and a buzzard took off out over the field with a clumsy flap before finally beginning to work itself up with regular, rigid wing beats. She shielded her eyes with her hand as she followed it up in the pale-blue sky. Her hair was gently lifted by the wind, and then it felt as though something broke in me. It wasn't something that hurt, just a weakness that finally surrendered, and for a moment it was difficult to breathe all the way down to my chest, and I wished she'd look at me again. Would turn her head in the same way and say it once more.

I actually had Utzon hanging on the wall of my room at home. A full-page cutting from the newspaper *Stiftstidende* about his work on the opera house in Australia. How he'd had all the white tiles sailed from Sweden to Sydney, and that the entire interior was pink granite. Pink granite! I had no idea what that looked like, but the words alone were simultaneously hard and soft . . . and that was what I wanted to do. Build houses in pink granite or green topaz with black tropical trees of the kind I had read about in *King Solomon's Mines*. Ebony with color like charcoal gray and green bamboo and mahogany, with grains of solidified dark caramel. Divine, flawless surfaces.

There was a shout from over by the cows. The young man had gone farther into the field, a tail of animals following him, and now he was surrounded by large bodies. A heifer rose clumsily onto her hind legs, and would have fallen on top of him if he hadn't taken a step back at the last minute. He yelled again, throwing out his arms to keep his balance. Then he turned around and tried to escape between the cows and to the fence. The heifer rose again behind him, and this time its hoof struck him on its way down, so he took a huge stumble.

Anders roared and cussed. Slapped the big, smooth body with a flat hand until he had broken up the flock and could help the bronzed man up onto his legs. He limped a bit on his way over to the fence.

The woman with the dark-blue eyes kept her mouth shut. There was a wild, forbidden laugh in her eyes.

"They do that sometimes," I said.

"What?"

I turned my back a little, rummaging in the almost-empty potato bucket as though I were looking for something. A bisected worm bled its entrails over my fingers, and a rolling, red-brown centipede darted down between the hard tubers. I lifted a few potatoes out of the bucket, found it and mashed it into the earth with a satisfying crunch using the tip of a stick.

"Trying to, you know . . . It's in heat. So you have to be careful when you go in among them."

She glared at me briefly, confused before the penny dropped.

"You're making fun of me," she said, sneaky laughter still in her eyes.

"Unfortunately not." I threw the potatoes back into the bucket and grabbed the fork again. "That heifer wanted your boyfriend."

Now she laughed properly and it made her look even younger. Like a girl of sixteen. It was confusing, but neither better nor worse than before. I liked her both old and young. In fact, I was almost sure I'd think she was beautiful no matter what form she presented herself to me.

"We really shouldn't be living out here at all," she said. Straightened up, and brushed the soil off her hands. "It can be fatal to people from the city. Do you laugh at us a lot?"

"All the time," I said. "There's not much else to do around here."

"No?"

The wind lifted her long hair again, and in that moment, I decided that she had to be one of the most beautiful women on the planet.

"Well . . ." She turned around and started walking. "I'd better go take care of the wounded warrior. It was nice meeting you."

"Goodbye."

She walked quickly, even began to jog slightly with the heavy shopping net dangling unevenly from one hand, and met her boyfriend down by the corner to the stable. Said something or other and laid her head against his shoulder. I could see him wince as he stretched out his arm so she could kiss it better and, chuckling, she bent forward so her long dark hair concealed her face.

1 9 7 8

"Come home with me. The rest of us would like to enjoy your company, too."

Dad had gotten out of the car before I'd even gotten off the bike. Stationed himself obstinately, legs apart, in the middle of the yard, and was hopeless to look at with his blue cap from Feed Stuffs and day-old stubble. He stank of beer and sweat, despite it being no later than eleven. He was supposed to be at work, but he must have spotted me with the bicycle man or when I'd cycled past Feed Stuffs, and remembered he had a son.

"I haven't heard from your mother, either," he said. "Not a word. That's a fine way to behave. Really fine."

He raised his voice so much that Anton, who had been doing something by the dung heap, appeared with hesitant steps, a barking Soffi on his heels.

Dad didn't pay any attention to him. Buried his hands deep in the pockets of his beige-colored work pants, with stiff arms and shoulders up in an unsuccessful attempt to seem relaxed.

He didn't take up much space where he stood beside Anton with his hair sticking out from underneath his cap. Dad was ruddy-faced and, in spite of his controlled calm, clearly upset. Mom's stay with her sister had obviously been extended. It was happening more and more often—a weekend became an entire week. Sometimes two.

Dad didn't like being on his own. I knew that well.

Both he and the house started to fall apart as soon as my mother closed the door behind her. Plants died in the windowsills, dirty dishes reeked, and the days dissolved into one another without rhythm. He began eating his food at night and early in the morning, if you could even call it food. My father without my mother was a man who lived on beer, fried eggs, fish cakes in tomato sauce, rye bread and dry biscuits with milk and cinnamon. In the evening, he would sit on the couch with his archaeological books and his little collection of arrow tips, pot shards, and bone fragments spread out on the table in front of him. Hair tousled and shirt open. The single sharply pointed flint axe, the pearl of his collection, which he'd found taking a shortcut over a plowed field fifteen years ago, was given pride of place beside the open beer. When he'd become so drunk that he could no longer read, he would let his fingers run across the ridges and valleys on a relief map of Zealand as though it were a pattern to be read in braille. Amateur archaeology, Mom called it, even though she knew he hated the phrase.

When I was younger, I often went with him down to the field where he'd found the axe. Or down to the bog, where we'd excavate from the black-as-coal, sewage-smelling soil while the red-white corks from our fishing rods bobbed on the water's surface and Dad drank a beer or two.

I was too old for all that now.

"I'm on vacation," I muttered.

He spat on the cobblestones and sulked.

"Vacation! I didn't get a vacation when I was a boy. I worked. Had an apprenticeship when I was your age. And most important, I always did what my father told me to. End of story!"

Anton rubbed his neck and nodded to my father without looking directly at him.

"Just let Jacob stay here, Erik. It's probably best for him when Birthe isn't home."

My father's shoulders sank a little. Rarely did anyone say anything to him about the beer. That it was too much, and too many, and he should stop. My mother did, of course, every so often, and then they quarreled and slammed doors. But Anton had confronted him, too. Once, at least. I'd heard them talking one afternoon in the spring at Feed Stuffs.

"If I were your father, you'd be getting a clip across the ear," Anton said. "You're drunk."

He clicked his tongue, and it sounded like it was for fun, but it was completely serious. And my father had laughed and said no, of course he wasn't. Anton had looked at my father for a long time without smiling before finally saying something ordinary like "well, so" and "where's the winter wheat shelved again?" and "how is everything else at home?"

That was why Dad didn't like Anton.

"Jacob and I have a fine time when Mom is away," said my father, looking over at me as if he was afraid I would protest. "We're fine."

"Of course you do," Anton said, still without looking at him. "Jacob is also fine here, and we can certainly use him over the summer. You know how it is. Everything that has to be done."

Dad bowed his head, shielding himself from the wind while he lit a match for his cigarette. Waved the smoke away from his eyes with an irritated movement.

"Well, the least you can do is call your mother and tell her she has to come home."

I nodded, knowing I wouldn't. He certainly knew it, too. He avoided looking at either me or Anton as he got into the Escort, crunching the gearbox as he accelerated and leaving us with the stench of burning clutch. Anton sent me a brief nod before turning around and disappearing back to the dung heap to resume his work with the muck fork.

"ANDERS!"

I found him in the kitchen, washing the dishes from lunch and whistling to the radio.

Little butterfly, flying from flower to flower . . .

"Do you go into town today?" He dried his hands on the dish towel.

"Yeah."

I threw off the backpack and poked around a bit in the front room. Ten *Donald Duck* comics from Bytte-Olsen, two with the Phantom and a few of the latest Sabotør Q5. And chocolate. Anders didn't really care for candy or licorice, that kind of thing. We walked into the lumber room next to the utility room. The wallpaper was green, and shelves wound around all four walls. There was silver polish, rag cloths, shoe polish and shoe horns; rusty kitchen scales, too; chipped plates and coffeepots and cookie jars and lamps that were missing a wire or a shade or both. It was also in here that Anders kept his treasures. Crumbling plastic bags on the floor held his collection of worn *Katzenjammer Kids* and *Donald Duck* comics, a magazine with a bikini-clad Lily Broberg on the front page, a little mermaid in brass glued clumsily onto a flat stone and a handful of glass beads, the kind used for bracelets and necklaces. And all his shards of glass. In a whole bag of their own, his collection from who knew since when.

He lifted the bags, muttering happily and swinging them back and forth as though to gauge how much they weighed.

"There's a lot," he said.

I nodded. I had procured most of the comics for him myself over the years. I bought them used or swapped them so we could read the continuous stories all the way to the end. Anders was still enthusiastic about it, but I didn't think it was the same anymore. The only ones I really wanted to read were *Silver Arrow*, *The Phantom*, and *Hudibras*, which could still get me to stand at attention if I brought them up to my room and locked the door.

"Here." I took a bag from him, took out the old ones, and started to put them in order for him. "Mind not to bungle them."

He nodded and gently smoothed the pages with his large hands. On the front page, of the one on top, Donald Duck was caught in a huge soap bubble. WIN MADAM MIM'S MAGIC RADIO. When he opened the comic, Donald and Daisy were sitting in a cloud of pink hearts. For once, Anders didn't smile to himself, just stood with his mouth open and lips dry while he scratched his scaly beard stubble. As though he'd suddenly thought of something.

"Do you have a girlfriend?" he asked.

I shook my head.

He stuck the tip of his tongue out between his teeth just like he did when we got pudding for dessert. There was something white and sticky in one corner of his mouth.

"Anton doesn't know what a girlfriend is," he said. "Anton can't understand that kind of thing."

There was something defiant in the way he said it. As if he were continuing a squabble that had been going on behind his thick forehead for a while.

"No," I said. "He can't."

I WENT WITH him to the marl pit.

The slopes were edged with large beech trees and closely over-grown ferns, hazel, and tangled hawthorn. The water at the bottom of the crater was black from the slimy, withering leaves, glossy and ice-cold and not good for fishing in, but Anders, who used to go with me when I was younger, had once told me a story of a giant pike that would be worth catching. Over three feet long, he said, and as black as the water she inhabited. If I got her up, said Anders, I'd be best to let her lie and die in peace and only touch her when her clear eyelid had dimmed. Otherwise, she could easily snatch a finger or maybe even a whole hand.

I didn't really believe it anymore. It was a monster that had sprung out of Anders's limited imagination, boy talk from his own obscure youth. The brothers weren't fishermen, and the one time a neighbor had come by and set a bucket of living eels on the kitchen table, Anton had sworn and spluttered over the cleaning of the slimy creatures in the sink. In spite of it all, he couldn't get himself to throw them out.

I lit a cigarette, closed my eyes, and laid my head back with my face toward the flickering sunlight in the crowns of the trees. Fish or not, it was nice to lie here with a line in the water and a whole pack of cigarettes that I'd swiped from Dad on my way out.

I often stole things from him. Loose change, even bills that he had in his pockets. I'd buy rum balls from the baker—sixteen for four kroner—cigarettes, disposable razors, chips and soda, which I used to share with Sten because he'd neither money nor the balls to get himself some.

My dad was both too drunk and too stupid to grasp my little acts of revenge, but it didn't matter much. It was the thought that counted, as the saying goes, and Hemingway would probably have done the same thing. Or Churchill or John Wayne. Or Utzon. Real men who had lived in reality and hadn't wasted their lives putting red crosses on archaeological treasure maps.

I opened my book and read a few passages.

"On April sixth, 1735, Nicolai Eigtved left Rome, and on May seventh, he arrived in Vienna . . ."

The accompanying drawing was a beautiful, slightly blurred rendering of Capitoline Hill in Rome seen from the Piazza Aracoeli in 1709. I'd already looked the word "piazza" up at the library, and knew it meant square. There were hundreds of squares and monuments in Rome. Maybe thousands. Eigtved had been the son of a gardener, but somehow he'd begun drawing. That in itself was a kind of miracle back then. His sketches were filled with tiny details and curlicues, buildings and gardens and grounds, not humans, because he couldn't figure out how to give them life. Only buildings. And people had held up his drawings and made them real. Amalienborg's four palaces and the Marble Bridge, which I'd seen on the school tour last year. Christiansborg Castle Church and the Royal Theater. Limestone, and Norwegian marble, and French stucco masons.

I shut the book and looked up into the treetops weaving above me. Zipped open my pants, grabbed my dick and let my inner picture gallery change from Rome to our dusty classroom. My ability to concentrate was, to put it mildly, limited for the time being. There wasn't a girl in the class I hadn't ripped the clothes off and screwed at least ten times within the last month. All in my dirty imagination, of course, but that had its own demands. And although I didn't do it three times a day, which was apparently Jørgen's preferred cadence—he had a fairly ignorant theory that his balls would swell up and explode without scheduled emptyings morning, noon and night—the skin on my dick was sometimes red and stinging. I'd just forced myself to take a day's break for that very reason.

I closed my eyes and conjured up our classroom. Taxidermied animals in glass mounts and worn blue high school songbooks in a pile under a poster with ABBA that the girls had hung up with pins and tape, and me, letting a hand slide between the legs of buxom Sussi. She was the most annoying of the girls in many ways, but there was something terribly exciting about the way she moved. A distinct rocking of her hips, and when she slid into the chair in front of me in class, I always imagined how her panties, under her dress, rubbed against the wooden seat in an arousing tug.

And then there was her smile.

She had a gap between her front teeth and when she laughed, she sometimes pressed a little pink, wet tongue tip out through there, and it was . . . I was going to show her that—dammit, screw her hard, until she screamed from joy . . . hard and over Mr. Madsen's desk—now—and I was in from the front and from the back, the images changing at a tremendous pace. Oh, love, love . . . and I came in the grass in a long, warm spurt and carefully wiped myself with fallen beech leaves.

The sky was a little cloudy now, and the wind was rushing louder in the crowns of the trees. There were voices at the edge of the field, a man and a woman, and something told me the man wasn't one of the farmers. First, farmers didn't go for walks with women, not even their wives, and second, these people were too loud. I had yet to hear people out here raise their voices to anything but a dog or cows when they held back and refused to move.

". . . you were gone for . . ." I heard the man say. "You can't—"

He didn't get to finish as she raised her voice. I could hear she was angry, shouting at him, but some of the words were carried off by the wind and the dry rustling of the grass.

"Let me go . . . that hurts!"

Had he hit her?

I crawled up the slope and spotted the man first. The guy from the commune, tall and furious, heading across the field of knee-high barley. His upper body was bare, and just like the time with the cows, there was something wild about him as he walked, his long hair fluttering in the wind. When he turned his head to look back, his face seemed distorted.

The woman sat at the edge, watching him go, plucked a long blade of grass and wound it around her fingers. She was wearing sunglasses, and her long hair was pulled up into a messy ponytail. But it was her. Anton had said she was called Ellen. She seemed fine, and I tried to retreat back between the trees while buttoning my shorts, but she'd already seen me. Lifted her sunglasses and waved.

"You're the architect . . ." She smiled that thin smile that adults did when they weren't happy enough to smile properly. My mother did it all the time. "Come and sit. You don't happen to have a cigarette, do you?"

I slapped the pockets of my pants like I'd seen real men do. Then I took out the packet and offered her one. The matches, too.

"What are you doing?" she said. She squinted at the first drag, looking at me over the rim of her dark eyeglasses. Her eyes were clear and still an intimidatingly dark blue.

"Fishing," I said. "And reading a little."

"Is there anything to catch down there?" She turned her head and leaned back to get a glimpse of the water between the trees.

"Nah, not really."

She laughed.

"I've always suspected that men only go fishing so they can sit and do nothing—maybe jerk off—out in God's free nature. Is there something to that, do you think?"

My cheeks burned. No adult had ever said anything like that to me. Her words and expressions felt like conductive cables to my hypersensitive dick, and she just sat there, looking as though it were all completely normal. Her eyes filled with a kind of friendly fun as she observed me through the smoke from her cigarette.

"I don't know anything about that," I said, turning away. Feeling both excited and deeply offended. "But it's relaxing, at least. Was that . . . ?"

I nodded toward the trampled grain.

"Karsten. My boyfriend. Sort of."

Sort of? I would have liked her to explain a little more, but didn't dare ask. So I settled for nodding knowingly. She got up and brushed the twigs and grass from her loose corduroy pants, still with the cigarette clasped between her lips. Rubbed one slim wrist with the other hand and cussed quietly before straightening up and shooting me a crooked, half-apologetic smile.

"Promise me you won't be such an idiot when you grow up," she said. "You have to be nice to your lovers, right?"

"Well . . ."

I blushed like a complete idiot and must have looked confused.

She took off her sunglasses, tilted her head and looked at me with a mischievous glint in her dark-blue eyes.

"I believe in you, Utzon," she said. "I can already tell you're a good guy. Pure, unsullied love. The girl who moves into your architect-drawn villa is going to be a lucky one. Well . . ."

She sighed and looked out over the field toward the commune, turned around, and began to walk along the edge in the direction she'd come from. I didn't say anything, just stood there, heart throbbing in my throat and chest, not knowing what to do with myself. And then, as though she knew I was gawking at her, she raised her hand to wave goodbye without turning around.

"See you, Utzon," she shouted. "And try not to fish too much. I've heard you can go blind."

I took the train.

I sat sweating with the day's newspaper in a sluggish compartment with brown spots on the blue seat cover. *Berlingske*. There were drowning refugees on the front page, a little girl floating in an azure sea. A butterfly had beaten its wings somewhere in the Amazon and released chaos into the universe.

The Danish summer countryside passed by outside—savannah brown and dark yellow with wide stripes of dusty dark green. Windbreakers and Mirabelle cherry plum trees, and linden, and ash, and dried pieces of moss with small, warm, flickering forests of willows and reeds.

Although the sky was cloud-free, the light was hazy like in a smoky pub or a murky sunset in Beijing. I ate a hot dog in the nicotine-colored arrivals hall at Aarhus Central Station, bought a bottle of water and a Snickers and went down to the platform for the local train. Jacob Errbo Nielsen, age fifty-three, in shorts, sandals and sweaty shirt. Divorced. With grown children and a relatively respectable life behind him, if you ignored a few slip-ups. Nothing much to talk about. Everyone makes mistakes, no one is perfect, and the nausea—which felt like something between hunger and disease—had more to do with the heat and the few too many beers I'd drunk in Nørrebro than the name of the city on the departures board.

Bullshit.

I could almost hear Kirsten whisper it in my ear, but she was also the world champion of guilt and shame. If no one stopped her at a dinner party, she would take on the blame for everything from

the Western world's early imperialism to famine in southern
Sudan.

"We've been terrible," she said. "And we really need to stop the
war in Syria now." At night she cried tears of honesty and humanity, but her guilty conscience was more of the decorative kind. One
that crowns the well-groomed hair of middle-aged women who
don't have true misfortune in their lives. By contrast, there were
other, more carnivorous variants of guilt to be found that festered
in open wounds and required partial amputation. Those weren't
something you should invite in.

And yet here I was, on my way to doing just that.

The train could have been the same one I rumbled back and
forth on when I started high school. The seats had been reuphol-
stered, of course, and the bitter stink of ashtrays was completely
gone, but apart from that, it was strikingly similar. The walls were
grayed from engraved names and hearts and hopeful time cap-
sules: I WANT YOU, CAMILLA and YOU ONLY LIVE ONCE and I WILL
LIVE FOREVER!!!

There was something overwhelmingly defiant and universal in
young people's need to express themselves. The first time they
understood one of life's very obvious truths, it was carved with
violence and power into tables and chairs. Even the stupid hand
dryers in toilets were ornamented with heartache and stiff cocks.
I let them be. Remembered how well-intentioned it had been trying to share modest, completely newly realized life wisdom with
the part of humanity who took the train or shat in public toilets. I
myself had transcribed poems by Emil Årestrup there. Something
about shadows and swollen lips. Erotica. A true intellectual. I now
knew all that wasn't too far from the cheerfully ejaculating dick
and YOLO. Once a young man discovered his cock was God, it might
be a small step for humanity, but it was a quantum leap for
Frederik, age fourteen.

Well-maintained houses and gardens appeared along the

smooth curves of the tracks—fields with straight, machine-cut lines. I had the afternoon sun on my back, and the sky was a dusty gray to the east as the train stopped and I alighted into the flickering heat with two shopping bags in my hands and my computer over my shoulder.

The station building looked mostly the same. Red stone, two-story. There had been a post office the last time I'd been here that smelled of stamp ink and paper. Now there were flowers in the windows of the first floor, three satellite dishes, and a temporary wire fence around half of the building. The weeds were growing through the fence, as well as on the separate platform and in the empty parking lot.

I crossed the road to Brugsen, which was exactly where it had been back then, between the gray concrete of Feed Stuffs and a narrow road leading up to the main street. I walked through the glass doors past the department with flowers in pots and cut tulips to the shelves in back. In my childhood, Brugsen had been the major store. Bigger than Hansen's Drugstore, and much larger than Nora's in Gammel Tostrup. Now it seemed claustrophobically small, the range of vegetables and bread exhausted as if there'd just been a long period of drought.

I could feel the eyes of the sole woman at the counter on my back while I carefully selected an ice cream and a pack of biscuits for the walk out of town. After a moment's hesitation, I threw a six-pack of Carlsberg into the basket, too. For me and the old men.

The lady scanned it all in, caught my cash with a flat hand and threw the coins into the register with an effective movement. Her nails were cut down to the soft pulp, red and scoured clean, and even though she was sitting, you could tell she was tall and lanky in an almost boyish kind of way, despite her being my age or even a little older. The red Brugsen T-shirt sat over her bony shoulders and minimalistic bosom like it would have sat on a twelve-year-old, but I liked the twinkle in her eyes. Curious. As if I were the first person she'd met in one hundred years. I tried to figure out if she was someone I'd once known, maybe even gone to school with, but gave up looking for similarities. The name tag—Birgitte—didn't tell me anything. And, actually, I didn't want to talk to anyone. I had more pressing needs. For example, I needed to take a piss. Urgently.

"Do you have a bathroom for customers?"

She sent me a knowing smile and nodded toward a heavy plastic curtain on the other side of the shelves of dog food and birdseed. Pulled me a key from somewhere under the counter.

"Make yourself at home," she said.

I TRUDGED OUT into the glistening sunshine with a lighter bladder, sat on the edge of the narrow ramp where the shopping carts were and looked around.

I'd lived in Copenhagen since I'd moved there for college. As I sat outside Brugsen, I couldn't remember having been in a little Danish town since. At least, not for any longer than it took to park a car and buy a Coke and Mars bar in the shop closest to the highway.

The silence was deafening. Like I'd been placed in the set of an empty village. Cars appeared now and then on the main street, but there was no sign of life for as far as I could see up and down Stationsvej. The only things moving were the half-withered flowers in the stone pots outside Brugsen, where hot gusts of wind tore the dull pink petals in all directions.

In the building where the general store had been, the window facing the street was plastered with paper and a FOR SALE sign, and the windows of the old butcher shop were blocked up with bricks three shades lighter than the old ones. A new town on top of the old one. Paint and asphalt and brickwork masking everything that still lay beneath.

I got up and started to walk down the road. Past Feed Stuffs, which still smelled like it had back then. Of grain and pesticide and the powdered milk that was mixed in large buckets for newborn calves, who only began drinking when they could suckle on three fingers after the hand was stuck down into the bucket. The large industrial doors were rolled down. The concrete loading ramp was gone, but there must still have been business happening in the store, because a few trucks loaded with dusty mountains of the year's first harvest were parked outside.

I walked farther down, past the family homes of two of my old classmates, Anna and Flemming.

My phone vibrated in my pocket.

"I've been thinking about it," said Kirsten. "I still think you should take the dining table and the two shelves from the living room."

"I don't want them, Kirsten. They're fine where they are."

"In my living room?"

"Yes, in the living room. Hell, what's wrong with them? Nothing. Just keep them."

She paused.

"Where are you?"

I felt the sting of irritation and a guilty conscience. Was she listening for signs of another woman, just like I used to listen for the clattering of bottles and hints of slur in my father's speech? Things you wouldn't ask about directly, but which were really the only things that interested you.

"I'm in Djursland, by myself," I said. "It's to do with my father's uncles. You don't know them."

"Okay." She sounded slightly less tense now. "But you still have to get your things."

"I don't want them."

"Then I'm going to throw them out."

"Can we talk about this when I get back to Copenhagen?"

"No. You have a week. I'll put them in the garage. If you want them, you can get them when you're back. Otherwise, I'll get someone to take your crap."

"Kirsten—"

"What do you expect me to wait for?"

I didn't know what to say to that. I saw Kirsten before me as I threw the last thing into the van. She'd gone out into the garden in the roasting midday sun and hacked the weeds between the herbs, looking like both herself and someone else entirely. The completely straight back and hair—blonde—which was always up in a loose, gray-speckled knot. I could recall every detail with my eyes closed: Kirsten, my once-so-cool wife. Her new demeanor was chilling. Unapproachable. She hadn't turned when I'd called her from the house. Instead, she remained standing with her back to me while she used the weeder to carve hard furrows in the earth among the rosemary, thyme and oregano.

It had been a hot, dusty summer. The leaves of the trees were already tired and withered, and rustled dry in the wind. The grass beneath the large birch tree on the lawn was yellow and prickly, and drunk wasps droned over prematurely ripe and fallen plums by the gable. Kirsten's red T-shirt was dark from sweat between her shoulder blades.

"I'm leaving now," I shouted, but she didn't answer or turn around, not even when I accelerated and slowly drove past the hedge with rolled-down windows.

The boundaries of separation were as blurred at the edges as an amputation with a blunt knife.

"Nothing," I said, exhausted. "But, shit, can't you just leave it there until I come back?"

She hung up without another word. I thought about calling her back for a brief moment, but let it go.

I stuck the phone in my pocket and picked up the pace, passed the showy town sign. WELCOME TO TOSTRUP—the town in the middle. The asphalt road was narrower than I remembered, bordered by a withered green jumble of wild carrots, plantains, nettles, and tall couch grass. In the spring, the heavens had opened in warm cascades of rain across the entire country, but now there wasn't a drop left, and you could see the drought everywhere. Even the corn had stopped waving, stiff and clattering in the dry wind.

The roof of the brothers' farm rose gray and rusty against the blue sky. The weather vane still sat above the rounded vent shaft on the roof of the cowshed, but other than that, the windswept horizon was unfamiliar and bare. The tall trees behind the farm were gone, and when the wind stopped for a moment, I could hear the aggressive buzz of cars approaching and disappearing on the smooth black asphalt-paved highway nearby. On the other side, a few dark-green factories rose on flat squares of asphalt, and next to them was now a blob of red-painted houses in a web of desolate roads and provincial town ordinariness.

My brain tried to cut and paste old and new pictures together as I reached the driveway. The front yard was completely overgrown. Clusters of ragged dark-green nettles grew in the shadows under cherry, apple and self-sown elderberry trees. The rusty Ferguson parked in the driveway had been impaled by thistles and errant peonies, winding themselves through the holes in the windshield and hood. Although the brothers had—as far as I knew—always been good to both their land and animals, a silent, vengeful nature was slowly enveloping the house in withering vegetation. Everything was so dry, and there still wasn't a cloud in the blue sky above.

I let the door knocker fall three times and listened for a moment. It was quiet inside. No barking dog, no footsteps. I put the bags down on the steps and wiped my forehead before knocking again, harder, suddenly hoping that no one would open. I could already see myself on my way back to the station, an open beer can in my hand. There were probably more trains to Aarhus, or else a bus.

Or I could score a ride on the highway and turn off my phone. Crawl back to my cave in Nørrebro and get wasted like I'd originally planned.

"You should've called."

I turned around and met his gaze.

Anton.

I recognized his voice and presence more than body and face. I remembered him as a giant. Over six feet tall, with wrists like fence posts. Now there was significantly less of him. His enormous body had sagged, the shoulders thin and bony under his shirt. He stood in the stable doorway in a pair of work pants that were far too big and reached out his hand as though we could touch each other across the sun-warmed yard. Then he gave up and walked slowly toward me.

"I didn't think you were so formal out here in the country," I said, smiling slightly. "But I've brought provisions."

As I pulled the six-pack from the bag, Anton clicked his tongue and grinned. It wasn't just his body that had faded away, but also that inexplicable radiance from almost forty years ago. The light some people are blessed with that draws others to them like freezing nomads around a campfire. The world had been safe and calm around Anton; I'd seen him soothe children and dogs and startled horses with merely his gaze and a heavy hand on their head. But whatever it was he'd had then, it was gone now.

He hesitantly removed his cap and squinted at the sun. Wrinkles cut fine, right-angled squares into the tanned skin of his throat.

"The bed's still upstairs," he said. "Other than that . . . just a cup of coffee. That much we have. Will you be staying?"

I nodded.

1 9 7 8

It sounded like a traffic accident, or a car chase like the ones in American movies. A car that sped up and then braked hard, hot rubber screeching on the asphalt.

Anders and I had been mucking out the chicken house all morning.

The perches were no longer perches, but poles of petrified chicken shit; the chickens had long since left the nesting boxes, which were stuffed with trampled cakes of straw and dung and lice. Instead, they laid their eggs in hollows scratched out in the chicken farm and found time to brood, their mothers' warmth making the eggs inedible. Anders grunted and cursed, calling them "little assholes."

"They'll get a fever," he said. "And then they'll stop laying eggs. We can't afford that. And we have enough chickens for this year."

I'd heard it all before, but it didn't matter. I just let him go on, as Anton called it. He would start with long, convoluted monologues about the pigs and chickens—the number of chickens last year and the year before—and if you interrupted and asked him about a detail, he'd answer about something else entirely.

I was wearing long pants, and had tied a bandana around my mouth before prying the dark pies of straw and chicken shit off the wet concrete floor. Every step we took released fleas in a dancing cloud over the straw.

The whining tires and the slam of a car door made Anders cower. Someone was shouting outside now. First a man, then a woman, whose higher-pitched voice broke into a scream.

"Who . . . ?"

Anders wiped his face and stared at the door, eyes wide, breathing heavily through his wet mouth.

Another furious exchange of words. Now the man and the woman were talking over each other. Anders put his hand over his face and pulled the corners of his mouth up into a strange grin. Both excited and frightened. I laid a hand on his shoulder like I'd seen Anton do.

"I'll go out and look," I said, setting the fork down. "You can stay here if you don't want to come."

He nodded, seeming calmer already, but now there was nothing to hear except the wind's whistling under the rafters.

I left Anders and jogged through the pigpen in Anton's heavy rubber boots, but I didn't see the man. Just the car spraying gravel up the driveway, then speeding away onto the road. A light-blue Volkswagen with a flower garland over the bumper that had spilled Ellen out into the yard as a kind of gift from providence.

I'd already jerked off three times to a new fantasy about her. The plot was simple: me with a fishing rod over my shoulder whistling when I surprised her, naked in the marl pit, after which she smiled at me frivolously, freed me from my shorts and underpants and said something like, "You won't become blind from this, at least."

Why she was naked to begin with, my overexcited imagination hadn't found a way to rationalize, but that hadn't mattered so far. I had thought of her often and even cycled past the commune a couple of times, but hadn't seen anything other than a pair of dirty boys sitting and splashing their bare feet in a hole they'd dug in the mud in the front yard.

Now Ellen seemed both more and less disheveled than when

I'd last seen her. As though she'd just woken up and hadn't had the time to get dressed and put herself together. Out of it, as Mom would say. She was bleeding a little from her lower lip, but wiped it away with the back of her hand in a careless motion while blinking forcedly out at the road. Her sunglasses had slid so far down her nose that it was impossible for her to see anything through them, and she looked only half-finished, with one arm in a long, moss-green woolen coat that was far too warm for the sunshine. Large tufts had broken free from the long braid hanging over her shoulder. When she saw me, she pushed the glasses up into place, turned around and picked up the backpack sitting next to her.

"Not now, Utzon," she said, turning her back to me, and I paused, unsure what to do with the soft voice and turned-away face. Anton appeared in the back door and hesitated, but stuck on his wooden clogs and walked through the yard.

"Well, Ellen."

She just shook her head, and Anton sent me a meaningful look over her half-covered shoulder. The unseasonable green wool coat had fallen even farther down and was now dragging on the ground.

"Jacob, maybe you should . . ." he said.

Reluctantly, I turned around and began walking while Ellen said something I couldn't hear.

"I don't think this is a good idea," said Anton.

"Just a couple of days," she said. "I have nowhere else to go . . ."

Despite me walking as slowly as I could, the last of the conversation disappeared under my creaking rubber boots and a tractor that drove past. I half turned while entering the stable and saw Ellen wipe her eyes several times with a green coat arm scrunched up in her hand as Anton took her backpack. There was something despairing in his hunched shoulders—as though something had gone seriously, irreparably wrong when he'd carried her suitcase across the yard to the farmhouse. Ellen followed after him without saying another word.

1 9 7 8

Anton repurposed Great-Grandmother's bed for Ellen, so I moved onto the living room sofa, which didn't bother me. When the brothers had washed up after dinner, we ate cake and drank coffee and watched the news. And then they went upstairs, leaving me in peace with the faint whistling of the water pipes and the hum of the kitchen fridge.

I didn't see much of Ellen for the first few days. Only if I woke up in the middle of the night was I lucky enough to sense a shadow passing through the living room, hear the flush of the toilet or the running of the shower or the crying, which sounded like my mother's. Muffled by a pillow or comforter, or whatever it was that women and girls found to cry into.

During the day, I whitewashed the pig house, working myself sweaty and sore with the skim-milk-thin solution, which I had to stir regularly with a thick stick. The wet layers gradually masked the stink of shit and piss, the greasy deposits of skin and fur and slobber, until it all dried into porous chalk and the wall was clean, cool and smooth under my fingertips.

The pigs stirred restlessly when I came out to them in the morning. The agitated grunts became giddier squeals as they stood snout to snout, chewing the bars over the trough. Their small, intelligent eyes beamed at me in pent-up amusement, and they willingly let me place a flat hand on their wet, hard snouts, still covered in the first compound feed of the day.

Anders threw things to the slaughter pigs so they had something to do. Shredded elderberry branches, turnips that they could roll across the floor and knotty, heavy fragments of rope that they pulled like playful puppies, their tails standing vertically, with abrupt hiccupping grunts that I swear were laughter. Anders stood there, smiling wide-eyed like a child.

"Just look at the little assholes."

I thought of Ellen. Living with a woman who wasn't my mother was new. When I walked into the bathroom just after she'd washed herself, I inhaled the steam still hanging in the air, saturated with her Lux soap and the new shampoo Anton had bought, its scent tinged with chamomile. I felt at once high from fever and lightning sharp. To my surprise, I began to crazily and feverishly seek out dark pubic hair in the drain. Stood in front of the mirror with my head tilted in an absurd, impossible attempt to recreate her naked reflection as it might have looked when she considered herself a half hour earlier. Perhaps she had touched her nipples, wearing only the loose jingling bracelets on her wrist and the leather cord with the smooth white mussel shell around her neck. The black hair between her legs moist after the shower.

I stopped whitewashing. Lowered my arm.

"How's it coming along?"

Anders had once again appeared in the white square of the barn door, and I nodded and waved, fished my cigarettes out of my back pocket. Unlike my parents, the brothers didn't care that I smoked, as long as I was careful with the butts and made sure to stamp them out completely with my heel.

"It's fine, Anders. Do you want one?"

I offered him the packet, and he carefully removed a cigarette with his big fingers.

"Thanks."

He leaned over the edge of the box, lit his own, and pointed at a young sow standing alone in the corner box. I could tell he was happy today. His movements were big and unrestrained, and his water-blue eyes clear.

"Boar-Clausen is coming today."

Everyone in the area knew Boar-Clausen. A guy who drove his truck around with a boar every time a sow was in heat and had to be seen to couldn't hide in a small town. The man himself was a bachelor and had a smaller, somewhat run-down farm at Ommestrup, but earned no money from it. It was too small, and Boar-Clausen was a farmer without the right knack, which everyone knew. But boars, he could figure out. I occasionally saw him at Feed Stuffs, where he stood with heavy, wheezing breath, talking nonsense with the other men. Afterward, he went home and shoved a pig with soccer-ball-sized testicles into his car, then drove out to his next customer. Sten almost always doubled over in laughter whenever we talked about him.

Anders didn't laugh. He stood so close to me that his scent mixed with the ones from the cowshed: pig, chalk wash, straw and dried clover. His bland mixture was of sweat and salt and something sweet that I only knew from him, and that I imagined was his own. Like we'd smelled as pack animals on the savannah before water and laundry. His short-sleeved work shirt was soft with smudges of fine dirt.

"So . . ." He pulled up his pants with one hand and cleared his throat, troubled.

Through the open door, I could hear the truck parking in the yard and its doors slamming. Men greeted each other with one-syllable words that grated on the ear. A brief conversation without superficial frills. I knew Anton well enough to know that in his business, all the practicalities were discussed first. Coffee was offered afterward if he decided to invite you in. Anders waved through the open stall door and trampled purposefully down the center aisle. Moved the wheelbarrow aside and put a few hay bales up to guard the feed bags.

Out in the yard, the truck's tailgate rattled, metal on metal, and Boar-Clausen cursed in his deep, gravelly voice. Cloven hooves had hit the loading ramp hard and unevenly.

"Dammit, not again!"

Anders had positioned himself by the young gilt's box with his hand on the bolt. Ready to open at the right moment and armed with the broom so he could push the gilt back if she tried to escape. The slaughter pigs had begun to squeal excitedly, and the mood was thick with anticipation. They could smell him, the stranger, and maybe what was about to happen, too. The beast finally appeared in the doorway. Enormous and hunched, with a body that was hard and lean under the coarse bristles, he was clearly eager. Knew exactly what to do, stumbling blindly ahead down the center aisle with white foam dripping from his mouth.

Behind him, Boar-Clausen walked with a rod, which he used to hit the swine on the sides as he shouted and whistled the boar down toward the gilt. If Boar-Clausen was embarrassed by his work, he hid it well. Silent with his jaw jutted forward, he gave Anders the sign to open the gate and the beast followed its snout, trudging directly into the young animal.

"Would you like to see it?"

Anders let his heavy forearms rest on the edge of the box while he followed the two pigs with his eyes. I positioned beside him, trying to look as relaxed as Boar-Clausen, who hopped over the partition and stood between the large animals. Rubbed the gilt on her back as he gazed inattentively out the window. The boar stuck his snout between the gilt's hind legs and fervently smacked his lips. The size difference between the two animals was terrifying. The boar was almost twice as large as the gilt, who stood there stiffly, her expression implying she was listening.

"That was the smallest . . . you had?" Anders said, tilting his head toward Boar-Clausen's truck in the yard. He moved his hands restlessly on the edge of the box.

"Him here? No, he's big, but the others are almost as big—I picked him 'cause he's usually good with the ladies. Not so aggressive. Since she's a gilt."

The balls on the boar were enormous. I'd seen such things before, of course, but they still managed to surprise me every time. Their weight and exposed position near the animal's ass. They rocked heftily when, with a start, it suddenly placed itself on the gilt's back. She stood still as stone.

"Looks like she's taking it well," said Boar-Clausen. It was nothing other than a dry statement of fact, and neither he nor Anders blinked an eye when the boar's thin, twisted penis swelled under his stomach. The boar thrust forward aimlessly and missed his target. The boar let himself fall; his hooves left two long, red marks down the gilt's sides, but she remained standing there, patient.

Anders clicked his tongue, and Boar-Clausen pushed the boar again with the rod, letting it slide along the animal's neck and then whacking it lightly on the side of its head to make it turn back toward the gilt.

"Come on, you big bastard. We don't have all day."

The boar jumped up again, huge testicles swinging underneath—a spastic jerk in the air. Boar-Clausen struck him on the back.

"You damned moron!"

He bent down breathlessly over his own large paunch, glaring at the boar's protruding dick. Then he moved laboriously onto his knees, grabbed the boar's cock and placed it between the gilt's dirty red flaps. The boar thrust again as the flesh under his pig bristles trembled. Slobbering and grunting, his snout was pressed against the gilt's neck for what seemed like an eternity.

I should have gone about my business, but it was impossible to look away now, and even if I could, it seemed more childish and embarrassing than staying. Neither of the men seemed to be bothered by it, but I felt a terrible, deep shame as the pig emptied itself, still with Boar-Clausen's hand around the root of his corkscrew cock, a tired-of-life expression on his face.

"That's her seen to," said Anders, clicking his tongue. "That's how it goes, Jacob. But you knew that well already?"

AFTER BOAR-CLAUS HAD gotten the boar back in the truck, drunk a cup of coffee, and driven off again, Anders rubbed the gilt's scratched back with cow udder cream. He mumbled low and comfortingly, smiling at me as the gilt leaned against him, letting him scratch her behind the ears. "A good boy," as my mother always said. "Anders is such a good boy."

But his body was sharp and hard under his shirt, as if he were made of wood and iron and stone.

I followed the old routines. Ducked when I walked under the door frame, set my shoes next to Anton's in the narrow hallway and continued on into the kitchen.

The old, thinly veneered cupboards and drawers had been replaced with gray laminate, and the smell of cigar smoke and some indeterminable dish with fried or cooked meat hung in the air. But there was also an acrid whiff of chlorine and vinegar and cleaning solution, which someone, probably a housekeeper, had brought with them from one of the nearby nursing homes. The steel sink was spotless, and a clean rag hung over the tap. There was now a woman in the house.

Anders sat at the modest dining table, back against the wall, looking lopsidedly out the window. He'd gotten thinner, cheekbones clearly protruding, and his skull seemed sharp under the bit of hair still on his head. There was no recognition in his eyes.

I offered him my hand without looking at him, and he accepted it without objection. His handshake was as lifeless as the rest of him.

"Jacob is here," said Anton loudly as he rattled the coffee machine. "He's come to help us."

Anders nodded. Reached for his cup and overturned it so cold coffee ran over the tablecloth and down onto the soft linoleum. I turned around and got the dishrag from the sink. Got onto my knees and patted around the worn, woolen slippers while Anders sat motionless, staring at me, his eyes nothing but troubled glimpses into the hollows of his skull.

"Thanks."

Anton took the coffeepot to the kitchen table and poured water into the machine. Opened a can and spooned bitter-smelling coffee into the filter with shaking hands.

LATER, WHEN ANDERS had been settled in the living room with the television turned on, Anton and I sat alone in the darkening kitchen.

"You still look like yourself," he said. "I recognized you right away. You just look a little tired. You're not sick, are you?"

"I'm an old man, Anton. Just like you."

I tried to laugh, but of course it wasn't funny, and he didn't smile, either. He just continued to stare as though he had to make sure it was really me.

"It's not that," he said. The way he was looking at me made me feel like a child again, defiant and defensive.

"I was just a kid when you knew me, Anton," I said lightly. "It'd be odd if nothing had happened to me in the meantime."

"Yes." He hesitated, as if wanting to protest. "You have a wife and children?"

I nodded without meeting his gaze.

"Right. It was nice of you to come, after all this time," he said.

"Of course." Sweat had pasted my shirt to my back and stomach. This bloody heat. "And it's Ellen that we have to find?"

Anton nodded, and his eyes finally left me. The edge of his large hand stroked the oilcloth, carefully collecting a pile of nonexistent crumbs. He coughed from somewhere deep down in his chest.

"Yes. Anders has begun to ask for her. Høgh. That was her surname," he said.

I took my little notebook out of my jacket pocket and wrote down her name, mostly so I had something to do. *Ellen Høgh.* Then I opened my laptop and placed it on the table. Anton was silent, and I gave him some time. After all, he was an old man. But apparently, he had nothing else to say.

"She could have gone off to college," I said carefully. "She wasn't that old."

"It's true, she wasn't. Twenty-nine. She could certainly have gone to college. She spoke about it at one point, at least."

I typed her name into the browser search box. There was no match on the full name, but quite a few for either Ellen or Høgh articles and Krak references for both. I selected the image search only, and the screen filled with unknown faces of all ages. I believed I'd recognize her if she were there. But there was nothing.

She could have married and changed her name—be dead, or be living a life off of the online radar. But I suspected that such a person as lively as Ellen would have left even a single beckoning clue somewhere in cyberspace. If nothing else, in the form of a few words on the screen. It was just a matter of finding that gateway.

I smiled at Anton.

"But you've no idea where she could've gone? Family or friends?"

He shook his head.

"She was from Aarhus and named Ellen Høgh. That's all I know," he repeated. "She didn't say where she was going. Didn't even say goodbye, but there could be quite a few reasons for that."

That sharp look again, as if he was trying to catch every single one of the movements in my face and body. The corners of his mouth twitched a little, and in the living room, Anders had turned up the volume on a talk show with an enthusiastic, clapping audience.

I thought of warm blood in my mouth and nose, the stench of pigs and chicken shit. I knew what he was thinking, what he was trying to get me to say, but I'd come, and that had to be enough.

Everything has its limits.

THE LIGHT IN Anders's old attic was softened by the dense spiderweb in the skylight window. A remodel in the '60s had left the room with sloping walls in a dark-yellow pine with knots like black raisin eyes.

I couldn't remember ever being up here as a boy. Anton and Anders had used the narrow staircase behind the door in the hall when they had come down from their one-and-a-half-hour naps. It had apparently been a long time since they'd been up here; there was a lingering mildewy smell of disuse and rodents. A thick, sticky layer of dust covered the single bookcase and the old television, standing with the antenna cable dangling loosely over the room's only source of light: a floor lamp with a green-lacquered metal shade.

The room was microscopic. The bed was squeezed under the sloping wall, and the end wall consisted of four brown-veneered cupboards that had been cut according to the falling ceiling height.

I sat down on the bed and felt the fatigue overtake me. As if I'd run five or six miles. For dinner, we'd had the two servings delivered to the brothers every day, which Anton heated in a microwave on the kitchen table. Powdered mashed potatoes, green peas and pork chops in a dark, sour sauce. Anton also found some canned food in the cupboard: a tin of minced beef and a jar of potatoes, which I heated while Anton helped Anders eat, one painstaking mouthful at a time. Half a beer in an old mustard jar. For dessert, we had soft, dark-yellow cherry plums from the tree by the gable.

Downstairs, the brothers puttered around, following the steps of their joint bedtime ritual. The toilet flushed, and the water ran in the sink. Someone, probably Anton, growled something, and the floorboards creaked under the weight of the two old men seeking their beds for the night. Anton had moved into Great-Grandmother's old bedroom, while a bed had been made up for Anders in what had once been the good living room. It was because the stairs had become too steep. And because they were saving energy, as Anton had said. Both the heating and their own.

I waited until it was quiet before I crept down to the kitchen and got a beer from the fridge. Then I went out to the yard, where the cobblestones were still warm from the sun under my bare feet. The evening sky above me was velvet-black and strewn with the kind of stars you didn't see in the city. Ice-cold, clear perforations of darkness.

I walked through the tall grass by the gable, where there was once a path to the garden, and stood there for a while. The new road had eaten the tangled hedge of red currants and elderflower and nettles at the bottom border of the formerly abundant soil, but the stump of the large chestnut tree had been allowed for some reason to remain as an amputated memento on the edge of the roadside drainage ditch. There was also the little pavilion in imitation timber, the upper half door open, and I could sense the flowers on the wallpaper, resembling black splotches of mold on the walls in the dark inside. I remembered them so clearly from back then. Deep rose and picture-perfect, around abandoned garden chairs with rotten cushions on the floor.

I pulled one of the chairs outside and sat down. Listened.

There was a longer time between cars and trucks on the bypass road, islands of silence in the dark.

I typed in the number for Bjarne. My company partner. Soon to be an ex, like the wife. I knew he'd already looked at the possibilities of buying my share, and thus far had asked me to stay out of things.

I didn't call, just like I'd stopped myself when I'd run over Janne's number with my fingertips for God knew what time. Reminded myself how little I'd liked her the day she first entered the office. There was an instinctive reluctance that I'd have held on to if I'd been wiser. I'd had several near-fatal experiences with her very kind. Petite and dark-haired, poisonously sharp-eyed with bizarre, defiantly girlish manners. She smacked chewing gum, moody and pouting. Crimson-red Marilyn Monroe lipstick, a blouse and a neat skirt—'50s retro—and a self-importance as unbecoming as an all-too-sharp fashion choice on a young woman. I didn't like her and couldn't take my eyes off her, which should have been warning enough. But she wasn't one of those girls who made it easy. She greeted me nicely and was seated at an open desk by a window, looking out over Kultorvet, which she immediately opened and leaned out of. Her transparent black stockings had a nice, strong seam that I was able to follow from her dark-green shoes with a heel up to the edge of her tight, gray-pilled skirt.

I stubbed my cigarette into the ground and went out onto the road toward the dazzling white car lights. A few miles farther down was the new on-ramp to the freeway, with new asphalt and white reflex strips. The unmistakable odor of human waste wafted up from the ditch, and long strips of semidissolved toilet paper lay in the dry grass. Last time I'd stood here, cows had grazed just a few yards away, and Ellen had sat with her sketchbook in her lap under a now long-ago-felled tree. Head laid back, eyes closed. Her neck smooth and flawless, a hand resting on the bent knee and slightly spread legs, even though she was wearing a dress and knew I was there. I felt the burning ache and the rage adjacent to it, because she was doing it on purpose.

Or wasn't.

Both were biting defeat in a battle she won, dozing lightly under the chestnut tree.

1 9 7 8

"Is she living here?"

Sten and I were sitting on the stone steps to the stable, watching Ellen. It was the first time she'd left the house in four days, and now she was standing barefoot in the middle of the yard, playing with Soffi as if it were the most natural thing in the world. She was wearing a pair of loose long pants and one of the brothers' checked shirts, which almost reached her knees, and when she turned around with her arms out to the side, the shirt unfolded like a sail in the wind.

"I don't know," I said. "Anton hasn't said anything about it."

"Nice?"

I shrugged. It wasn't a good idea to share your innermost thoughts with Sten. You never knew what he got out of them, and there was something in him that I didn't understand. Sudden inclinations that consumed him briefly from within. Snail races. Playing cards with naked women. Fishing trips to Følle Strand, where we never caught a thing. And then there were the dangerous ones, like when he'd stabbed a pencil into the buttocks of a first grader he'd caught in the schoolyard and thrown over his shoulder. He did it again and again as the boy screamed and fought, tearing desperately at Sten's hair, and he probably would have done it a few times more if it hadn't been for the teacher on recess duty, who freed the boy and furiously hurled Sten to the ball wall. Sten just laughed while he saw to his punishment.

"She looks nice," he said, pursing his lips. And then, as if he'd thought of something, "Look at these."

He took a jelly jar out of his jacket pocket and held it up against the light. Two smooth, blue-white lumps, each about the size of a walnut, slid along the edge of the jar as he slowly turned it around.

"Gross."

He unscrewed the lid from the jar and stuck it right under my nose.

"Cut it out!"

I pushed his hand so hard he nearly dropped the jar, then pulled it back with an offended expression. Anders and Anton had castrated seven piglets that morning. Just hearing the screams from the stalls had made me nauseous and put me into a cold sweat, but naturally, Sten couldn't stay away. He'd sniffed around it like a dog would a dung heap.

Ellen had found a stick that she was throwing for Soffi, but the dog didn't understand the game and remained there, stupid and happy, sniffing her hands. She looked over at us and laughed.

"Hey, Soffi!"

Sten put his thumb and middle finger in his mouth and whistled sharply, then reached out a flat hand. Soffi came running, wagging her tail a little hesitantly. He had once bitten her ear for fun, and she hadn't forgotten it. He stuck his fingers into the jar and fished out one of the testicles. The gleaming lump was covered in a clear, red juice, and its white flossy tail clung to his wrist.

"Would you like a treat?" he said. "Come and get a treat from Uncle Sten."

He stuck the lump in Soffi's face and pulled it back again, then pressed it into the licorice-black snout before finally letting her sink her teeth into it and slowly pull it from his hand. Soffi wagged her tail in thanks before running to the other side of the stables, her teeth still gently closed around the lump.

"What was that?"

Ellen, who had come over to us, looked for the dog, and Sten smiled pleasantly.

"A little delicacy," he said. "You should try it sometime. They taste best when you lick them."

She sent me a quick, questioning look, which I didn't dare return. I fervently wished Sten had stayed away. Ellen walked back over the yard to the cow fence, where she pulled up long tufts of grass as she snuck in to visit the munching animals.

"She's hot," said Sten. "How old is she?"

"I don't know."

"If she stays here all summer, you may be allowed to find out. There's nothing wrong with an older woman. Nothing at all."

"Shut your mouth, Sten."

He fell quiet and sat there pouting, poking an earwig between the cobblestones. He'd gotten it to raise the hind part of its body and snip hot-temperedly with the little pincers on its ass. There had been no news on Lise. He never said anything and I didn't ask, but he looked tired. Had been alone with the chickens until two o'clock in the morning, he said. There was still vaporized chicken shit in his hair and under his nails.

"And here comes the retard."

He straightened up and pointed, then sniggered like he always did when he wanted to draw attention to something that wasn't really funny. A younger boy who had fallen over and had hurt himself in the schoolyard. Or someone who had dropped their lunch. Without fail, he'd nudge someone with that idiotic snigger as though we were still twelve years old. I hated when he did it in school, and I hated it now.

"Look," he said. "Anders is in love."

Anders had gone over to Ellen. He had picked some strawberries, which he offered her with a flat hand and lowered eyes. Sten laughed and made a quick movement with his hand over his crotch.

"What do you think Anders does with girls?" he asked. "Has there ever been anyone?"

There was something both hurtful and curious in his eyes. Sten's own success with girls was limited—it was those teeth and the fact that he was so small. His dick was still microscopic and almost hairless.

"Think about it," he said. "A whole life without any . . . Do you think he does it with the pigs?"

Again that stammering laugh, asking for trouble, that I could never quite manage.

"Shut up. You're disgusting," I said.

I could tell I was getting angry. Not only because of what Sten said, but also because of what had happened in the yard. Ellen's hand on Anders's shoulder while she chose and ate a berry with the other. She should take better care of herself, keep more of a distance, because just like with Sten, there was something about Anders that was incomprehensible. He stood there, towering over her like a giant.

Ellen turned around and looked at me. Smiled and waved us over, but we both stayed sitting. Sten cast me a sidelong glance. Took a packet of cigarettes out of his back pocket and lit one without offering me any. His cheeks went completely hollow when he took a drag.

"Maybe Anders isn't so stupid to girls when it comes down to it."

LATER, WHEN STEN had finally pedaled home, I pulled off my T-shirt in the narrow bathroom. Filled the washbasin, lathered my hair, face and upper body with a washcloth and soap and rinsed off with boiling hot water. Then I went into the living room and rummaged around in my bag for a clean T-shirt.

The door to Great-Grandmother's room was ajar, but I didn't

give it a second thought until I heard weak scratching against the wallpaper and a coat hook on the floor. A shift of weight and something moving.

"Hello?"

There was no answer. Only silence, as if both I and the person on the other side of the wall were holding our breath. Then I walked silently over to the entrance and pushed the door open.

Anders was standing in front of the bed. Unmoving, his arms hanging heavily by his sides. He still had on the overalls he usually wore in the pigpen, pant legs shrouding his stockinged feet. Light fell through the yellowish-white lace curtains, drawing gray shadows on the wall over the short double bed. The bedspread and comforter were pulled aside, and there was a creased hollow in the middle of the pillow, as if someone had just rested their head there.

"Oh, it's you."

He nodded, turned toward the bed and pulled the comforter and bedspread into place. Clapped it once with a flat hand and walked past me, his head lowered. I heard his wooden clogs on the stairs and farther out on the bumpy cobblestones to the pigpen.

1978

Sten's room was floating at the edges, the floor was rocking and on Sten's bed lay Toad, waiting. Completely still. All of a sudden, I saw that she was half-naked. A blouse, one of those thin, tight-fitting ones in an angry orange, but no pants, and she was lying on her back with one leg over the edge of the bed. The eyes were completely black in the dark under the sloped roof, and the place between her legs was hidden in shadow. My dick was sore, confined, and needed to be freed from my pants, but I was in Sten's room, and someone could come in and see us together. Someone could reveal and humiliate me. Nobody stuck it up into the Toad.

"Utzon!"

A hand on my shoulder and darkness around me. The first thing I sensed was the gray square of the living room window in the middle of all the black. I had to touch the rough cushions of the sofa before I realized where I was. That I was lying on the sofa in Anders and Anton's living room.

"Utzon!"

A pale face hovered over me, and although I knew it had to be Ellen because she'd called me Utzon, I didn't answer. The terror and bizarre sadness of the dream weighed heavily on me.

"Are you awake, Jacob?"

It felt different when she said my real name. More serious. And now I could see she was fully dressed: long pants and a loose white shirt that made her almost luminescent in the dark. She smelled like nighttime and lilies.

"What's happening?"

I sat up with the blanket still around me, suddenly embarrassed that I was wearing only underwear. Checkered ones that were a bit too small. My shorts were across the room on the chair. Far beyond my reach.

"I need your help with something," she said. "It won't take long, I promise."

I folded the blanket around my waist, noticing how my stiff cock was trapped embarrassingly in my tight underpants.

"Of course . . . yeah."

I rooted around for my clothes with my free hand and pulled on my shorts, standing with my back to her. My fingers were weak and clumsy after sleep. I pulled a T-shirt and sweatshirt over my head on my way to the kitchen, and when I'd stuck my feet into Anton's shoes, she put a hand on my shoulder and opened the door into the summer night.

"**WHAT ARE WE** doing?"

She threw a quick glance over her shoulder and started walking down the road in bare feet as she shook a little in the cool air.

"I still have some things down there," she said lowly. "My money and some . . . some personal things."

I caught up to her in three steps, awaiting further explanation, but she didn't seem to want to say any more at the moment. The problem had to be the ex-boyfriend. The long-haired hippie. He'd shouted at her and was probably responsible for the bleeding upper lip she'd had that day she'd been thrown out into the yard. I was sure I was taller than him, maybe stronger, too, and the thought of potentially having to fight him made my blood pump hot and fast.

There was something frightening about real fights. The serious ones, where people got beaten up and everything happened so fast. I'd only seen two of that kind in my entire life. One was in the schoolyard between Steffen and Mogens. At first, it had been quite normal. Mogens had said something smart about Steffen's mother without knowing she'd just died. A mistake that cost Mogens two front teeth and a bent rib. Steffen had kept on beating him, even though he was lying down, the sound of fists on bloody skin ringing loudly. Like when we smacked a wet blob of clay to mold it. And then there'd been when those two guys had stumbled out from a bar in the middle of the afternoon and begun to fight wildly, swinging their arms, until finally an uppercut knocked one backward and he cracked his head on the flagstones.

Neither of those fights resembled the slow, lazy tests of strength that Sten, Jørgen, Flemming and I gave in to, two and two, when boredom got the better of us in the boys' bathroom. One of us would inevitably be toppled onto his back while the others held his arms and legs tight, every muscle tense with resistance, a few quick jerks to get away and then long, sweaty pauses with heavy breathing and plenty of ridicule. "Wimp," and "You want your mommy?" and "What are you going to do now, cry?" An oozing blob of spit on the loser's throat and collarbones to complete the humiliation. Sharp, stinging slaps on the check that flared for half an hour.

"Thanks for coming with me." She smiled, but her attention was somewhere in front of us.

"I've always been afraid of the dark—it's so scary to wake up in the middle of the night," she said. "It's always a thought. Do you know what I mean? Whatever you think about at three o'clock in the morning is always terrible."

I shook my head and threw a stone between a pair of whispering beech trees. Found a stick lying like a thick, black snake in the grass and picked it up. It sat nicely in my hand, and I felt better about everything after hitting the heads of some gray-black thistles in the ditch. A knot of little toads crawled across the road in front of us on their stumpy, thin legs, and we had to step carefully so as not to crush any of them.

Ellen stopped to listen.

"A nightingale," she said. "Can you hear it? It's down in the bog."

We stood still, listening to its soft tones in the dark. I was starting to freeze a little now, as the cold dew settled on my bare arms.

"There," said Ellen, pointing. "It's just down there."

In a hollow in the curve before us, a warm, flaming flicker appeared by the dark trees and the house behind. I knew the place well. The houses in Pinderup stood with their backs to the forest and the stone wall that had once been built in the woods by the neighborhood's hunched farmers. My father had told me how all the stones in the yard had been plowed from the earth and gathered in piles that grew, year after year, in the damp, overgrown corners of the fields. Then, at some point, the farmers built fences with them so the animals in the common pasture didn't escape into the woods.

A campfire had been lit in the commune's neglected front yard. The flames were as tall as a man and smelled of burned rubber because someone had rolled a car tire halfway into the fire, where it glowed and pulsed like slow-flowing lava. As we got closer, I could hear singing and weak audio from a radio or tape recorder. A pair of long shadows danced on the wall of the house.

"Stay here," said Ellen. "I'll be back in a moment."

I remained standing in the cover of darkness and a very fragrant elderberry bush, watching Ellen's slight, fluttering figure disappear around the back of the house. I could see she'd turned the light on inside, but none of the people swaying slowly by the fire reacted. I recognized the boyfriend, Karsten, among the others. He had lost the shirt and was painting wide, dark stripes on his cheeks and down over his bare chest. A cigarette glowed at the corner of his mouth as he hummed and moved around the campfire. He threw his head back in a wild jerk. Behind the fire, I caught a glimpse of a group of young people with beer in hand and a couple of children, around six or seven years old, who sat poking the flames with long sticks as they leaned in, whispering secrets to one another.

The mosquitoes had begun to buzz around me because I was standing so still. One had already settled on my throat, and I slapped it instinctively, although my father always said it was best to let them be. I suddenly had to pee, but Ellen was nowhere to be seen, and someone had turned the music up. The women had begun to dance. They weren't so young, with sizable tummies and breasts, and danced in short judders as if constantly colliding with something hard, interrupting the movement they had begun. Their long, loose hair fell heavy and glossy around their pale moon faces.

Karsten was gone. Where he'd been dancing, a lanky boy in jeans was dragging a carton of beer through the grass to the group of teenagers. There were screams and shouts, an apelike jungle choir in the velvety-soft air.

Where was she? Uneasy, I looked at the illuminated window, but there was no visible movement there.

"Hey, man!"

I jumped. The music had been so loud that I hadn't registered anything before someone put a hand on my shoulder.

"Alone in the dark, comrade? Where'd you come from?"

Karsten stood behind me, looking like he was about to keel over; I involuntarily pulled back a little. Not because he seemed threatening—in fact, he was smiling crookedly as he heaved his tight jeans all the way up and zipped them with a firm grip on the waistband. He'd obviously been out to pee. But there was the sharp smell of alcohol and something else about him, stoned and strange. The eyes that both saw me and didn't. Once you've lived with an alcoholic all your life, it's easy to recognize the signs of an out-of-control stupor.

"What are you hanging out around here for?" he said.

I didn't know what to say. I just stood there, feeling my face turn red as I looked around for Ellen. She still hadn't come back.

"Do you want to come sit with us?" He rested a hand on my shoulder again. "Guests are welcome. You don't get too many of them out here in Boo-country."

He grinned a little to himself, like he'd said something incredibly funny, grabbed my arm, and pulled me into the flickering light of the fire. The two boys had thrown a plastic tub onto the flames. It melted slowly as black smoke drifted across the ground.

"Ugh!"

He pulled me out of the path of the smoke and sat down on a piece of severed tree trunk that had been placed by the fire.

"Come, sit and relax." He slapped the space next to him, and I obliged reluctantly. The trunk was damp and slimy under my bare thighs, but I didn't dare stand back up. I just sat there and watched the others dance across the fire from us.

I recognized a couple of the teenagers from school around the beer carton. They were about four or five years older than me. One of them was the big brother of Anna, a girl in my class. A beefy guy with a bowl cut, fluffy sideburns and tight jeans. I saw the others around regularly, too, in the students' center and the cafeteria. The girls worked at the nearby retirement home, I guessed. The five who sat there were part of the age group that had been left in the town while the rest went off to Aarhus or Randers or Rønde for high school or business school. And, as though to emphasize that point, Anna's brother lifted his beer and blew a long, deep note over the neck of the bottle that ended with a thunderstorm of a fart, which caused the entire group to roll around laughing.

They drank like alcoholics.

None of them seemed to have noticed me. Only one little boy watched me long and persistently, the wide, dark eyes in his pale face illuminated by his homemade torch.

"Do you want a smoke?"

Karsten handed me a little packet of hand-rolled cigarettes, long and thin in gray paper, and I accepted without really wanting to. I should have left, but Ellen hadn't come out yet, and she was why I was there. If it really was that she was afraid to go home alone.

Ellen's boyfriend had lit a cigarette for himself and apparently sunk into his own train of thought while watching the dancers. We sat there for a while without saying anything. The cigarette tasted sweet and spicy and good because I'd started to freeze in spite of the heat from the fire. The mosquitoes had found me again, too, and I slapped a few on my thighs, fidgeting.

"We're red," he said suddenly, pointing at a slightly stocky young man with the tip of his cigarette. "He looks beefy enough to be a communist, doesn't he? Those round cheeks . . ."

I laughed politely, but it didn't seem like he'd said it for fun. Or to me, for that matter. He just sat there, stone-faced and staring.

The slightly too-large guy was still dancing with the ladies. His long hair smacked his round face hard, the whites of his eyes were very white and his gaze seemed to have moved on to me. I suddenly felt dizzy. Hovered a little over the rotten trunk I'd been sitting on.

"Is there something wrong with him?" I carefully formulated the words with my lips, but my voice was distorted.

Karsten didn't answer. He leaned forward and rested his head in his hands. I could smell him very clearly. His hair was so greasy that a cross-parting had materialized, maggot white in the midst of the thick, curly strands. I turned away, forcing myself to look at the guy by the fire again. His pupils had slid up under his eyelids and his mouth was open. He was no longer dancing in time with the drummed rhythm.

"Hey," I said again. Much louder this time. "Is there something wrong with him?"

The guy by the fire lost his balance, falling forward heavily.

Away from the fire and half over one of the younger boys. The boy pulled away quickly, his little face vexed and distorted by pain. He whispered something to his brother, and the two boys disappeared into the darkness.

The man remained outstretched with his face in the wet grass.

The way he was lying there wasn't right. My father hadn't acted so strangely even during his worst trips—I wasn't sure if the guy could breathe. I felt like I was being suffocated myself as I looked on. My mouth was dry, my heart banging against my ribs with its own little hammer.

None of the adults seemed to have noticed the crashing fall. The two women half sat, half lay on a quilt next to the guy. One lit a match, shielded it with her hand and let the other one, the blonde, light her cigarette with the flame. The blonde suckled the cigarette like a baby would its bottle, pouted and blew fancy smoke rings into the summer night.

I got up on unsteady legs and went over to the guy who had fallen. He was still lying motionless with his face to the ground. It wasn't natural to fall like he had, without defending yourself. I got down on my knees, gently took hold of his shoulder, and pulled him over onto his back. A dark splotch had spread across the front of the tight velvet pants, and he stank of warm piss, but he was breathing deeply through his half-open mouth. He had a home-made ring in his ear, steel wire wrapped around a titmouse feather and stuck through the lobe.

"What's your name, anyway?"

I turned my head. Karsten was sitting, looking at us with narrowed eyes. I looked around for Ellen again, but something about it was all wrong. There were colors in the dark that I'd never seen before.

"Utzon," I said, wanting to get up. Wanting to go home.

Just then, I felt a violent pressure on my Adam's apple. The force of it was so painful and sudden that at first I thought I'd been hit by something. Struck in the throat with a club. But then I was being pulled backward, and I instinctively reached out behind me so as not to overbalance. My hands groped over warm, wet velvet pants and skin. Then the guy moved, toppled backward, and I fell backward, too, and landed on him, still with his hands gripping my throat.

I uttered a kind of muted grunt, but my organs and vocal cords had no air, and the rest of the fight was a silent struggle as I wrestled, trying to loosen his fingers and free myself with wild, directionless blows. He was kneeling behind me, my head in his lap, face over mine and a black, unconscious look. His mouth, still open, was breathing heavily, and a thin thread of saliva hung from it.

Air.

I had to breathe, but there was only that terrible pressure in my chest and his wild, black-as-coal eyes floating just above me.

"Don't touch me," he whispered.

"Sorry."

It hurt to spit out the word, and dark spots formed at the sides of my vision. I slipped into the outer edge of consciousness; sounds washed over me like waves and retreated again.

A shout. Angry voices.

Then I felt a jerk and my head thumped to the ground, making the same sound as falling apples. The grip on my neck was loosened and the pressure in my chest and head stung briefly before subsiding, leaving only a strong throbbing pulse in my temples. I breathed in painful, irregular gasps.

Karsten had grabbed the guy's shoulders and pulled him away. Shoved him, shouting in his face. "Let go. Let go, dammit." And behind him, the two women, petrified, hands in front of their mouths. A child screamed.

On the ground, in the wet grass, the guy turned onto his side, curled up and vomited.

"Ugh! Disgusting." Ellen's boyfriend looked away.

I was helped up onto my trembling legs and felt an uncomfortable damp spot in my underpants. I didn't know what to say, so I just took a hesitant step in the direction of the road.

"Hey, you." Karsten patted me hard on the arms like you do with someone who's just come up out of ice-cold water. Pat, pat, pat. "He's just having a bad trip. You don't look too good yourself. Stay here for a few minutes so you can . . ."

He took a deep breath, spread his arms and exhaled. Smiled encouragingly. Already had a new, sweet-smelling cigarette in his mouth. My heart pounded. My breath was warm and putrid. My throat hurt, too. There was something wrong, something wrong with me, and I had to get away now. I staggered in the direction of the road and began to walk. One foot rambling in front of the other.

SHE CAUGHT UP to me in the dark and hugged me hard.

"I'm sorry," she said. "I shouldn't have asked you to come. He's really crazy."

Cool fingertips over my face.

"Sorry, Utzon. Sorry, sorry, sorry."

I almost lost my balance and reached out for her. My hands brushed the fabric over her breasts, and for a short, quivering moment, she stiffened and stood leaning against me. As if she was waiting for something. My thumb slipped over her nipple. Again.

Then she uncoiled herself, took my hand and pulled me on.

1 9 7 8

I woke up late with a brutal, shooting headache.

The door to Great-Grandmother's room was open for the first time since Ellen had moved in, and the bed had been made up with neat, sharp folds. The windows to the garden were wide open, and the thin curtains fluttered over the boys and girls in white porcelain on the windowsill. I could see her bag, shoved under the bed. The thick green wool coat was on a hanger on the edge of the darkly varnished wardrobe. Most important, she was still here.

The feeling of her warm, pert breast was still on my fingertips, as if I had developed a new set of senses for things that were no longer there. I had to find out exactly where she was now, whether she was happy or sad. Hear her voice. I looked around quickly and noted that my shorts and T-shirt had fallen haphazardly in the brothers' bookcase. My new Adidas sweatshirt was nowhere to be seen, and I half remembered the grass and dirt on my bare arms while I'd tried to free myself. I must have gotten out of the pullover one way or the other. I swore at myself. It had cost a fortune.

It was almost ten, and the breakfast things had been cleared, apart from a lonely plate with two pieces of dry bread and an empty coffee cup. Outside, the sun shone warmly, and white clouds drifted slowly over the glistening roof of the stable.

I took burned coffee from the pot and sat at the table under the loudly ticking clock. It hurt to swallow the coffee, and I was sure

it was going to hurt even more to eat, but I was so hungry. After
a minute, I carefully peeled off a soft bit of white bread, chewed
it thoroughly and flushed it down my sore throat with a small
sip of coffee. I was tired and felt pins and needles in my face—
an unusual sensation, since I usually only had them in my foot
when it fell asleep. I had a long, thin cut on my forearm,
undoubtedly an injury from my encounter with the elderberry
bush I'd waded through in my panicked escape. Apart from that,
I felt pretty okay.

"Utzon, are you awake?"

I didn't recognize her when she came into the kitchen. Her
clothes were the same as when she'd arrived—checked shirt and
bell bottoms—but from the neck up, she was a different person.
Gone was her long hair, and her dark-blue gaze peered out from
under a machine-trimmed crown. She let her hand slide over the
fluffy crop and smiled sleepily.

"New architecture," she said. "Don't you think it highlights the
vertical lines of the throat and accentuates the dome of the skull?"

She turned her head so I could see her in profile, and I
couldn't remember ever looking at a woman like that before.
She smelled like something sweet and appetizing that I couldn't
put my finger on.

"I'm so sorry about last night," she said. "I didn't think it would
be like that. They're normally really nice—they only party like that
once in a while."

I nodded, still struggling not to stare at her crew cut. She looked
like a boy, yet not at all. It was as if the masculine hairstyle highlighted her soft femininity. Her narrow face, the big eyes behind
her glasses and her soft, full lips. Her neck that was sleek and
curved and made me think of a swan's down. The beautiful, cruel
cheekbones came into their own now, too. I tried to catch her eye,
but she didn't notice, and I wondered for a brief moment if it was
something I'd imagined. Her breast under my hand and the

expectant look. The silence in both of us. A kind of defiant chal-
lenge. Or maybe just doubt.

She moved around the room, easy and carefree. Rummaged
with the coffee machine and turned on the radio. "Rose" by Sebas-
tian, who'd made his bed.

"Did you find what you went there to get?" I asked, but she
looked away. Let her hand slide back over the crew-cut hair.

"Forget it, Utzon," she said. "And for God's sake, forget those
funny cigarettes. Oh God, I'm really sorry. You won't say anything
to Anton, will you?"

I shook my head.

"Nothing happened," I muttered.

"Hey." She lifted up my chin with her index finger and looked into
my eyes, just like my mother did when I pouted or felt sick or sad.

"You and I, we have a disgusting and cruel task today. Follow me."

ELLEN STOOD IN the chicken yard, arms outstretched, study-
ing the horde of squawking birds flocking around our feet. It was
hot, even though we were in the shade, and her smile was somewhere between laughter and unease.

"Look at them." She sighed. "How are we supposed to do this?
I love chickens, Utzon. They're so much fun to watch. I feel like a
commander in a concentration camp."

I wiped my forehead on my sleeve. I was already beginning to
sweat.

"Have you never done it?"

I nodded toward the chopping block and she laughed.

"No." And then, as if it had suddenly dawned on her, "I don't
know what you're supposed to do. All this is foreign to me, Utzon.
But I'm a quick study! Anton said we have to take the red ones.
They're the oldest. You can see it on their feet—they're not so nice.
So . . . the three red chickens with the ugliest feet will die."

She pointed to a red hen standing by a clump of nettles, picking hot-temperedly at the last unraveled remains of a brownish rat skull.

"We'll take that one, then," I said, driving the hen toward the fence. Its long neck moved in rigid jerks, and it raised its voice from a cluck to a frightened cackle as it stuck its head through the holes in the chicken wire and pushed against it, flapping its wings. Around us, the chicken farm had become a torrent and screech of panic-stricken chickens, geese and turkeys. I reached out for the chicken, grabbed a wing and held on tight.

"First step accomplished!" I said triumphantly. Ellen made a V with both hands over her head, like a soccer player who'd just scored a goal.

"Are you used to this?" she asked.

I shook my head. "But I've seen my friend do it a few times. They have a chicken farm."

I'd never cared for the way Sten killed them. He didn't use an axe, but held the chicken into his body with one arm as he tickled them under the beak or scratched their comb or stroked them over the eye with the hand he held the knife in. *There, there, little chick.* They couldn't understand anything, of course, but still. He always put on such an act. And Sten had a penchant for unfeeling destruction. Slid the knife blade at a slant down through the animal's throat so the head popped off like the cork of a champagne bottle in the black-and-white movies aired on New Year's Eve.

I placed the chicken on the chopping block so its throat was stretched taut and its body slightly lifted, and waited until it was completely calm, staring back at us. Ellen gripped the axe as I held the animal tight.

"What do you think she's thinking about?" she asked.

"Do it now."

She lifted the axe.

"Anton and Anders have fed it every day of its life. It thought it had a good idea of what people were like, but now we're killing it. Experiences lie."

"Come on!"

She sent me a half smile and wiped her eyes before grabbing the axe again with both hands and swinging it hard. It came down precisely on its mark. I took hold of the decapitated head by its pale comb and threw it down to Soffi, who stood beside us, wagging her tail.

"From the queen's table."

There was blood on the chopping block, and more dripping from the open neck cavity. I held the body away from me, my arm outstretched, so I didn't get any on my clothes as the headless animal leaked the last bit of life from its body.

"And what about you?" I said. "How'd you really end up out here on Heinrich Dünscheisse's field?"

Ellen shot me a look of surprise. Grinning, her eyes still shiny.

"Dünscheisse? Where in the world did you pick up that sort of German, Utzon? Maybe you're a little too smart for all this. And I'm the adult here."

Disquiet ran through my body, and I had to move to let it out so I wouldn't explode. I made a few sportsmanlike swings with my arms, stretching my sore muscles.

AFTERWARD, WE EACH sat on a chair in the yard, plucking the dead chickens over steamy buckets of scalding water. She cast me a sidelong glance.

"Do you draw? Since you're going to be an architect?"

"A little."

I thought of the sketchbook in my backpack: page after page of stark naked women, pussies and breasts. It suddenly all seemed so childish and unprofessional. I doubted Michelangelo or Schiele or Picasso had painted with a hard-on like I did.

"I draw a lot myself," she said. "We could go out together some-day, if you want?"

The warm, wet down clung to my hands and forearms. The smell in the air was of burned meat and feathers, as well as the soaked newspapers, which we'd put under the tubs. Anton came out with a kitchen knife and cut the first of the pale chicken bodies open just above its hindquarters. He showed us how our hands should slide up along the breastbone and loosen the wind-pipe and esophagus, pull out the violet entrails, together with the rock-hard gizzard, the liver and the little black-green gallbladder, which for the love of God wasn't to burst. A skinny, gray-striped mother cat circled around us with her wispy kittens before running off with the gizzard in her mouth. Ellen laughed and absentmind-edly drew a wide, bloody stroke down her cheek.

We rinsed off our hands and arms in a bucket of soapy water that Anton had carried out to us, and all three of us sat on the staircase afterward, smoking, as we stared at the bare cadavers on the baking tray. I placed myself close to Ellen so that our bare legs touched. When she moved, I could feel the warm, gentle pres-sure against my skin, and I couldn't think of anything other than her elbow against my thigh and the warm twinge in my shorts.

It was so blessedly calm in my head.

LATER, I SAW them walking out across the field. Anton and Ellen. I watched them from a distance as they walked side by side, only their upper bodies visible over the soft green veil of barley. Anton marked off the lark nests in advance of the arrival of the combine harvester from the machine station. He planted tall, thin sticks with red fabric strips that fluttered under the ragged sky.

Ellen walked with her head tilted, but once in a while she turned her face toward Anton and moved her hands and arms in fast, eager movements, explaining something or other to him. And although I wasn't close enough to see her face, I was sure she was laughing.

I already knew exactly how that sounded. There was a slight hoarseness in that laugh that I knew and could replay in my head, just like the guitar solo from "Stairway to Heaven." I had her inside me.

"God, it's heavy today!"

The housekeeper slammed the door to the bathroom behind her, obstinate and ruddy from the heat and steam. She was still barefoot, her loose harem pants rolled up over her knees. Her sweater was soaked through, glued heavily to her sunbaked upper body.

I had greeted Jette the day before. A gaunt lady in her midfifties, she had her gray-brown hair pulled up into a bristly, stumpy ponytail. She was a former nanny, she'd told me, but had been fired after thirty years. Fair enough, she'd said. Small children were exhausting, and it was hard to mind them at home in the end. Old people, at least they didn't run out onto the road and get themselves killed while you were out having a cigarette. And, she said pointedly, she looked after those she was told to look after.

"Has Anders been difficult?" Anton asked as I put on more coffee and stacked the weekly newspapers into a little pile by the door. She smiled gratefully.

"No. Most of the time, he's gentle as a lamb." She'd pulled out a cigarette stump from the packet on the kitchen table and was turning it between her thin fingers. "It doesn't take a lot to get him to do things. It's more . . ." She exhaled heavily. "He can get so terribly angry sometimes."

Her lighter clicked furiously when she lit her half cigarette. Her cheeks were hollow and acne-scarred under the sharp cheekbones.

Anton shook his head ruefully.

"I've tried talking to him—"

"Yeah, like that's going to help."

Jette clenched her narrow lips together in a thin line, stubbed out her cigarette as fast as she'd lit it and began to fill up the bucket for washing the floor.

"It's a good thing people like me still exist in Denmark. But I almost end up wishing for a back injury and early retirement after a bath day out there with him."

"I understand."

Anton fiddled with his packet of cheroots, and I felt this was a conversation they'd had before. Undoubtedly verbatim. Jette venting frustration and anger, and Anton accepting it.

"There're those who just scrounge off the system nowadays, Anton. But *I* set the limit. I have my dignity. I do my job properly and have never mooched off of anyone."

She exposed her long teeth, grinning at her own cheekiness as she found a floor rag in the closet and threw it into the hot water.

"I don't have enough time to do the living room today. But there's a young man in the house now, too. He might be able to swing the vacuum cleaner at some point during the day."

I nodded.

"Of course. I'm here to help out a little."

She sent me a distrustful look.

"Yeah, what do I know? I've never seen you before. But once I've sorted out the utility room, I'll get a little lunch ready for you, and then that'll be it for today."

"That's very nice of you, Jette. Thank you," said Anton.

He was calm, his open palms a sign of peace and surrender. I had only ever seen Anton angry once in my life, but it had left a lasting impression. Like Atlas dropping the earth from his shoulders.

I opened my laptop and went to our website—my old company's website.

They hadn't removed my name yet, and my likeness was unbearably smug. A graying academic trying to keep his head at an angle so the skin under his chin looked somewhat tight. Found Janne listed among the staff and contemplated her beautiful, pious half smile. There was no surrender or even a suggestion of the desire to please in the way she sat with her chin protruding and the little curl at the corner of her mouth—one that someone should kiss softly, indulgently.

The first time I invited her to coffee, I'd already weighed up the advantages and disadvantages. I'd scrutinized my own motives and concluded each time that my interest in her was purely professional. It was her talent that interested me. Her creative, intricate mind. It would quite logically be a crazy thought not to develop that talent just because she happened to be a young woman. I'd been a mentor for several young people to whom I'd felt attached before. Rasmus five years ago. And Tilde, who had been with us for nearly three years, before she flew onward. So I invited Janne to coffee and museums. The Glyptotek, with all its smooth, naked bodies and vines and marble columns. Louisiana, on the lawn in the sunshine with the view of snapping waves on the rocky beach.

I wrote far more emails to her than I strictly needed to. Sat up late at night, drawing up new suggestions just so I could ask her to comment on them.

Janne, I think we can win by increasing the masonry surface and openings in the body of the building. Cuts, new surfaces. Have a look at it and let me know what you think . . .

Janne, what's your opinion on this?

Sometimes her answers were blunt, bordering on rude: *Are you fucking kidding me?*

Other times, she rose to the bait and came to my office, pulled a chair up to my desk and outlined her own suggestions. Took apart my ideas and let new ones flow across the gridded paper. Here and here, the two ellipses should run through each other. Glass and brick in the half spiral that formed the entrance.

Jesus. I let on that I'd handle the expenditures, despite knowing that none of it was possible given our budget. I could tell she was flattered by my interest. The hard shell was nothing more than just that—a shell.

Anders had come out of the bathroom and sat down heavily at the kitchen table. He let the nail of his thick index finger trace the pattern of the oilcloth and didn't look at any of us as Anton buttered a slice of bread and poured some coffee for him.

"Is there anything I can do for you while I'm here?" I asked. "Grocery shopping?"

Anton leaned forward, resting his shaking hands on the back of the chair, and stopped to catch his breath.

"No," he said. "Jette buys whatever we need. But if you'd like to go up and see the town, you can check whether there's still life left in the car out there. There shouldn't be anything wrong with it, since I go out and start it once a week, but it needs to be driven a little."

THE HEAVY GATE to the barn slid reluctantly on its rusty tracks, and I had to lean my full weight against it to push it all the way over and let sunlight spill in onto the concrete floor. The dust danced up and down with the wind in heavy, swirling spirals.

The grain room to the left was empty and swept, but the old machinery was still there. The rusty auger, hoe and quern stone, which stood where I'd left them, and a completely rotten transmission belt secured to the engine of an old moped. The dusty, dove-gray Ford Taunus stood in the tractor's spot, unlocked and with the keys inside. I slid into the driver's seat, which was upholstered in turquoise leather, worn soft and thin—all the way through to the dark padding in some places. The steering wheel felt hard and slippery in my hands, and there was rust on the doors, but the engine hummed effortlessly when I turned the key in the ignition, put the car in reverse and rolled out into the yard. My phone vibrated discreetly in my back pocket, but I was sure it wasn't anybody I was in a hurry to talk to.

Letting my physical memory guide me, I turned left on the narrow road and drove toward Pinderup along the fields of brown rapeseed and pale-yellow wheat.

1 9 7 8

Out on the road, cars passed by, one after the other. Patrol cars with dead sirens on their roofs, a few ordinary-looking white station cars and finally a dark-blue van with big white letters on its side.

The police.

I'd only seen those kinds of vans on the television and in *The Olsen Gang*—they didn't seem so dramatic in real life. Their pace was almost leisurely, and one of the policemen sat with his arm out the open window, his hand resting on the side of the car. I went out onto the road and saw the long tail of cars turning off toward Ommestrup and disappearing as the larks sang undisturbed high, high up.

It had to be Toad. It couldn't be anyone other than her. I took my Bianchi from the garage and followed. I could still see the motorcade a little farther ahead on a hill, and I put all my weight into the pedals, feeling my pulse in my chest and thighs, lungs burning when I increased my speed. I passed Damgården and continued through the flickering narrow bit of forest where the water stood black as coal, shiny puddles between the trunks. Mosquitoes danced in the shadows, and I had to reduce my speed several times so I could wipe them from my face and throat.

The strip of cars had parked alongside the gravel road down to the chicken farm, and a pair of uniformed men had already let a few big German Shepherds out of the first vehicle. The animals trotted excitedly around themselves, sniffing the wind and wagging heavy, swinging tails. Sten's father was there, too. I recognized him with his blue suit, crossed arms and slightly rounded back. He'd never been a big man. The rare times he took off the suit and walked around in the kitchen in his ratty T-shirt, he was small and bony and weird to look at, and his breastbone stuck out as though someone had stabbed a spear into his back and pulled it out on the other side. But I thought he looked even smaller today; he stood so oddly alone among the other men. Uneasy in his body, his curly hair alternating between wild bristles and lying flat in the wind. He nodded at something the officer said, rubbed the corners of his mouth with his thumb and forefinger and looked out across the fields. Threw out his arm and rubbed his face with a flat hand. His eyes squinted against the sun.

Things had gone wrong after Toad had disappeared. Even I could see that.

The wind stank of liquid manure, dry soil and sweet, fermenting gray hay on the field because he hadn't collected it in time. The hay tedder was covered with long, curly, sticky burdocks, snow-in-summer, and couch grass at the end of the mechanical house, and the stench of putrid chicken dung from the coop spoke of far worse neglect. Over time, it had come to stand as tall as a man under the cages.

He saw me but didn't as I slowly walked my bike along the line of cars.

"Is Sten home?"

"Yeah, yeah, Jacob. He is," he said, grimacing. An attempt at a smile, I assumed. "Thank God he hasn't scuttled off anywhere."

"I DON'T WANT to talk about it," said Sten.

We were sitting up in his room, gazing out the window. Dark

panels in plastic wood, a bookcase with tanks and plastic soldiers, a few soccer posters adorned the room, offset by the penetrating odor of feet and the omnipresent stench of chicken shit that hung in his dad's boiler suit and hair and skin, and sometimes even in Sten's when he was out working the cages. When the wind blew from the right direction, we even got the reek from the gray industrial hall on the west side of the farm in through the window, but that didn't seem to have ever bothered Sten. Sometimes I thought his sense of smell had simply been sautéed away at a young age.

"We can go for a bike ride," I said.

The police had spread out across the farmyard, and now they were striding over the creek on the boundary to the neighboring field and walking in through the corn. The dogs' tails stood up among empty ears as the stalks were trampled down in brutal straight lines.

"They've already searched over by the stable, and in the garage, and the mechanical house, and all that," Sten said. "It's crazy when she's only gone to Aarhus. I'll fucking kill her when she comes back."

He'd always had acne and breakouts, but now his face was almost exploding in red, inflamed craters, which he kept touching with his fingertips.

I nodded. Mostly because I didn't know what to say, but also because I could see that he needed to be right. He'd been crying. His eyes were red and swollen, and down in the kitchen, his skeletal mother was walking around, looking just about the same. His aunt was there, too, probably to help out, but the two women had somehow managed to make the place even messier than it had been before.

The cupboards in the kitchen had been emptied of pots and pans, which lay soaking on the kitchen counter alongside old dishes and half-filled plates of open-topped sandwiches glistening with fat. Salami and other cold-cut meats, gray and shiny from the heat, caused the flies to dance in the dusk.

Sten walked away from the window and sat down on the bed. He furiously combed his short hair with his fingers, then pinched one of the big red swellings on his forehead, grimacing.

"We didn't get the hay in. At all. Dad went crazy when Mathisen offered to bring it in for him. He doesn't want any machines driving around out there because of Toad. But we're going to have to at some point. It's just lying out there. And we need to empty the cages, but Dad is completely . . ." The edge of his mouth quivered. "The new chickens have already been ordered. The slaughterhouse is ready, too. It's all going to hell."

I could vaguely make out the back of the blue boiler suit out in the field where Sten's dad walked with the family collie on a leash, putting his hand up to his mouth from time to time and calling for Toad. They were all doing it.

It just seemed so crazy.

If Toad was out there in the fields somewhere, she probably wouldn't be able to answer. Still, we could hear the weak cries bleat through the open window.

"Maybe we should go out and help them search," I said, but Sten just shook his head and hunted under the comforter for a moment for a Donald Duck comic. His bedding was shabby and stank of sweat.

"Are you crazy?" he said. "She's not lying dead in a field. It's *Toad*. She never goes anywhere if the grass is taller than her."

He stuck out his foot in its holey sock and held it about six inches above the floor. His feet were long and thin and flat.

"She's afraid of everything. Bees, and beetles, and flies. Everything. She'd never go out there, and even if she did . . ." He gave me a quick, searching look. "Just think what she'd look like now, after all that time in this weather. No, thanks!"

I shifted, uneasy.

There was something about the way he'd said it that made it real. I'd seen loads of dead animals. Including ones that had been left lying there for a long time. Piglets thrown onto the roadside to be picked up by the truck on its way to the soap factory. Once, a sow had lain there for weeks down by Damgården, stiff and swollen, with its crooked yellow canines sticking out from its dissolving jaw. The reek was awful, but no worse than the fact that Sten and I had had fun poking sticks into its jelly-filled eye sockets and piercing its spotted paunch with a pointed stick so gray intestines and a clearish, dark-red liquid ran out over the ground.

That could now be Toad—Lise. I decided to call her by her real name in my mind from now on, as a kind of belated respect.

"Just tell me when you're going to empty the cages," I said. "I can help."

"Yeah, yeah." He looked down at his hands. Picked at a frayed nail bed. "We'll see, Jacob."

I suddenly wanted to put my arm around him, just like Mom had done with me when I was younger and couldn't stop crying over something. Even though Sten was so irritating in so many ways. We weren't great friends, and I wasn't even sure I really liked him, but he was there, and he'd always been there. He seemed so small at that moment, sitting there. Completely alone and without his family.

"It'll be all right," I said, hoping I sounded convincing. "Like the way she yelled at your mom sometimes, she's just trying to give you a real fright."

He looked up at me and smiled weakly.

"Exactly," he said. "That's what I'm saying. But I'm going to fucking kill her when they find her."

1978

"Do you know the girl? The one they're searching for?"

I straightened up with the posthole digger and wiped my forehead with the back of a muddy hand. Squinted at the sun and followed Anton's eyes over the field. Two dark figures had appeared at the edge of the woods on the other side of Damgården. And more had materialized after them, most of them dressed in long trousers and long-sleeved sweaters, so that they could wade through thistles and hip-high clumps of nettles there. As far as I could tell, it was just another search party, the third one we'd seen in the last few days. It wasn't just the police fine-combing the terrain anymore. A team of volunteers now met every evening in the village hall for a status update. A few from the community watch and some local hunters who knew the area headed up everything in conjunction with the police. A few days ago they'd been in the marsh, and now they'd reached our farm with their shouts, dogs, thermos bottles and cakes baked by the mothers in the town.

Anton had seemed uncomfortable all morning.

"Her name's Lise," I said.

He lifted up a stake from the high grass and slammed it so hard into the hole that it stood mostly upright. Then he got the sledgehammer, swung it high above his head and let it fall on the stake. It hit with a dull crunch.

"I know. But do you know her? Beyond that?"

I rubbed a bead of sweat off my nose as I lifted the posthole digger, measured three long steps and pushed it down into the soft soil. Both Anton and I were soaked with sweat after walking in the hot sun all morning. The division of labor was clear: I dug, and Anton hammered the stakes into place, pushed earth around them and stamped it all down with the heels of his wooden clogs. It was nearly noon, and it wouldn't do any harm if we went in soon to eat something.

"Is she—is she nice to look at?"

I couldn't help sending him a quick look over my most recently dug posthole. Anton had set down the sledgehammer again and turned his attention to the stooped figures on the hill. A group of about fifteen men and women were still out in the field. Spread into a fan and armed with long, thin sticks, which they used to separate the grain on both sides of the path they were trampling. Their weak shouts to one another drowned in the wind.

"Em . . . I don't know?"

I wasn't sure what to say. It seemed disrespectful to call Lise ugly. Just as bad as using the nickname Toad. It wasn't right to speak badly of people who might be dead.

"But have you heard anything? About where they think she is?"

"Not other than what they've been saying in town," I said. "The usual things. She had an apprenticeship in an office in Auning, and so on. But that she'd started going to the bar."

These snippets of information I hadn't gotten directly from Sten, but I'd heard them the one time I'd ridden my bike to the butcher for Ellen. That had gotten me two pounds of minced pork wrapped in wax paper with an elastic around it and a feeling of subdued panic. The police had been around to interrogate people again, and they'd talked to Lise's only real friend, a tall, thin, bespectacled girl named Laurel. As in Laurel and Hardy—because she hung out with little, fat Lise. But she couldn't help them because she didn't know anything.

Anton frowned.

"They'll come here, too," he said. "Trample our corn. But that's how it is. Of course, they have to, when a young girl is missing."

I hesitated. I didn't want to talk about it. And certainly not with Anton.

"Yes, of course. But she wasn't so sweet to look at, you say?" Anton said absentmindedly, as if he hadn't heard my earlier response.

"Well . . ."

I shook my head, picturing Lise the last time I'd seen her. It had been a warm spring day, probably even warmer at the office in Auning and afterward on the bus home, because when she'd shown up, she was red-faced and shiny in a slightly too-tight blue office skirt that went halfway down her tree-trunk thighs. Her shoes were new, with little heels that had already buckled under her weight. A white blouse and a blue blazer jacket. If she'd ever seen one of those women's magazines, like my own mom read, then it must only have been at the doctor's or hairdresser. And her clothes were, like Sten's, mail-order and of the same practical nature as her mother's. This was obviously an attempt to try something new, but even I could see that it was wrong.

The skirt had become disheveled and curled in the heat, and under the tight-fitting blazer and blouse, her bra had cut a deep furrow into the flesh just below her heavy breasts. She looked like a wife. A farmer's wife, or a little girl dressing up as a lady. Her sullen mouth was painted crimson, and her bangs stuck out awkwardly, despite her securing most of them with two childishly colorful butterfly clips. But she looked beautiful in a way that I couldn't fully explain to Anton, that made me want to cry when I thought about it. Because she'd seemed so . . . happy. Because she thought she'd waved a magic wand over her head, like the fairy godmother in Cinderella, and had actually smiled when she saw me.

Maybe it was because of the new clothes and the sunshine. Perhaps it was because Sten, whom she hated, had gone behind the gable to piss, so for once we were alone. She sat next to me on the stairs and told me a joke she'd heard at work. Something about a Norwegian, a Dane and a Swede, a plane and packed lunches. I thought there was something sweet about all girls when they smiled the way she had that day.

"She's nice enough," I said.

Anton nodded, took the hammer and put it up into the truck with the stakes and fencing wire, and as soon as the weight left his large hands, they began to shake. Anton's hands always shook. A quiet man with unquiet hands.

Over the ridge, the sky was bright blue, and far out toward the marsh, you could see figures moving across yet another field while the dogs yapped happily.

"If you hear something," he said, drying his hands on his muddy blue work pants, "something or other about it, then I'd like to know."

He didn't usually talk so much, and he certainly never asked for help with anything other than what had to be done. Mending fences, feeding pigs, carrying milk buckets, handling the rats in the barn.

"I don't know who'd say anything," I said.

"People talk," said Anton. "They'll certainly talk about this."

ELLEN AND I walked through the woods with our sketch pads. We followed the dusty forest path that smelled of red forest ants, dark honey fungi and sour beech leaves along the stone wall until we came to the troll oak. The tree was ancient and didn't really look like a tree anymore. Its huge trunk was split, cleaved into several smaller ones that turned upward, outward and even downward so the branches rested heavily on the soft forest floor. Part of the oak tree was gray and dead, the transition between dead and living wood an invisible line under my hands. Seven hundred years old, maybe more. Our biology teacher dragged us down here every fall to gather acorns.

Ellen crawled up to the place where the trunk split, cursed mildly because of her long, orange-red skirt, which she eventually ended up tying into a knot at the front so she wouldn't step on it. She was wearing a loose black undershirt that gave access to a glimpse of the dark, straight hair under her arms and bare skin on her stomach when she reached up for a new place to grab.

I crawled after her and sat down on one of the big branches. So close that I could touch her if I stretched out my arm. Could she really *not* feel it?

"The fight for women's rights is lost as long as these are our fashion," she said, irritatedly pulling up her orange skirt. "Our vanity will cost us the final victory."

"I didn't know we were at war."

I wanted to hold her, to protect her. It was hard to resist the impulse, and I was sure she felt it, too. At least, it felt as though the warmth in my midriff was radiating out, causing the air between us to whirl in waves of pressure. I edged a little closer, but she didn't seem to notice. She half turned away from me and laughed.

"No, you wouldn't." She broke off a twig and threw it at me. "You are a big, stupid boy who will one day become a big, stupid man."

"Okay." I smiled, moving a few inches closer. "And what is it we're fighting about?"

"Everything."

She hopped down, landing on the soft forest floor with a firm thump. Loosened her skirt and shook it into place with a few soft swings of her hips. I grabbed a branch and swung off, hovering a little in the air before jumping off and landing right behind her.

"Let's fight, then."

She looked at me and laughed.

"You're too small, Utzon. If I hit you, you'd end up badly hurt."

We sat with our backs against a slender, blue-green beech tree, each drawing. We threw our only eraser back and forth when one of us—mostly me—needed it. Ellen had a dainty wrinkle of concentration on her forehead as her pencil danced in quick jerks across the paper.

Red ants started to bite me under my T-shirt and on my ankles, and I squished a few of them with the tip of my pencil.

Ellen looked over at me with a crooked smile.

"You have to suffer for both art and beauty," she said. She contented herself with absentmindedly shooing away her angry attackers from around her sandals.

"Why are you really out here and not with your friends during summer vacation?" she asked.

I shrugged.

"Only Sten is home."

She grew serious.

"How's he doing? Sten?"

Something in the way she said it made me wince. I didn't know how Sten was doing. The road to the chicken farm had become strange and overwhelming since Ellen had moved in. I honestly tried not to think about it all so much, and avoided looking in that direction. But of course, Sten was still down there, alone with his elderly parents.

"He's managing," I said, hearing how stiff it sounded. "He and Lise were always fighting . . ."

She glanced at me out of the corner of her eye.

"What do you mean?"

"Well, they didn't like each other."

Her hand froze in the air above the sketch pad.

"Come on, Utzon. What a thing to say." She smiled in the way she sometimes did. Like an adult to an overexhausted child.

I bent over and rooted around for the cigarettes in my back-pack, then gave her one, enjoying the light touch of her hand as she accepted it, her eyes both teasing and schoolteacher strict.

"You smoke too much, Utzon. Your fresh, pink lungs will be ruined."

"I'm an old soul. It all has to fit."

She smiled. "Yes, you are."

I wanted to reach out and touch her. To say something more. There were so many things I wanted to talk to her about. I wanted to tell her about all the things inside me, the ones that no one really noticed. Books I'd read and what I thought of them. The architectural book of Eigtved. But I couldn't figure out where to start.

We smoked in silence and drew a little more, and at one point she got up and sat on her knees next to me, so close that I could sense the smell of her soap and fresh sweat.

I stiffened.

"No, no. Keep going." She touched the edge of my paper. "I just want to see how you work."

And later, when she'd considered my nervous strokes a little, "You're not all that bad, Utzon. But you've never had lessons, right?"

I shook my head.

"It doesn't matter," she said. "You can get them anytime."

Carefully, I leaned over and looked at her sketch pad.

Her drawing was wilder than mine, the strokes looser and with less detail. On the other hand, I could see that the few details she had included—fissures in the bark, leaves in the foreground that dissolved into diffuse, dark shadows against the sky—were far more precise. My shapes seemed crooked and overdrawn in comparison to her shadows, suggested in primitive, careful shading.

We sat so close that her breast brushed up against my arm, and

I briefly felt the soft weight of her head against my shoulder. My erection was immediate and painfully restrained by my shorts.

"Here and here," she said, creating an almost invisible line through the trunk of my oak tree. "Look at the main line, the inclination. Details are important, but it's the big lines that create the movement. The truth of the oak tree lies in the way it's chosen to stretch and bend according to the light. All that which has made time pass over the last thousand years."

"Trees don't do much."

I was short of breath and certainly red as a berry, but Ellen didn't seem to notice. She narrowed her eyes, looking up from my drawing to the tree and back again. She drew a loose, choppy line.

"You're wrong, Utzon," she said. "That tree has been moving for almost a thousand years, only in slow motion. Very, very slow."

She stuck both of her forearms into the air and rotated them slightly.

"Even stones are in motion before petrifying. You can tell from their lines and colors that they've been twisted and pressed and turned, and have been softened and plied in the red-hot hands of a great god. That's what you have to draw—the movement. Always look for the movement."

I gaped at the distorted trunks and drew in a few more lines before she grabbed my hand and added a new one. Her cheek was so close to mine that I could feel the heat radiating from her.

It wasn't a conscious decision; it was just how it was. I turned my head and let my lips graze her soft cheek. It seemed like the most natural thing to do, almost inevitable. As if we'd been involved in a complicated dance that had stretched over several days, and had finally reached its logical finale.

For every move she made, there was a response from me. Her cheek against mine hadn't been a coincidence.

I gently stroked her neck, the black leather cord and the white mussel shell smooth between my fingers. And then I kissed both her throat and the shellfish. Her skin was salty and warm against my dry lips.

"Utzon . . ."

I closed my eyes and waited for her next move. That she would kiss me on the mouth with slightly separated lips. The tip of her damp tongue against my teeth. But it didn't happen.

In fact, she sat utterly, utterly still with her head a little slanted, as if she were listening for something far away. One of her hands and one of mine were still in the air in front of my drawing, hers closed around mine in a loose grip, and I thought she had to be able to feel my pulse through our fingertips. Decoded and followed my heart rate.

Then she laid her head upon my shoulder.

"Ah, hell, Utzon . . ."

She pulled away, and the dance disintegrated. Her eyes were blurry and impossible to read.

"It's whispering," she said, nodding up at the tree crowns.

The sky above us had turned dark blue, and the light was the color of sulfur. As we packed our sketch pads into my backpack, I saw something move out in the thin undergrowth. At first, I couldn't see exactly where the movement was coming from; I thought the man was something nonliving. A tree or a stone. But then the contours stepped out from between the branches. Arms and legs. The face was nothing but shadow, or at least, that was the only thing I could see. Branches broke and a couple of birds flew sharply upward as something dark moved in the flickering light among the leaves.

Ellen had seen him, too, and her face shone in wonder. The same little wrinkle in her forehead appeared as when she concentrated on the sketch pad. She stood still for a long moment before vigorously swinging the backpack over her shoulder and starting to walk. I walked backward after her, my heart pulsing in my throat.

"Just let him be," said Ellen quietly. "He walks down around by the commune, too. Looks in through the windows. He doesn't do anything."

"Do you know who he is?"

I didn't realize she could process things so calmly. Somebody had been standing there, watching us through the underwood. A madman, maybe. It happened regularly—calls on the radio for missing people who'd run away from the hospital in Aarhus. People who heard voices and walked around with a knife, that kind of thing. People the police said you shouldn't approach.

"Maybe."

She looked at me and laughed. Not in an unfriendly way, but as if I'd said something both stupid and funny. I nodded and threw one last glance in the direction we'd come from, but now there were only the muffled mumblings of the forest. We sped up just as the first heavy drops lashed through the leaves.

"Damn!"

Ellen laughed, pulled up her skirt and ran with the backpack bobbing up and down on her back. I followed after her, driven by the rain and the fright still in my body, and we sought out the eaves of the barn en route to Pinderup, pushing ourselves up against the wall. She up against me, out of breath and smiling, while the large raindrops fell, leaving tiny craters on the sandy road. Like a meteor shower in a desert.

"Maybe we should tell the police," I said slowly. "That there's a man like that, a peeping Tom. Now that Lise . . ."

Ellen leaned against the wall and shot me an inquisitive look. Her forehead and cheeks were wet from the rain, droplets of water sparkling in her short hair. Her slender hands worked with a beech leaf that she must have torn off while we were on the move. She pulled it apart carefully, so only the thin ribs remained.

"You shouldn't be so worried," she said. "It doesn't suit you, and she might still show up."

She laughed, stroking my cheek so I felt like a child. But I didn't say anything else. She had to know that I couldn't help but worry. That it was *her* I needed to take care of and protect from evil. She had to know. But she just smiled, squinting against the rain and the gray sky.

"It's died down," she said. "Let's go back."

Pinderup wasn't a town, nor was it just a village. It was full of single-story houses with uneven buds of garages, living rooms, family rooms with high vaulted ceilings, raised attics and sparkling new bathrooms. The walls were freshly plastered and painted in blue, rusty red and Skagen's yellow, and the planed lawns were neatly framed by tightly cut hedges and wooden fences. Where there had once been a commune was now a long, low-rise farmhouse with a newly tiled roof. Its stone walls were plastered and painted a dazzling white. The windows were new, too, and the little band of front yard was trimmed and neat, with pink flowers in baskets and a row of lush peonies along the white picket fence. The outhouse with the old toilet had been leveled to the ground and replaced with a lawn and a plastic swing set. The old trees had been felled, and an aggressive edge trimmer had left the flowers in the ditch with bleeding, open stems.

What was I doing here?

The doorbell sounded like I'd just walked into a bakery, and the door was opened after a few seconds by a young woman with a two-year-old boy sitting firmly on her hip. She seemed to have all the time in the world, and was calm and perfumed in an organized way that you associated with the provincial middle class. Fabric softener, plank floors, new electrical installations and children who were pudgy and scoured clean, drank fruit juice and ate white bread.

She smiled.

"Yes?"

"Yeah, sorry if I'm disturbing you," I said. "But I lived in Tostrup as a child and had a friend who used to live here. In the commune. I was just curious about whether you know what's become if it."

"In the commune. That was a long time ago—a lot has happened."

She was young and beautiful and tall. Broad-shouldered, with solid hips, baggy jeans and a lace undershirt that bulged unevenly over her stomach. Her hair was long and brown and straightened, like in a low-budget American television series. Without doubt, she'd been in the disco in Rønde four years ago with a bunch of Bacardi Breezers, tapping her foot while her boyfriend—now husband—danced, his upper body bare under the disco ball light. That was then, and this was now. She looked like the type who'd become an adult early on, and with fitting seriousness.

"I was hoping you could help me with the names of the people who used to live here."

I couldn't tell if she had any concerns about inviting me in, but I looked exactly like what I was. A middle-aged, well-groomed academic with grayed temples. There was no residue of Jutland in my dialect, and I was quite sure that I possessed the comportment of a big city, making me the most civilized of white men.

She showed me into the hall with her free arm and swung the child down to the floor with impressive ease. Clearly a woman who'd retained both shape and composure after giving birth. Kirsten had turned into a stick insect, working herself lopsided and gaunt and smoking neurotically during the five years we had small children.

"Well, come on in, then. I actually grew up here in the town. My parents live just over there." She nodded toward the house on the other side of the road. "Grandpa and Grandma lived on a farm a little farther out. Frederikslund, if you know it?"

I nodded and looked around. Walls had been knocked down and rebuilt elsewhere; new layers covered the old. Everything was painted white. Children's squiggly drawings on the wall and pictures of happy families on the refrigerator, just like in every other Danish home. Ordered and clean, the opposite of mine and Kirsten's house in Valby, where everything had been ruled by Kirsten's love for vintage and wear and tear and academic antiestablishment. She'd spent enormous amounts of energy not to resemble her orderly parents in Slagelse. Listened to loud jazz and cleaned to the overture from *Carmen*. She was still able to sit down with a glass of red wine and stare defiantly at the gardens of Valby and the newly built carports, saw herself as an agent of chaos in a regular suburb, but when it came down to it, she was like her mother and most other women in everything that was essential. Classic mildness, which had been her most distinguishing characteristic as a young girl, had long been replaced with the blunt pragmatism that my father consistently referred to as women's "postloveliness period."

"As soon as they're no longer beautiful enough to pull you around by the dick, they put a ring in your nose instead. You fall asleep next to a gentle honey-scented creature and wake up beside a witch."

I could see my own warlike Valkyrie in front of me at home in the house. Her loose, tangled jewelry in a box out on the street for five kroner apiece. The dining chairs in a dark photograph on a secondhand website, going for nothing. The children's drawings and bead plates in the garbage. Our marriage and family life wiped out in the time it took others to cut their hedges.

The young woman threw out her arms and spun around once.

"Well, this is how it looks now. Do you recognize it?"

I shook my head. "I was only here a couple of times. Do you know how long they lived here?"

"The people from the commune?" She frowned. "They were

here when my mom was older, maybe into the late seventies. Grandpa and Grandma had a little to do with them, just after they moved here, but it was a wild place. My mother wasn't allowed to go in."

She crossed her arms so her breasts were pushed together a little in her loose undershirt, and I wondered if it was on purpose. Whether standing in front of a man would make any woman consider what position her breasts should be presented in. It was a real bra with a lace trim, not one of the soft-elasticated, unbleached cotton ones for breastfeeding women. This one had thin, black straps and provided a significant boost to the soft attributes, and I appreciated her gesture. There was comfort in a woman's bosom, but luckily she wasn't my type. It was a relief.

She brushed a hair from her forehead with her fingers. Moderately long nails, femininely painted, like they should be everywhere except in academia.

"Who is it you're looking for?"

"A woman named Ellen. Or someone who knows her."

"Your mother or sister or something like that? Just like in *Without a Trace*." She gave me a cheeky look.

"Too young to be my mother and too old to be my sister," I said. "I'm trying to track her down for a friend."

"Okay. I can probably find some names in the papers we have on the house. If you give me your number, I can call you."

"Thanks. Your grandmother and grandfather—are they still alive?"

"My grandfather is Åge Jensen. He still lives on the farm. You can visit him if you want—his memory is still sharp."

She got her cell phone from the windowsill and let her fingers run over the screen. She tapped in my number while we walked out to the hall together, the baby tottering after us.

"You wouldn't like a glass of water before you go?" She looked at me with a slightly furrowed brow.

"No, thanks."

"You don't look the best, which is why I offered. It's easy to feel unwell in this heat."

I turned and caught an unwelcome glimpse of myself in the hallway mirror. Unfortunately, it was one of those moments where you haven't gotten to prepare yourself for meeting with your own reflection. Where you can't straighten your posture, lift the edges of your mouth and call forth the sparkle in your eye. And I immediately understood her concern. Despite the heat, I was paler than usual, my skin thin and fatigued in the light from the open door.

I REMEMBERED FREDERIKSLUND well.

It was one of the larger properties on the road to Auning, built around a graveled square courtyard with an arched entryway.

Several of the windows in the barn buildings were broken, and the property was empty, if you didn't count the pickup from Auning Carpentry Company and some Rockwool fiber balls pushed into the rearmost corner. There had once been dairy cattle here, I guessed. A daily, lively stream of cows being driven out to pasture and back again for milking three times a day. A clatter of heavy milk cans and clumsy, cloven hooves.

Now the buildings lay like a collapsed foreign object in the middle of a cornfield that was growing all the way in to the flaky stable walls and stretching for as far as the eye could see on the other side of the huge farmhouse.

I let the door knocker fall heavily against its brass plate, and shortly thereafter a shadow appeared through the patterned green glass in the door. Åge Jensen. He led me into a dim room and pulled the curtains aside, then pointed toward the farm's old boundary to the south. I couldn't see anything other than the withering corn plants and a hot-tempered rotating sprinkler, which breathed steam and fog to the farthest corner. He drew them closed again.

His grandchild had called and warned him of my arrival.

"They were some bastards, especially the two chaps. Communists or something, they reminded me of. Came and told us everything we did was wrong, but what did they know? Nothing. Couldn't poke a stick in shit without destroying both."

Åge Jensen sat on the sofa with his hands in his lap and a pained expression on his lips that seemed chronic and unsolvable. Neither the bottle of schnapps nor the filled chocolates I'd picked up in Brugsen evoked anything but tired grunts. He couldn't remember much and hadn't had anything to do with them. Not after the incident with the sheep. Three animals had died of thirst in the summer of '76 in the commune's miserable fencing at the back of the stable.

"I'll never forget it, I can tell you that. The day they dragged over the dead animals and asked if they could still use the meat. They wanted them skinned and dismembered, despite it being clear that they'd been dead for at least a day. It was a warm summer, and they hadn't sheared them or given them water." Åge Jensen's thin lips curled upward in contempt.

"And what then?"

"What then? I told them to go to hell with their dead animals. They were drunk. Or worse. Probably drugs. I didn't talk to them after that."

It was dark and stifling in the living room. I glanced at the dark shelves, which had no books, but a cemetery of capsized picture frames, dark silhouettes of what were probably children, grandchildren, and great-grandchildren.

"Should I turn on the light?" I said, already standing up to do so.

"No."

I sat back down. Studied the old man's shadowy face, trying to discern how old he was. Eighty or maybe ninety? I couldn't remember him, but there were farm owners you saw and others you didn't. The most solid friendships from back then were built on borrowing one another's machinery in a pinch and rounding up runaway livestock together. Frederikslund had been a big farm where they didn't have to borrow anything.

"A girl named Ellen Høgh lived there once," I said. "Do you remember her?"

He nodded.

"A happy girl," he said. "Sweet, but like the others." He twirled his index finger around at his temple. Leaned so far back that a ray of light from the window hit his face. A big nose, wide jaw and astute expression.

"You come from Svenningsens', you say? Anton and Anders. They're probably well on in years now."

"Eighty-seven and ninety-three, yes. They're still going strong."

Åge Jensen grunted.

"Thanks, but I'm up to date on the living and the dead here. That's what the obituaries are for."

"They send their regards," I said.

"Yes, well."

He moaned again. Thin, frail arms and legs and a distended soccer-ball-sized stomach. Liver problems, cancer or some other malignant thing had filled his insides with fluid or tumors.

"May I ask how you know the two brothers?" He reached out for the bottle of schnapps and unscrewed the lid. Sniffed it.

"They're my father's uncles. Can I get you a glass?"

He shook his head and put the bottle down again. Waved an aggressively buzzing fly away from his forehead. He sized me up again. Whatever might be wrong with Åge Jensen, it wasn't his mind.

"Anton and Anders. They were a pretty pair."

"What do you mean?"

"Well, they stood out after what happened. It was an awful story, and it only got worse and worse."

I leaned forward a little to hear him better. "We've never had much contact with the rest of my father's family."

Åge Jensen shifted on the sofa in obvious physical discomfort. Something was hurting somewhere, and the movement apparently gave no relief. He clenched his teeth.

"Well, the mother . . . she had Anders too late. Forty-six, I think she was. Bit of a scandal back then, so it was talked about. My mother was still offended twenty years later. And then there was the boy himself."

"Sorry?"

"Loopy. A bit off."

I'd never known exactly what was wrong with Anders, and it had never occurred to me to ask anyone. He just was the way he was.

"And Anders was difficult in his young years. A little too fond of the girls, if you know what I mean. Cycled around to the farms in the evening and stood outside, staring. I had an older sister, Johanne, who was pretty. After he besieged us for two weeks, Father went up and spoke with Anton. Then it was over."

I frowned.

"How?"

Åge Jensen shrugged his shoulders.

"He sorted it out, like how you usually sorted things out back then. Gave the lad a telling-off or maybe something a bit harsher. I don't know if he was locked in, but we didn't see Anders at Pinderup anymore after that. And Johanne certainly hadn't been the first."

I flashed to Anders and myself in the yard one day long ago. The smile as he bent down over Soffi and scratched behind her ears. Blew on the mucky muzzle. His collection of glass shards, the oldest of which had been worn round and dull by sand and waves from Følle Strand.

"I have to go," I said, and Åge Jensen nodded.

"Karsten Villadsen," he said calmly. "One of the boys down there was called Karsten Villadsen. And he's not a communist anymore, that much I do know."

1978

Soffi barked furiously in the yard, and even though the wind sang through the rafters and metal sheeting, both Anders and I could hear car doors slam. Brief shouts and another dog barking in competition with Soffi.

Anders glowered at me, a little short of breath after our joint effort to clear out the hayloft. The dust sat in dry black splotches in our nostrils and ears, and our lungs stung like after a long run. Old bales of straw at the back, gray and half-rotten from age, had been pushed, pulled and swept out over the edge and down the loading platform. Blind, transparent young mice, no bigger than the tip of my little finger, whirled down with the crumbling moldy load. Their closed, bulging eyes resembled blood-filled tumors under their thin lids.

Some of the straw could be salvaged and used as bedding, but Anton wanted most of it out on the dung heap so it could be driven out onto the field and plowed down. This had taken all morning, and we still weren't done.

"Who is that?"

Anders's mouth stood open as he eagerly moved the tip of his thick, blue-red tongue over his lips. Smacked them. Anders loved when guests came. Hearing the neighbors tell their stories to pound cake and black coffee with three teaspoons of sugar, which he carefully stirred with the teaspoon grating against the bottom. It was often he who set the table and made the coffee.

He was standing completely still now with his pitchfork up in the air and a faraway look, listening attentively. He had balanced an entire straw bale on the upright fork, and when he set off heaving, I could sense the formidable back muscles working under his shirt. He had been annoying me all morning. The way he spoke, the stupid Donald Duck comics that he kept going on about, his smell when he came too close to me—which he did all the time—of cigarette smoke and sweat and pigpen and dead shrews and dead horned beetles in the windowsill.

"It's not a tractor or a Volvo. Not the mail . . ."

I didn't bother answering him. Instead, I went over to the open hatch and began to climb down. Through the barn door I saw what was left of Lise's search team. A handful of persistent men waiting silently, leaning on their cars while one of them spoke to Anton.

"We can't just stop now . . . There are a few of us helping the police . . ."

Anton, who had been in the garage for most of the day rummaging under the hood of his car, stood with his head lowered, listening as he rubbed his hands on a piece of frayed cotton cloth.

His movements seemed tired. His whole body was rigid in a way that I'd never seen before. Three of the piglets had died in the stable during the night, stiff and trampled down into the straw. Something had also changed that summer since the day I'd followed the police cars on my bicycle out to the chicken farm. It rained every day, sometimes with thunder, sometimes without. Afternoons of steady, pouring rain had given the cornfields a dull grayish sheen, and the wind was hard and wet, tearing the green apples from the trees. Peony and poppy and dahlia petals whirled out over the road on the way into town.

The three men were in army green, and one had a rifle hanging over his shoulder and a Cocker Spaniel beside him. More hunters.

Or maybe from the community watch. There was a field exercise ground with burned-down ruins somewhere on the road to Randers where they usually played war, crawling around with gas masks and helmets and potbellies, setting fire to an already ruined town. All three of them looked tired. Windswept and ruddy-faced after several days of hiking in the sun and rain over the fields.

"But we're just asking for permission first. It's your land . . ."

The man paused briefly to see if Anton would say anything, but he kept quiet, so the man nodded to the others. They scrambled across the fence and disappeared behind the stable as one.

Anders looked disappointed. Would probably have liked to have seen one of the guns, but Anton was already on his way back into the garage with heavy footsteps.

"What did they want?" asked Anders, and I realized he knew nothing about Lise. He didn't listen to the news or read the papers.

"They're looking for a girl," I replied.

"Why?"

I shrugged and suddenly caught sight of Sten.

He sat astride his bike in the driveway, all the way out in the road, looking—at first glance—like he used to. Short, bright hair bristling wildly in the wind, flushed cheeks and tanned legs in too-short shorts. He was trying to keep his balance on the bike without putting his feet on the ground, then relaxed and began to topple. Pushed off, let go with his feet and toppled again. I think you had to know him well to see that something was wrong. But there was a slightly glazed look in his eye, as though he had a fever, and he'd lost weight, too, despite it being difficult to believe that possible. His face pulled upward in sharp new lines.

I lifted my hand and he waved back. He was still balancing precariously on the bike with an expression that was both distant and focused.

"Why are they looking for a girl, Jacob?"

Anders hadn't released the furrow in his brow. Sometimes, his complete ignorance about everything was terribly annoying. Mostly when he tried to understand something he never would. I sighed.

"Because she ran away from home."

"A little girl?"

"No, a big one. Lise, from the chicken farm."

He lit up and nodded eagerly. Stuck his hand in his pocket and jingled his new shards of glass.

"I know her," he said.

I looked at Sten, who had gotten off the bike and stood shaking in the cool wind. He was in a T-shirt and shorts. Did he ever get any food at home? His knees were big and bony below his long, thin thighs, which were beginning to bend the wrong way.

He made a quick, sharp toss of his head toward the road, and I set off alongside him without looking back.

"**THEY'RE STILL LOOKING** for her," I said dumbly. "Maybe we should go with them."

Sten rubbed his eyes like someone who hadn't slept in a century. Pushed his bike slowly beside me.

"We don't need to," he said, scraping the toes of his shoes on the roadside. The sole of his rubber boot was cracked, so he had to shake out stones on a regular basis. "Just let it go on. Most of them are part of the community watch. They do it on their own time, and if something has happened to her—if somebody did do something—they'll kill the idiot when they find him. He won't live long enough to go to jail. That's what they told my father."

And I nodded, not really sure that was a good thing. That they would kill someone. Of course, it appealed to me on a purely theoretical level. A fitting punishment for the crime, it seemed fair, but it was like most violence. Fun to fantasize about, frightening in reality. And when I tried to imagine one of these completely ordinary men with his comb-over flapping in the wind and a sinewy finger on the trigger, it seemed ridiculous. Most of them had safe, comfortable lives, with jobs at Carletti or up at the furniture factory. How could they be the guardians of justice?

"Just wait, I guarantee you she's just in Aarhus with some friend. And now she won't show her face because she's embarrassed this has become such a big deal," I said.

He laughed, and for a moment he almost looked hopeful.

"Yeah, that'd be a pretty sight, wouldn't it?"

We walked a little farther without speaking. The light drizzle in the air settled coolly on our foreheads and necks.

"I dream about her," said Sten, giving me a sidelong glance as if to gauge whether I'd start laughing at him. "In my dreams, she's dead. Every time. She just lies there, dead, but I think that somehow I can change it. Reverse time. And in my dreams, I can, but then I wake up again."

He blinked a few times and seemed to collect himself. I could see him mentally slapping his cheeks, just like boxing trainers smacked their bruised, groggy fighters. The only thing I could think to do was give him an awkward pat on the shoulder, which caused him to cower and laugh weakly.

"Yeah, yeah," he said. "There's nothing we can do. We'll just have to wait and see."

He sounded like he'd said the same thing to himself hundreds of times. Mechanical, and without conviction.

"We'll just have to wait and see."

1978

It had begun to rain again.

Not in warm thunder showers, but ice-cold, horizontal cascades that beat the leaves of the trees to the ground and made the air we were breathing raw and cold. The water soaked through my jacket and ran into Anders's too-wide rubber boots. Farther on, Pinderup came into view through the blanket of rain. The low houses lay pressed under the gray sky, the commune with its curtains drawn and the driveway and front yard overgrown with thistles, field scabious and yellow bedstraw around the improvised campfire.

The blue Volkswagen T2 was still parked outside, but there were no signs of anyone by sight or sound. No lights in the windows.

I approached carefully, stepping into the front yard and wading through the damp, knee-high weeds. Garden snails, chocolate-colored with hard-candy striped shells in yellow and black and orange, crawled over the house's black-tarred plinth with soft, semitransparent bodies and eyes hovering on stalks. Toads the size of my little fingernail sat along the wall, and I had to step carefully not to crush any of them under my heavy boots. At one of the covered windows, I leaned in and tried to look through the narrow slit in the curtain. It was dark inside, but then I remembered it was also Monday—they might be at work, if they did such a thing. Karsten and the little stocky guy and the two women.

The other houses had dark, shiny windows under the wet sky, too, so I followed the driveway around behind the farmhouse to a narrow, chaotic patch of land. A bathtub with a hole sat with its bottom in the air, and down by the wall were a pair of rusty Dutch hoes and a spade with a broken shaft that had fallen into an ankle-deep puddle. In the corner by the stable, somebody had knocked a sandbox together that stank of cat shit. The sand was patterned by the raindrops in the brutal downpour, and the wooden box was filled with yellow grass and dead leaves. A pair of forgotten plastic shovels, a sieve and a faded yellow bucket seemed to have been through a few too many summers. On the uneven cobblestones near the back door stood pots, a stack of plates and a pair of old cart wheels threatening to collapse against the stable wing. A fat black cat sat in the open barn door, staring hatefully out into the rain.

"Hey! Looking for someone?"

I turned around and saw Karsten standing in the doorway to the back hall, leaning against the frame. He looked normal, if it was possible to judge such a thing from his attire. Worn jeans, bare feet and a white turtleneck sweater. His long hair set in an impressive puff, big like a movie star's.

I cleared my throat. My sense of invincibility had shrunk significantly with the reality and rain.

"I think I forgot my sweatshirt here. It's a blue Adidas one."

He squinted at me through the dense rain.

"You were the one who had the bad trip," he said.

I hesitated. I didn't really care for the way he was looking at me. His head slightly tilted, awaiting an answer.

"Yes. I just came to get my sweatshirt."

"Of course," he said. "I saw it somewhere." He smiled, and I felt fairly sure it was out of kindness.

"If you come inside, it might be a little easier to talk about everything. I've just put some water on the stove. It should only take a few minutes to find your sweatshirt."

I stayed in the heavy rain and looked from the fat cat to the open door.

"No, I . . . have to go. I'll get it later."

"You do? Right now?"

I nodded, starting to walk away with my heart pounding all the way up into my throat.

"Hey, you." He was on his way through the rain after me. "I know exactly who you are. I've seen you with Ellen, too. You know her. Did she send you here?"

I turned around and saw him standing right behind me. He looked strangely hopeful, standing there in his bare feet in the rain. His wild mane was already hanging heavy and wet around his face. Full lips and a sharp chin, dark eyelashes. He wasn't a big guy—just slender and long-limbed in an almost feminine way, like the members of the Rolling Stones.

"You're not afraid of me, are you?"

I looked down at my rubber boots, which were whitewashed with lime and had cracks in the toes.

"Nope," I said, trying to sound brazen and indifferent. "I have to—I'm—"

"Have to get back to Ellen?" He tilted his head back and considered me from under the dark eyelashes. "Tell me about her. What she's doing with the old men."

His voice was still friendly and normal. Like he'd said something banal about the weather, but there it was again, that corrosive, inquisitive look. Just for a second. Then he smiled and ran a hand over his face.

"Sorry," he said. "That was a stupid thing to say."

"I have to go home," I said in a sure voice.

"Of course you do." He clapped a hand on my shoulder. "But damn, at least wait until it stops raining. Anything else'd be crazy. I've got some dry clothes that you can borrow, too. Come on. We have important things to talk about."

"JUST LEAVE YOUR boots on."

He walked ahead of me into the narrow hall, where there was a mountain of shoes in every color and size. Haphazard red children's shoes with black laces, several pairs of sandals, scratched clogs and rubber boots. And under them dried cakes of mud on the hard, dirty concrete floor.

"Yeah, sorry." Karsten glanced over his shoulder while striding over the chaos. He lit a cigarette. "There's just no—it's the damn kids, too, dragging all this shit in every day. Do you smoke?"

He threw a crunched-up cigarette packet to me and continued on. The kitchen was worse than the hallway. An old door balancing on a pair of sawhorses served as a kitchen countertop. Some creative soul had even tacked a flowered curtain up along the edge so the splintered horses were partially hidden. There was no sink, which explained the stack of dirty plates out in the rain, but it still seemed quite strange. The stove stood freely on the floor, its sticky cord running across the room to a socket by the door into the living room. In the area by the socket where it had once stood, the worm-eaten floorboards were savagely broken.

"Nikolaj and I are tinkering with the kitchen," said Karsten, tossing out his hand. "The wood is almost pulverized from worms. See? It's all old shit."

He bent over, picked up a piece of wood and held it out to me.

I stared at the crumbling beam without knowing what to say.

"Soft as old cookies." Karsten pressed with his thumb and index finger, transforming the wood into dust under a little pressure. "It's bullshit."

He shoveled mint tea leaves directly into a mug and poured hot water over them, then handed me the cup.

"I don't think we have milk or sugar, but maybe the ladies will bring some back with them. They're out doing a grocery run with the boys. Sit down and I'll find your sweatshirt."

He pointed with his cigarette toward the sofa in the dark room, then went over to the record player and began flipping through the pile of LPs on the floor.

Crumbs littered the coffee table and a patchwork blanket was thrown over the threadbare sofa to cover its holes. They'd moved the furniture around since I'd last been here, but the smell was the same. Wet and cold and like a summer cottage, as if the house had never been heated.

"Here. This is exactly what we need."

He put a record on, carefully placed the needle in one of the grooves and began to sway to Joe Cocker's hoarse vocals in "Something's Coming On." He'd apparently forgotten all about my sweatshirt.

"There was something else," I said, almost having to shout to make myself heard over the music.

He scraped a few crumbs together in a pile on the table, leaned back and threw his feet up. "What is it?"

"Ellen said you had a peeping Tom here. I know the younger brother of the girl who's disappeared, so I thought maybe you might've seen something. Or talked to the police about it?"

"No," he said, laughing. "I'm not a fan of the system's henchmen. And I don't think those things are connected. There're loads of people who like to spy on others and jerk off in God's free nature. You should read a few books. Be a little more open and a little less box-shaped. It'd do you some good."

He got up with a start, left the living room and came back with a pair of velvet trousers and my blue sweatshirt, which he handed me along with a towel.

"I am curious," he said. "How does Ellen pass the time up there? Long walks with the retard?"

The downpour started again, flailing like heavy gray curtains outside the windows. I took a sip of my tea while I watched him over the edge of the mug. I left the clothes lying there, despite both my pants and T-shirt sticking to my skin and the fact that I was

freezing like a dog. I didn't want to take my eyes off him for as long
it would take to pull a sweater over my head. Must be paranoia.
I'd heard you could get that after smoking weed.

"I have to go home."

"Yeah, yeah." He shook his head, annoyed. "You'll get there. What
do the old folks say to suddenly having a young woman in the
house? She's not screwing either of them, but I know damn well
what they're thinking. Especially the retard. Always standing there,
drooling over her."

I didn't answer.

"And what about you? What's your name?"

"Jacob."

"And how old are you, Jacob?"

"Fifteen."

"Aha." He plopped down on the sofa next to me and fished a
hand-rolled cigarette out of a crumpled Camel packet on the table.
"You could easily pass for seventeen or eighteen, couldn't you?
Muscles and all."

I sat as though plastered to the sofa, caught in a panic that made
me play dumb and dead at the same time while Karsten handed me
the packet.

I hesitated, remembering quite vividly my senses putting the
world into strange colors and patterns. Marijuana. I was almost
sure that's what it had been, despite Ellen not saying so.

"No, thanks."

"Come on, have one. I don't trust people who don't smoke and
drink."

"I—no, thanks."

He shrugged, leaned back again and picked a tobacco leaf off
his tongue. Tapped his foot to the rhythm of Joe Cocker's wild,
jagged guitar.

"Let me guess," he said finally. "You love Ellen with all your
young, warm-blooded heart. Am I right?"

His words and the teasing smile on his beautiful Mick Jagger lips caused blood to rush to my cheeks.

"It's nothing to be ashamed of. Women are good at making us love them, and Ellen is one of the best I've met. It's biology, mein Freund. Just like this weed. It works, and everyone loves Ellen. *I* love Ellen, dammit, even though I really, really hate her. Believe me. I know exactly how you feel. Love hurts."

He took a long drag of his joint, holding the smoke in for a long while before slowly letting it seep out of his nose.

My entire body felt the discomfort now. My stomach and head and chest.

"Here. Take one. You'll feel better."

He pushed the packet of roll-ups back to me. And I took one because I didn't know what else to do, but I didn't light it.

"You're averse to believing me now, because she's hit you with a hard left. You want to defend her to your last drop of blood. I can see it in you. And I also know why you feel that way."

He reached out his hand and tousled my hair.

"That beautiful, beautiful body she pretends not to show off, but does anyway. When she wears men's shirts, you can always see something. It's unbuttoned all the way down to her breasts, right? And her ass . . . so clear through the soft material of her skirt. First you think it's by chance, a slapdash peek that you can enjoy in secret. But she's the one wearing the trousers. Those blue eyes. The little nicknames she bestows on all the guys she meets. What'd she come up with for you?"

I sat completely still with his strange, crystal-clear gaze honed in on me. Then he whistled softly and stared up at the ceiling. He actually looked like he was about to start crying until he smiled instead. A small, crooked grimace that didn't look like a genuine grin.

"What if there *is* a man out there killing girls? What about Ellen? Did you get a good look at the peeping Tom?"

He nodded in the direction of the living room window that faced the front yard. "It was in the winter, and it was pitch-black. That was probably why he dared to come so close. Normally he just putters around down by the hedge between us and the neighbor, like a hedgehog."

"But did you see him?"

"No. Only his back, because he bolted into the woods and I didn't make it that far. Thought that run-in was enough to scare him."

I nodded.

"I said all that about Ellen because I want to look after you. Be careful with your heart—it's hard to be fifteen. Do you know why women hate us, Jacob?"

I shook my head.

"Women hate men because we only want to screw them for twenty years of their lives. They know it and we know it. And they get revenge while they can, by any means they can."

He went over to the record player again. Put a new record on with music I didn't know. Acid guitars and a keyboard woven together with a wailing male voice. I somehow managed to make it all the way to the door.

"Is there a woman-murdering monster out there? Is that what your friend says? The boy down at the chicken farm." He turned to assess my expression.

"I don't know," I said. "The police believe she was murdered. By a man. That's what everyone is saying."

Karsten nodded.

"People like that should have their damn balls cut off. Isn't that right, Jacob? We have to take care of our women."

"I don't want to. I don't want to!"

Anders's shout from the living room grew louder. Through the open door, I could see him sitting with his white legs swinging over the edge of the hospital bed and his arms wrapped protectively around himself.

The morning had been gray and stagnant. The old men were still sound asleep when I'd gotten up around eight o'clock and closed the window. Cursed at the flies that had woken me as soon as the sun had begun to rise. I'd drunk my morning coffee alone to the ticking of the clock.

Anton stood in front of Anders, looking like someone who wanted to hit something.

"But you have to, Anders. You have to go to the toilet, and then you can come out and have a cup of coffee. Jette will be here soon."

Anders looked uncertain. His glance flicked over to me and out to the living room window, where it stopped on a distant point as he stroked his hand over his hard, white beard stubble.

"Anders . . ." Anton shot me an awkward look, pulling the door shut so the rest of the conversation became a woolly mumble.

I took a sip of my coffee and turned on my phone. Nothing from either Kirsten or the kids. The last sign of life from my daughter was a text that Kirsten had been magnanimous enough to send on to me. She and her boyfriend floating in a swimming pool somewhere sunny in southern Europe, followed by *XOXOXO*, whatever that was supposed to mean. My son, as far as I could tell, might still be lying half-unconscious under the beer keg I'd bought him for his college party, unwilling to talk to or even look at me.

The living room door opened, and Anders trotted past me on his way to the toilet. His pants zipper was open and his shirt worn thin, with only the two top buttons fastened. Anton sat down in front of me and rubbed his face with a flat hand, then began to butter a slice of toast.

"Have you eaten?"

I nodded, took down the last cold dregs of my coffee and got up. Outside, a combine harvester made its subsonic hum under the noise of the cars from the bypass. The floor vibrated until the sound of the machine disappeared toward old Pinderup. An old Volvo rolled slowly past the driveway, decelerated a few blocks down and returned shortly thereafter. Its rims had been incurably damaged by rust, and the bumper was caked in dried mud. In the dusty side window, I caught a glimpse of the driver's face as the pale, contourless oval turned to look at me.

I suddenly felt a new restlessness that had to be walked off.

I WENT IN the direction of the old highway and struggled up the windswept hill, already covered in sweat on my back and under my arms. The landscape breathed hot dust.

Cars drove by, long gaps between them, tires singing on the coarse asphalt. But apart from that, the first life I spotted was a hysterical little dog that barked angrily as it followed me along a newly painted picket fence. The lawn was stained yellow, and behind it was a piggery gasping for air, all its windows wide open.

"Shut up, Mille."

A woman stood in the flower bed with a watering can. She was the same age as me—a redhead, plagued by the sun, in white gaiters up to the middle of her shins and a sleeveless turquoise top draped over her round stomach. She put down the watering can and strode after the hyperactive, yapping dog.

"Sorry about that. People don't come around here so often. She's not used to it."

I nodded, leaned my head back and studied the property again.

"There weren't pigs on this farm forty years ago, were there?"

"No, no." She bent down, breathless, over the dog and finally got ahold of its collar, swinging the creature up into her arms. "No, it was a cowshed when we took over. We tore it all down and built a new one. Are you from around here?"

"I used to come here a lot . . . to the Svenningsens'."

She squinted against the strong light.

"The brothers?"

I nodded.

She looked slightly apprehensive, trying to figure out what she could say.

"Yes, they're not so . . . We don't socialize with them. The youngest, Anders, I don't think we've ever seen him."

"What about the man down there?"

I pointed at the stone sign marking the dusty avenue on the other side. Felt the same nausea that had overwhelmed me on the train here.

She kissed the little dog on the nose with a loud smacking sound then put it back down, and it began to bark again, its thin legs trembling with rage.

"No," she said decisively. She had to talk loudly to drown out the dog. "He's very private. Men can become a bit odd out here in the country. They need a woman, otherwise they end up peculiar."

She laughed and tilted her head, blinking knowingly to prove her point. She had on mascara and a discreet reddish lipstick that the dog had completely licked off the left side of her mouth. She picked up the troubled, scuttling mutt again. The creature twisted in her arms, revealing its little carnivorous teeth in a snarl. Salty sweat burned my eyes, and suddenly I felt light-headed, as though I were floating and falling at once. I hadn't gone any farther than the point where I could still see the roof and weather vane on the brothers' farm, but this was no-man's-land. In the wavering air over the wheat field was a mirage of two figures—a man and a woman planting fluttering red pennants in the sandy soil.

WHEN I RETURNED, a fat, black smoke column rose toward the sky, waving up under the corrosive sun from the back of the stable. I could already hear the small, hard cracks from the combustion of wood, hot glass and plastic from the edge of the yard.

"Anton?"

I walked around the building through the already trampled nettles and spotted him by the wall beyond the old dung heap, feet wide apart and a pitchfork in his hand to stoke the flames. He pushed a few black-and-white picture frames further into the fire, shielding his face against the heat with the other hand. It reeked of gasoline and poisonous gas.

"What's going on?"

He sent me a sidelong glance before turning his attention back to the fire.

"Housecleaning," he said. "Best to do that kind of thing yourself."

He threw a couple of old phone books onto the fire and prodded the pages with the tip of his fork. He'd been working hard while I was away. He'd dragged a small chest of drawers through the gray-green nettle stems. A plaster sketch of a boy in a shirt and lederhosen, offering an apple to a little girl with yellow hair. Old black-and-white photo albums with crackling tissue paper between the pages. An ivory letter opener and a brass matchbox with a clumsily cast image of the Trundholm sun chariot.

Everything went on the fire, which Anton, short of breath, but with conspicuously safe movements, poured a half canister of diesel over. Even the Amager shelf from the parlor, Great-Grandmother's old armchair and the coffee table from under the living room window. We stood beside each other, watching it all burn, melt and blacken in a fire that was almost invisible in the strong sun.

"I'm doing someone a favor," he said. "Old shit. Will you get me a beer?"

"Is it okay to drink this early in the day when you're an old man?"

He laid a heavy hand on my shoulder and smiled.

"When you're an old man, you're allowed to do anything you're still able to."

Afterward, I sat with a cup of coffee on the stairs while the brothers took a midday nap. The heat had turned the air into vibrating glass over the yard's cobblestones while I sipped my thin, bitter coffee. I Googled Karsten Villadsen on my cell phone, just like I had the night before.

The man in a tie, posed in a cavalcade of men in a conference room, as well as on the company roster and in a separate photo behind a very wide, tidy desk, barely resembled the Karsten I remembered.

"Well-off" was the first adjective that came to mind.

He was slim but still muscular, despite being around seventy. His intellectual glasses had a bright-green frame, and his white hair was trimmed in a military buzz cut. Still, I had no doubts. I recognized the eyes behind the polished lenses and the self-confident, jovial smile from the living room a thousand years ago. When I clicked on the older photographs, I was taken to profile articles in *Stiftstidende* and *Berlingske Business*. "From hippie to international businessman: A fairy tale" and "The magnate who stepped out of his own shadow."

My second adjective was "impure."

Karsten Villadsen's components didn't fit together. Not with who he was now, and not at all with what he'd been like almost forty years ago. If he were a painting or a building, you would have talked about compositional disharmony. Uneven lines and angles that were too sharp.

He was the founder and CEO of a medium-sized company that researched enzymes and other biological components. They made deliveries to a few of the major pharmaceutical companies, and it seemed to be going well. Their headquarters were in Fredericia, and the photographer had shot a shiny glass façade that mirrored the sky, had its image doubled in the iron-gray water encircling the building in a modern-day moat. A piece of city in the country, and an abomination in a pesticide-created desert of former cornfields to boot.

Do you know why women hate us?

If he asked me today, I would have pointed to the symbolism of the massive phallic sculpture he had planted in front of the main entrance of his capitalist cave, but I had a feeling that not only did he know the answer, he'd learned to live with it, too.

I called the main number.

"Can you say what it's regarding?"

The secretary had a professional smile in her voice.

"Yes." I hesitated. "Say it's regarding Ellen. Ellen Høgh."

"One moment."

There was a brief pause with soft waiting music. A painfully muted version of "The Girl from Ipanema." Then a clatter and a deep, male voice clearing itself.

"Karsten Villadsen."

The impatience of an important man laced his words. He was busy and was on his way somewhere.

"Jacob Errbo. You may remember me from Tostrup. The summer of 1978."

There was a short silence on the line.

". . . No, honestly. That was a long time ago. What is this about?"

"Ellen. I haven't had any contact with her since then, but I'm trying to find her. For an old friend."

Silence.

"I'd like to help you," he said. "But I moved from the town around that time as well, and haven't had anything to do with her since, unfortunately. I tried to find her a couple of times myself. Who was it you said you were again?"

"Jacob Errbo."

"That doesn't ring any bells."

"We met a couple of times . . . I'd like to talk to you. In person."

Papers rustled somewhere in the background. A jumble of voices.

"I'm on my way to a meeting. If you leave your name and number with my secretary, I'll get back to you if anything comes to mind."

He hung up, and I called the secretary back and dutifully left my name and number without any illusions. When men like Karsten Villadsen said they might call back, it was nothing more than the most courteous brush-off in their repertoire. After that, the most persistent were allowed to argue in vain with the secretary.

I checked my messages. Nothing from Kirsten, and not from Janne, either. Hopefully it was all over now, but it had certainly had its moment. Both at work and in the city. I couldn't protect Kirsten from the whispers, which, I presumed, were seeping like a chemical spill from the city center down to Valby. The story couldn't be rewritten.

In the living room, Anders breathed heavily in his hospital bed. I was supposed to get going. I scribbled a note to Anton and put it on the kitchen counter before heading back out into the burning sun.

1 9 7 8

I got up at five o'clock in the morning and listened at Ellen's door for a moment, which had gradually become a habit. She was breathing quietly, but I remained standing there until I'd heard the springs of the bed creak as she turned over in her sleep. Until I could be sure she hadn't disappeared in the night. Gone back to the commune or, even worse, to Aarhus, where I'd never be able to find her again.

The sun was a dazzling white splotch behind a haze of clouds, and the wind was cold against my bare legs as I cycled down the long gravel road to the chicken farm. The air was damp, and the forecast had promised heavy local showers. Anders and Anton were crossing their fingers for them to pass; maybe we'd be lucky, despite the swallows flying low over the gray buildings of the chicken farm.

"WE GET TWENTY kroner an hour. Each. But we have to keep going until we're finished."

Sten was leaning against the hall's rusty metal gable wall, a cigarette hanging from his lower lip. He'd smoked for ages, but not like this—relaxed, but with an undercurrent of fury. It was the same Sten I'd glimpsed the last time we'd seen each other. Narrowed eyes with a hint of mistrust that hadn't been there before.

He offered me one from the packet and lit my cigarette with his own as he let the smoke slowly drift out from between his lips. Like a gangster or a movie star.

"That's fine," I said.

"We could probably have asked for more. The old man is pretty desperate right now."

"No, no, it's fine."

To be honest, my hourly wage was the last thing I was worried about right now. As things were, I would have worked for Sten's father for free if he'd asked, and Sten knew that. Or he should have, because I'd never tried to lead him—or his father, for that matter—down the garden path when I'd done work at their farm.

"Good!" Sten threw his cigarette into the tall, wet grass and clapped his hands. "Let's go, then."

The blue pair of overalls he was wearing was adult-sized and sagged off his narrow shoulders, arms and thighs. The sinews of his light-brown throat and neck protruded clearly, making him look like a vulture in a Bugs Bunny cartoon, but he still moved lightly and energetically in his old rubber boots. I followed him into the gable, immediately spotting the Volkswagen T2. Light blue, with flowers primitively painted over the fender. A new HAPPY had been painted in big orange letters over the side door.

"Who's here?"

Sten followed my gaze and shrugged.

"The guys from the commune. They never have any money. They're loading the truck."

I nodded silently and followed him as he opened the door into the hall and went into the small room where he and his father hung up their work clothes. The waiting room to hell, as Sten called it.

I'd been in here loads of times before, just to stare in horror when Sten selected a single rooster sentenced to death and slaughtered it in front of its mother. I'd worked here a couple of long afternoons last year, when things had to be done quickly and one of the usual helpers had backed out. Still, the noise and the stench of ammonia hit me like a kick in the face as though it were the first time, making me dizzyingly light-headed.

"Here."

Sten took another pair of overalls from a hook inside the door and threw it to me. Waited patiently as I pulled on the cold, stiff getup and buttoned it all the way up to my throat. Then we walked up the steel staircase to the floor with the cages.

"Is the truck here?"

Sten nodded.

"It's parked out front. Dad'll take them and pack the boxes."

He pointed at the big open hatch in one side of the hall, where his father was already standing on the truck's loading ramp, sorting the plastic boxes. To get down there, you had to balance on the narrow walkways that went from the wire cages over a sea of chicken shit. The stench was indescribable, as was the feeling of sticking a hand into the first cage and pulling a chicken up by the leg. One at a time, I pulled them through the narrow opening at the top while they flapped their gaunt wings and uttered sad, angry sounds from their throats. Then I walked on to the next one. I could carry four chickens in each hand as I jogged along the narrow walkway in a strange, irregular line dance in an effort to keep up with Sten on the other side. Down by the opening to the truck, I handed my feeble chicken bouquets to Sten's father, who threw them into boxes so hard that I could hear their wings and legs break.

This wasn't Anders and Anton's place; lark nests weren't marked off here. Sten and his father had their own way of doing things.

"Oy . . ."

The hall was lit by a cool, blue light from the fluorescent bulbs under the dusty rafters, which cast dark lines on Sten's father's face as he leaned over the box and pushed down with a flat hand. He cursed like I'd never heard him curse before. His pale face and receding chin were already streaked with dirt and sweat, and the expression in his eyes was somewhere between rage and fatal exhaustion. Sten had told me his father hadn't slept since Lise had disappeared, and I believed him.

"Oy . . ." He dragged the box out to the ramp and handed it over to the guys from the commune. I caught a glimpse of the chubby guy's wet, curly hair, his head jerking slightly every time he shoved a box over to Karsten. I returned to the cages.

Trampled-flat black cadavers lay in the bottoms of some of them. The chickens had pecked each other bloody in others, so my hands sometimes met open wounds and naked, bare skin. I couldn't keep up with Sten. His movements were accustomed and sure, and he didn't care whether he broke a wing or a pair of legs when he pulled the animals from their cages. I'd seen him play tennis with some of the new chicks. He'd stick his hand into the box they were in, throw one up in the air, and hit it with a tetherball racket as though he were bloody Jimmy Connors. Blood, feathers and entrails everywhere.

"I'm just used to this," he said when I protested. "You'd be doing the same thing if you lived on a chicken farm."

I doubted that, but he was right in that I *had* become tougher after the first few times. I didn't break anything, or I tried not to, but it was still bad. And the chickens screeched and flapped with their half-bare wings, shitting all over my pants in fear. The smell always lingered in my skin for days, no matter how much Lux soap I scrubbed myself with.

I lost my grip on a hen that fluttered between the cages and ended up in the gooey, rocking sea of shit under us. Sten whistled and laughed.

"She'll be sorry for that in the long run," he said, pointing. The hen, which had collapsed on its folded wings, sat with open, blinking eyes, looking around. There was no movement, only the eyes and the head, which was tilted slightly as if the hen were somewhat surprised by the situation.

A little to the right of the death-sentenced wretch, something bright stuck up out of the thick mass. It could have been anything. A branch or a bucket handle or something that Sten's father had lost on one of his lonely cage inspections. But for some reason, I was sure at first glance.

It was a hand.

My brain refused to understand what it was seeing, so I took a few steps back to get a look from another angle. It looked like a hand from there, too, and I walked back a little along the narrow path between the cages. Until I was standing just over the spot, and it was no longer just a hand. The contours of a face were just discernible below the grainy surface. Nose, cheeks and eyes like a cast molded in a stiff crust of shit, and the absurd outline of a butterfly hair clip.

Lise.

And as I thought it, I walked a few steps and threw up all over the cages, chickens and sea of shit.

I HUNG AROUND the yard for a few hours after they'd pulled Lise out and driven her away.

It was pouring now, and the water dug deep furrows into the coarse gravel of the yard as the police spread out in all directions. Men in yellow raincoats with plastic bags and barrier tape went in and out of the hall while what should have been day grayed and darkened under the heavy clouds. I sat with Sten up in his room, watching the stream of people coming and going.

One of the officers had asked Sten's father how he usually emptied the huge slurry tank under the cages and hadn't been satisfied with the answer. Shit couldn't just be sucked up in a slurry spreader and driven out to the field, because then important clues could be lost. Now the tank was to be emptied one truck at a time, and the whole lot run through some kind of filter out at the sewage treatment plant.

Sten's father had stood in the yard for the first hour, directing traffic to the hall with vague, indecisive movements. But nobody really took notice of him, and now he was just standing there, the thin gray hair stuck to his cheeks and forehead and the boots black and heavy with water. Someone should have gotten him and sat him down at the kitchen table, poured him coffee and forced a slice of bread on him, but Sten's mom was in the kitchen, and even though we were a floor above, we could hear her dry, moaning sob, and who would want to sit with that?

Sten sat chewing a fingernail while he looked out. "There's going to be some mess with the chickens," he said, nodding to the truck still parked next to the big hall. The driver hadn't been allowed to leave with his cargo of rejected animals, so he was huddled with the two guys from the commune under the shelter of the cab instead. The glow from their cigarettes could be seen behind the still-moving windshield wipers.

"Do you think somebody murdered her?" I glanced at Sten, who'd moved on to the next nail bed. Still chewing slowly and methodically. He shrugged.

"I don't know," he said. "Maybe. Toad never went in there, but she might've been drunk. People do crazy things when they're drunk, don't they?"

I couldn't imagine Lise going out to see the chickens. Not even in a drunken stupor. She hated that place, especially its stench, and she was deathly afraid of all birds. A sparrow on the stairs made her scream like she'd seen a two-headed monster. There was no logical explanation for how she'd ended up lying there with a white, dissolved face, eyes staring at the dusty gray sky of the chicken coop hallway.

Someone, a strong person maybe, might have dragged or forced her in there, up the stairs, and farther along the rocky boards between the cages. Someone who'd thrown her down, and when I imagined it, I heard Lise begging for her life. Heard her scream, and suddenly it was Ellen. Her eyes that were covered with dark crusts of shit, and her body that was soft and yielding in a way that made you afraid it would suddenly erupt.

There was slightly less than a mile between the brothers' farm and the chicken farm—ten minutes on foot and five minutes by bike—and Ellen was visible from the road when she picked peas in the garden or fed the chickens or walked along the fence with her sketch pad, long skirt pulled up so you could see her tanned legs.

I got up a little too quickly and dried my palms on my bare thighs. Cleared my throat.

"I think I'm going to go home."

Sten turned his head toward me with a glazed, uninterested look.

"Of course. Yeah."

"But you can come and get me when—when they get to the last part."

"Yeah, thanks."

I smiled stupidly and rapped my knuckles on the single Bayern Munich poster that Sten had attached to the sloping wall with pins. I didn't know what else to do, and had reached the door when he said something.

"People will talk about her," he said. His lips were pulled tightly downward at the edges. "They'll say she was going around, fucking all sorts."

"I don't think—"

"Of course they will," he said quietly. "They'll say she was a prostitute. But I'll clear her of all that. We have to find the pig who did it. We can do it together."

His voice was cold; it reminded me of how he'd acted that morning with the cigarette in his mouth, a new, hard expression in his jaw.

"Of course," I said. "You can count on me."

1 9 7 8

"Isn't it weird that it's so beautiful out, when somebody's just been found dead like that?"

Ellen and I walked beside each other, she with an outstretched arm to run her hand through the reddish light-green oats. The sun was shining again, but it was cool, and the sky above us was a light, indifferent shade of gray. I didn't know what to say. I'd never thought of the landscape as being beautiful, just ordinary, and right now the only thing I noticed was the moisture on her long, tanned neck. The scent of soap on her hair and body, mixed with the natural salty smell she had, hurt me a little every time it hit me.

"Yeah, it's strange."

"The Vikings called July the month of the worm because everything rotted in the heat. Worms in flesh. But everything is so beautiful in July."

I smiled, despite my boyish discomfort around her. She was so serious about it.

"The Vikings were crazy," I said. "Too much mead and blood. Probably too many women, too."

She laughed just long enough for me to glimpse her beautiful teeth. Over her shoulder was a bag with her sketch pad and pencils.

"They were definitely crazy," she said. "But they were also very practical. March was manure month, April was grazing month, June

. . . I don't remember what June was, but July was the month for decay and maggots."

We reached the area near the railway station, and she strode over what almost resembled a barbed-wire fence. Its thread was rusty and tangled in grass and wild bushes. That kind was no longer used for livestock, so now it was only soft tufts of fur from hare and deer stuck to the sharp steel wire joints. Farther up the slope, cow parsnip grew with its juicy, hairy stalks, so we had to move carefully through the wilderness. And then there were the gooseberry bushes that Anton had promised us. Three of them, full of transparent green berries.

Ellen pulled a plastic bag from the pocket of her denim shorts and began to pick, and I joined her. Our hands met briefly when we put berries in the bag, but we'd stopped talking to each other. Concentrated on the task at hand and what would soon be marmalade and stewed fruit in Ellen's saucepan.

There were worms in plenty of the berries. The month of the worm.

She threw a berry at my neck and laughed.

"I don't think they're quite ripe yet," she said. "But it'll be fine if I use a bunch of sugar."

I crunched an acidic berry between my teeth, grabbed one of the old fence posts, and felt the soft crack all the way down at the ground when it released its hold and remained hanging on the thread. The next time I came up here, I'd have to bring a wheelbarrow with me for the old stakes and take down the fence. Maybe with Anders, but preferably with Ellen.

I could see us working side by side in the heat. Her in a T-shirt that clung to her back and small, pert breasts. I in my bare upper body, so there wouldn't be much in the way of clothes between us. My hand under her fine jaw, her mouth open and her tongue pointed and full of life against my teeth, and then the predictable tumble into the grass where I pressed my burning heat and rock-hard limb in toward her denim shorts and sweaty stomach until she wiggled herself out of her clothes and I could finally take her in the biblical sense. Dear God. I was about to faint or die or explode all over everything.

"Anyway, how are they sure Lise was murdered?" She stuck a long blade of grass into her mouth and bit it. It was enough to drive you crazy.

"Her clothes," I said. Sten had reluctantly shared a few details with me. "She wasn't wearing tights or a jacket. No shoes, either. Only a skirt and a thin blouse. The night she disappeared, it was cold, even though it was the end of May. And she'd never have voluntarily gone into the henhouse."

"I didn't know that," she said, shaking her head. "I was in Berlin all spring. Maybe that was just as well . . ."

I caught her eye and extended my hand to comfort her. But she didn't see it. She just continued her determined march through the high grass.

"Are you afraid because of what's happened?"

"No." She shook her head. "That kind of thing is rare. Like getting hit by lightning."

She gave a start and cursed quietly. Something had stung her foot, so she had to stand on one leg, leaning against me as she pulled off her other sandal and examined the soft sole. I took advantage of the chance to fix my suddenly too-tight pants. It seemed like she was trying to kill me by way of diverting the blood from my main internal organs.

"Have you ever gone up there?" She nodded up at the tracks.

I thought about it. Remembered jumping from sleeper to sleeper with Sten and Jørgen back when we'd been Danish saboteurs in enemy countries. Hands and arms dust gray from the ash and coal in the fire we'd lit at the foot of the slope. Jørgen had a plastic machine gun, so he'd been able to shout *ratatatatata* while the rest of us had to settle for a deep-throated rumble or a whistle as the imaginary bullet careened toward its target. Our laughter when the train came; we'd remained standing on the tracks until the conductor had blown the horn and shouted out through the open window.

Ellen had begun to climb the slope. She'd reached the pile of soot-blackened crushed stone she needed to boost herself up between the rails. I followed until we were side by side again, each walking with a cigarette, and it felt so nice. The sun was burning through the thin layer of clouds. A heron took off from the bog on the other side of Ingeborgs' farm, and it was like a totally different landscape, we were so high up. Ellen hopped up onto one of the tracks, walking along it parallel to me, smiling crookedly, the ciga-rette still in her mouth.

"I come from a station city, too, don't I? Aarhus. The locals who wished they could travel usually went down to the harbor to watch the ships, but I went to the train station and watched the trains go off to Hamburg and Berlin and Paris. Or even beyond that, to the Urals and the continent behind them."

"This goes to Grenå," I said dryly.

"Spoilsport."

"Oh, well, it stops at Aarhus, of course."

"Yes."

She jumped down from her rail, resuming a jumping gait between the tracks. You had to take a step that was either a little too short or a little too long to avoid slipping through.

We could hear a train in the distance on our way through the woods, and worked wordlessly down the slope on the other side to wait for it to pass. I scratched myself on some thorns on my way down, almost stumbling while Ellen moved surprisingly agilely to a short Mirabelle cherry tree. I picked one of the little fruits and took a bite. The peel was sour and bitter, and the rest of the fruit not ripe yet. Here, at the foot of the slope, it was silent and warm among elder, hawthorn and rowanberries, as well as invisible birds hopping between twigs, ruffling their wings and chirping lightly.

"That stuff Karsten smokes . . ." she said. "Stay away from it. From him. It's too much lately. And drugs are dangerous, especially when you're as young as you are."

"Okay."

"I mean it, Utzon!" She stopped and stared at me with the clearest blue eyes in the universe. "You have to mind yourself."

Her nipples were visible through her light T-shirt, and I couldn't help staring like the cursed, all-too-easy idiot I was. Because she was beautiful. A single buzzard circled above us on an ascending airstream. Didn't beat its wings once in the time I followed it with my eyes.

Ellen nodded at it. "The vultures are coming. I told you, it's worm month."

We could see the brothers' farm again. The tall chestnut trees, the stable and Anton's red Ferguson, crawling slowly across the meadow with the five worn-out milk cans he used to bring water to the cows.

I stood up and spotted Anders standing unnaturally straight, watching us from the crossing a ways behind us on the track.

"How long has he been there?" I don't know why I was whispering, but I was.

Ellen laughed, shrugging. "He's beating thistles," she said.

And Anders was indeed leaning on the scythe as though he'd had it with him and had just straightened up to catch his breath and stretch his back. But I couldn't see where he'd been. The grass and thistles were still standing at almost man height in the boundary between the railway line and cornfields.

He raised his hand and waved, but remained standing in the same spot as we began to walk toward the farm. Ellen, lost in her own thoughts, occasionally let the bag of berries heavily slap the wet grass, and I followed after.

Still behind us, Anders started walking along the railway fence with the scythe swinging in front of him in long, impressive pulls. Cutting down thistles and the long grass, common wild oats and all the other plants that made life difficult. Watching us with a hand shading his eyes.

RISSKOV

Trimmed hedges, wrought-iron gates and six-foot-high, white-painted walls surrounded the homes. The sidewalks were covered in newly cracked light-gray gravel with sharp edges, specially imported from Sicilian quarries. The tiles in the huge kitchens and bathrooms had been fired in Tuscany, and the dining tables were yard-long planks in dark American walnut, African mahogany and Carolina pine.

I was an architect and had seen it all a thousand times before. A panoramic view of the water, lots of natural light shining on modern furniture blended with classic design. Small, infantile clashes with even smaller short-lived waves of fashion. Ripples on a troubled surface of abundance that could be replaced at any time if someone started to feel bored. The rich people in Risskov and Hellerup were similar, and although they all spent exorbitant sums to stand out, their imagination didn't generally extend beyond their neighbor's interior designer.

By comparison, Kirsten's and my home in Valby was a museum of events that had played out twenty and thirty years ago. There were key rings with keys to locks that no longer existed. Gjøl trolls and miniature Rubik's Cubes. A small box containing a boy's baby teeth, a handful of worthless pesos from our vacation to the Philippines, and an unused laboratory jar for a stool screening that I'd received from the hospital on my fiftieth birthday.

Karsten Villadsen's address wasn't in the phone book, of course, but a longer profile in *Aarhus Stiftstidende* revealed that the successful business owner lived in Risskov with a direct view of the water. There were even pictures of him inside and outside a brand-new villa that resembled an old nobleman's house with a hipped, black-tiled roof, a balcony with a complicated balustrade, grapevines and plump cherubs on the brickwork. Not impossible to find if you had an eye for detail, and this street looked closer than the others. Prospects were starting to look good.

I switched my phone off and parked the Taunus in front of a driveway with a Porsche and a Mercedes behind another black iron gate. It was a private road. Below me, the water sparkled between the leaves, and a wooden staircase led farther down the steep slope. The year's heat had long ago transformed it into a lukewarm algae soup, but from up here, it was beautiful in the glow of the late-afternoon sun.

Houses and cars and water. Down on the beach, a bunch of teenagers cheered. The girls laughed hysterically, and the boys howled likes monkeys in a cave. They were playing volleyball, flexing their young muscles, and I could almost feel their strength in my own body. Remembered the sensation of taking off and soaring. The older you became, the more you felt the hazy, confused thoughts of your youth. You saw yourself through a fogged window of glass and time.

There was no name on the mailbox in front of the house closest to the water, but after scrutinizing the pictures on my phone, I could identify the top of the large chestnut tree that Karsten Villadsen had posed in front of in his large, overgrown garden.

It was easy enough to get to the front door. Karsten obviously had money, but not the neighbors' collective inclination to fortify their castles against a sultan's army of slaves. There was no electronic door, no six-foot-high wall with steel teeth and no digital intercom.

If you ignored the monstrous size of the house—over five thousand square feet, at least—and a single surveillance camera glowing red and angry above the door, the surroundings seemed almost friendly. The large yard in front of the house had an overgrown hedge around it and a lawn that had been allowed to turn into a forest several years ago. Self-sown beech and oak trees battled for light under a few old apple trees, and a beautiful lime tree cast dancing gray shadows over the house and tall grass. The driveway, on the other hand, was a neatly cleared path of freshly cut mulch with a single mailbox-red Audi S5 Sportback. Leather seats and a masculine finish on the dashboard, dark wood paneling, that were to give an illusion of Chesterfield and sherry bottles and British indignation. Unimaginativeness knew no bounds here, and that kind of car had never succeeded in making my blood boil. They were neither beautiful nor ugly. And if I were ever to build a house, it would be one of wood in the middle of a forest. I took the beautiful, winding staircase to the front door with firm steps and rang the doorbell.

It sounded like a church bell was ringing behind the door. One, two, three times. Then I heard quick steps, and it was opened by an older teenager, maybe seventeen or eighteen. And despite Karsten having been close to thirty when I met him, the similarity was striking. The boy was taller and broader than his father, but his face was the same. Strong, midlength hair, soft lips, dark lashes and pretty, slightly slanting eyes, which I would probably have interpreted as soulful if the boy hadn't continued to write a text while I stood there in the doorway.

"Yeah?"

He looked up at me, amused. Probably thought I was a Jehovah's Witness or from the city government. He didn't look like a young man afraid to slam the door in someone's face.

"I'd like to talk to Karsten Villadsen."

"What, now?" He glanced over his shoulder and tapped a few more words into the phone.

"Okay, yeah, but only for two seconds. Dad!"

There was no answer, and the boy sighed. It might have been apologetic, but was probably more out of irritation at being forced to do something active.

"He's here somewhere," he said. "I'll call him."

More typing on the phone, followed by a conversation that would have been better behind closed doors.

"Hey, Dad. There's someone here who wants to talk to you . . . No idea . . . a man, older . . . okay, one sec."

He looked at me without lowering the phone. "Does he know you?"

I nodded. "You can tell him it's about Ellen."

The boy rolled his broad, gym-trained shoulders, turned his back and walked a little into the beautiful hall. Mumbled something and threw another glance in my direction. Then he turned around again and shouted to me.

"It's fine, you can come in. He'll be down in a minute."

And then the young man disappeared into the huge house again, typing eagerly on his phone. His Ralph Lauren shirt and light-brown shorts had vanished, and he'd left the door ajar behind him.

There were indistinct voices and slammed doors somewhere above me in the lofty hall, but I continued on through the double doors into a living room that opened into three adjoining rooms. Through an open set of patio French windows, you could look out onto the large, overgrown backyard and farther out to the water that glistened between the trees. The built-in floor-to-ceiling shelves on the wall bordering the next room contained all the literature I'd ever wanted to read. *Ulysses. The Capital. The Idiot* and *War and Peace. Lolita. The Trial.* Hemingway's complete works, Kierkegaard and even a series of biographies of great men.

At the bottom of the garden, a well-groomed woman in her midforties appeared in my line of sight with a watering can in

her hand. The mother of the boy, I assumed—youthful in appear-
ance, at least from this distance, though a semitransparent white,
long-sleeved chiffon blouse revealed she had skin she no longer
wished to show off. I'd learned that from Kirsten, who generously
revealed the greatest secrets of the female sex as, drunk and snig-
gering, we went through the symptoms of creeping age from our
respective armchairs.

"See-through blouses and nylon stockings," she said. "They're
used to cover imperfect skin. Nothing else. Watch out for it, now.
Old, wrinkled women wear them. Forty-plus. Not younger than
that. Not if they're smart, at least."

She had reached her midforties at that time, having just bought
her first blouse with lace and transparent sleeves.

The woman with the watering can walked over the lawn, disappearing from the picture. Thirty years younger than her husband
and afraid of being discarded. But we all were, when it came down
to it. No one wanted to be reminded of impending death.

I pulled out a chair. Wegner. I couldn't help but stroke its smooth
lines before sitting down. Stood up again.

The furniture in the room was of Danish design, resting on rugs
with thick pile and clear colors. Modern art in strong, sprawling
shades and brushstrokes hung on the walls; a grayer, shy drawing
right next to the patio door caught my eye. No larger than an A5
page, but professionally framed. I walked over the parquet oak
flooring and gently touched the slender steel frame. On first glance,
the pencil drawing was a classic crucifixion motif. A suffering,
beardless Messiah on a white background and in detailed lines,
but the cross itself was missing. There was only a naked upper
body, outstretched arms, and wrists hammered into the nothingness of the white paper, and instead of the usual loincloth, the man
was standing in water to the middle of his sharp hip bones, revealing only a hint of genitals and pubic hair below the surface. His
long hair fell heavy and wet over his cheeks, making it difficult to

determine whether he was getting out of the water or drowning. It was signed *Ellen*.

"I was actually the model for that."

I hadn't heard him coming, but his voice instantly sparked forgotten impulses.

Tell me about her. What she's doing with the old men.

I turned around and spotted him in the double door out to the hall. Good-looking like in the pictures, and still with a boyish, unpolished charm. Despite being rich, he apparently wasn't one for pink polo shirts and smoothly ironed canvas pants. Instead, he was braving the summer warmth in jeans, threadbare in the right way, and a large checked cotton shirt.

He smiled.

"Sorry it took so long; I had to take off the statesman attire. When it's as hot as today, you almost need a tow bar and cable to pull it off me. But you are . . . ?"

"I called you earlier today," I said. "Jacob Errbo."

"Yes. Interesting. Jacob. Architect in Copenhagen, family man. I looked you up after our conversation." Karsten looked at me impassively. "I believe I asked you to wait until I'd had some time to think it over. Did Jytte give you my address? She doesn't usually do that."

"I found it myself."

He smiled with a microsecond's delay, then threw out his arms.

"And now here you are. I told you, I don't know where Ellen is, but of course I'm a little curious. You're younger than me . . ."

"Yeah, I didn't know her very well, either, but she lived with my father's uncles during the summer of seventy-eight. You and I met a couple of times, too."

"All right. If you say so." Something was obviously in motion behind the smiling, suntanned façade, and I instinctively knew that he hadn't settled for just Googling me. He knew everything. About me and Kirsten, and probably Janne, too, however he'd managed it.

"I think I do actually remember you. You were the boy."

I nodded, clearing my throat.

"Yes, and as I said, I'm looking for Ellen. Or someone who can tell what became of her. Did you have any contact with her after those years in the commune?"

"No. I never heard anything. But you say she traveled?"

"That's what I was told. She just disappeared."

"Yeah?" Karsten laughed quietly. "That sounds exactly like her. You didn't always know where you had her. Rarely did, actually."

"What do you mean?"

He nodded toward the garden, where his wife was still bent over the roses.

"There are two kinds of people, right? The ones who are stable and the ones who flip out. Take, for example, Mette, whom I married twenty-two years ago. She was young then, very young. Twenty-five. Almost thirty years younger than me, and if you'd been a nervous man, you might have feared that she'd have gone off with a younger man by now. But I knew she wouldn't. Do you know why?"

He didn't wait for an answer.

"Because she was already so calm when we met each other. Unexcitable, serene. She'd never think to break up a marriage, she doesn't harbor dreams of realizing herself and the thought of sex with other men gives her nausea. Literally. She told me that once. The only drawback is, you end up with such terribly boring children. When your childhood is as easy as it was for my three, you already know that you'll be good, but never great." He smiled and blinked teasingly.

"Ellen, on the other hand . . ." He shook his head slightly. "As beautiful and neurotic as a race horse. Fucked up. It can be appealing when you're young, but it's extremely difficult later. I should be glad she dumped me, because I hardly had the strength to do it myself."

I scrutinized the drawing of the crucified Karsten Villadsen. His mouth was drawn harder than the rest of his face, his eyes closed in almost blurred lines.

"Were there drugs, too?"

He nodded.

"Ellen was stoned whenever she drew. LSD. She did her best work on drugs. It didn't work the same way for me. I held up the camera and saw the wildest things through the lens, but when I got clear-headed and developed the film, it was boring as shit. Grass and half faces, all completely out of focus. I did drugs when I wasn't working; she did them when she was. At least, in the beginning. Then she stopped doing that, too. I don't think I've ever met someone who was so fucking hypersensitive about everything. Are they still alive, those two old codgers?"

"Yes."

He nodded and glanced at his cell phone. My visit was obviously coming to an end.

"You and Ellen had no mutual friends I could contact? People she was with before you dated. That'd be—"

He moved his arms apologetically, like he must have done a thousand times before at board meetings and with management. If my visit had shaken him, it wasn't visible. Like a modest, random geographical displacement at the bottom of the Pacific Ocean—tangible on the seismograph, but absorbed by the ocean.

He looked at me and smiled as he offered his hand in goodbye.

ON MY WAY home, I stopped at the ruins of Kalø Castle and bought beer and a hot dog, which I ate while heading out toward the narrow isthmus.

I'd come here in spring and fall as a boy, even stood on the slope and frozen my ass off, in tatters, one cold February day with crumpled ice twisted across the beach while my father slashed his spade through the snow and protected vegetation. I recognized the lonely church, the little forest and the paved medieval road to the point. Birds tumbled on the upthrust of the bay, which smelled rotten and tangy above the flowers and stinging grass in the salt meadow.

I went for a walk around the ruins, contemplating the tower that stood like an empty shell out toward the steep slope and the water. Jackdaws had built nests in the old joist holes on each floor, and at the bottom of the structure lay piles of the branches that they'd dropped during their work. Weeds had been wiped away at the bottom of the old dungeon. When they'd begun to restore the ruin many years ago, they'd found pitch-dark secret tunnels dug under the thick walls by unhappy prisoners with frayed, bleeding nails.

I sat in the shadow of the tower wall and opened the first beer, then took out my cell and scrolled through an unexpected wave of texts from Kirsten. Most were practical. A valuation of the house, papers from the little, persistent joint lawyer we had commissioned to draw up lists of our assets and suggestions for how they should be distributed. Something had to be signed. There were questions that had to be clarified and rounded off, and here I was in Jutland, completely useless. Her fury brewed with every message, finally erupting in the last.

Why the hell do I have to sort everything out? Really. It's your shit, your problems. And I haven't gotten anything that resembles an explanation.

Multiple calls from an unknown number, but no message.

She was right, of course. We'd spent more than thirty years together, had children, bought a house, had mutual friends and family, so of course I owed her an explanation. But I wasn't sure I had one.

Something had happened in the drafting room that day in June. The heat had melted the plastic and the candles in the windows, and for some reason everyone was out. They were taking classes or with clients; all the hopeful young people had gone home early or were at the beach or were bent over their assignments at homely kitchen tables or in garden chalet communities. The only ones left were me and Janne, who was hopelessly treading the awkwardness that had somehow developed between us. I told a funny story, sat as close to her as I possibly could.

"I'm going now," she said a while later, and I followed her with a sidelong look as she gathered her phone and keys into her purse and left the office on high platform sandals that highlighted her summer-brown calves, glistening with sweat.

I sat down on her chair and touched the mouse so the computer woke up with a weak hum. She hadn't logged out of her Facebook page, and I scrolled through her friends. Young women with their hair carelessly blown in front of their faces, funny grimaces, sunglasses, serious poses, or parodies of serious poses, ironic comments about the media and themselves to make them seem cooler and more genuine, when they did the opposite. The men were in running tights with mountain bikes and sunglasses in front of the Grand Canyon, at summer cottages or in a diffuse darkness with little stripes of disco light. Janne herself flashed pictures from China and more recent ones from New York's Brooklyn Bridge and Chinatown. Unsmiling and with a red pout, as usual. And I could neither look at it nor stop looking at it.

In a relationship with Stig Nielsen.

I went in and studied the tiresome amount of mobile uploads. Stig was a handsome and seemingly serious young man. A political science student with stubble and neat, straight jeans of the kind that didn't attract too much attention with holes nor sloppiness. Janne, I could see, had been invited to an event on Vesterbrogade on Friday evening. A party. I noted the place and time, sensing reality slip away from under me like loose gravel on a slope. I'd never been an alcoholic, but sometimes—in weak moments like this—I thought my father and I might have more in common than I'd normally admit. I sought my own drugs with as much proficiency as my dad taking his beer from the fridge.

Was that what I should tell Kirsten? That something had gotten stuck years ago and couldn't be healed? Pain signals that continued to run in long-since-severed nerve pathways. Or was that an explanation she'd rather be without?

I opened beer number two and leaned my head back against the wall, closing my eyes. A thought had slipped away from me—something to do with the station and Brugsen and the six-pack I'd bought the first day I'd been back in town.

The pale light over the cash register, the bony upper body, the blonde hair and the curious, water-blue eyes. Laurel. Why hadn't I seen it before now?

1 9 7 8

"You *said* I could count on you."

Sten's voice was low and tense, without any suggestion of the little fooling-around laugh that had accompanied everything he'd ever said before Lise had disappeared. It wasn't only his body that had become lean and hard. We pulled our bikes along one of the newer suburban streets behind the school, where the newly built gardens were naked. The trees were still too small to give shade, the grass on the lawns thin and pale and filled with fresh, green dandelion shoots.

"Ah, dammit, Sten . . ."

"What is it? Are you scared of her?"

"No, but why can't you do it yourself?"

I thought of Laurel, of how she'd looked when I'd met her at the bridge a couple of weeks ago. Ash gray in the face, with her long, tangled hair hanging down over her bright eyes. I wasn't afraid, but I certainly didn't want to talk to her. And definitely not about Lise. I was pretty sure there was an imminent risk of her crying. And what was I supposed to do then? I didn't know how to handle crying girls.

Sten ran his hand through his hair, which sat in greasy strips over his scalp, as he gave me a furious look over his shoulder.

"Because she hates me, and you know that. She won't tell me shit."

His nails audibly scratched against his scalp again. And I caved. Because I didn't want to get into a fight with him, and because it was true. Laurel hadn't spoken to him since that time she'd forgotten to lock the door to the upstairs toilet and he'd come barging in the second she was sitting with a protruding abdomen and was wiping her bottom. It was a picture he'd painted for me at least a thousand times. The spread legs, the glimpse of something pink in the mousy pubic hair and Laurel's furious attempt to slam the door with both hands while Sten remained paralyzed halfway into the bathroom.

He must have jerked off an infinite number of times to that image. I myself had done it a few times, but fortunately she knew nothing about that. According to Sten, Laurel had a memory like an elephant and was quite good at bearing a grudge, but she was always kind to me. Even used to smile at me if I met her on the main street.

A good start, said Sten.

We threw the bikes into the hedge in front of the detached house and stood for a minute, staring at the drawn curtains and the closed door. The garden was neat, half-barren and newly sown like all the others on the street. There were raised flower beds, greenhouse boxes and parsley and carrots in twisting rows, but light-green weeds had begun to wind their way among the newly planted saplings.

"Her parents have gone camping, but she didn't want to go with them. She's been hanging out at Crazy Horse in Hornslet and at the bar every single night since they left. Stupid cow. Most girls are smart enough to stay in at night at this point."

"Well, yeah." I stalled for time. "But you can't keep doing that, Sten. And maybe she needs to be with her friends, too."

"Friends?"

He spat on one of the smooth, light-gray tiles and nodded toward the front door. "I'll wait out here while you talk to her. She

has to confess that it was her. The alcohol, everything. And she has
to say it to the police, too. I won't stand for her going around and
saying rumors about Lise."

"We don't know if she is."

He shook his head, furious.

"But you *know* how she is. I've told you! She just can't tell anyone . . . and I want to know what men were staring at Lise. Every
single one of the sick bastards."

Of course, I already knew what he was thinking. He had repeat-
edly found beers and schnapps and cigarettes and used condoms
down near the bush by the road. Really disgusting. According to
Sten, the condoms could only be Laurel's because she was a prostitute, and I'd tactfully failed to point out the obvious. That
Lise—at least in theory—could also have had something to do with
those used condoms. It was fine with me if Sten didn't want to
think that.

"That's all she has to say," he said. "That it was all her."

He was so different, I thought. There was no longer even a hint
of the boy who'd blushed his way through the German accusative
masculine, feminine, and gender-neutral forms two months ago.
He'd aged a thousand years since they'd found Lise, had retreated
from the rest of us. From school, from trading cards, and cycling
to Kalø. I understood what had happened, but not quite what it
meant. What was going to become of him?

"Fine." I shrugged and walked reluctantly up to the door, throwing a last look at Sten before ringing the bell. He hid on the other
side of the hedge, staring at me with burning eyes. Feverishly
scratching his scalp.

"What?"

Laurel had opened the door and was glaring vacantly at me.
She was taller than I remembered. At least six feet, with long, pale
arms and legs. And despite her pulling down her T-shirt, which
was the only thing she had on, I managed to get a glimpse of her

fluffy pink underwear and a bit of pubic hair sticking out under-neath. It was impossible to keep my eyes from it, even now, when the circumstances were so serious. I silently cursed at myself.

"I came because I'm trying to find out . . . something about Lise."

Laurel's eyes narrowed. "Why?"

I glanced back briefly, but Sten was nowhere to be seen.

"I'm friends with Sten," I said. "And he . . . We're trying to find out something."

"Okay. Jacob, right?" She stepped aside, waving me toward the kitchen, and didn't seem angry or hysterical. Just tired.

"Yes."

Laurel nodded and went to the kitchen sink to fill the kettle with water. Her feet were bare, and there was a swarm of little birthmarks on her white legs.

"You can have a beer, too, if you feel like it," she said, nodding toward a box standing in a ray of sunlight on the floor by the fridge. Half the bottles were already drunk.

"No, thanks," I said. "It's fine. I won't be that long."

The kettle rumbled faintly on the stove, and Laurel sat down at the small four-seater by the window. She rubbed a thumb over a tabletop full of crumbs and began to diligently split a hunk of bread into pieces with a frayed polished nail. Her fingers were long and red, and her knuckles bent the wrong way, rubberlike, when she pressed them against the surface. There was something about her that reminded me of a creeper plant. Like she had to lean against and seize creatures with more vitality to remain upright. Her not-very-big breasts were two pointed tops under the oversized T-shirt, and she smelled of night and sweat and sleep, even though it was only late afternoon.

"What would you like to know?" she asked, blinking her long, colorless lashes.

"Lise . . . Sten doesn't want you going around saying all sorts of things about her. That she was with a lot of men."

Laurel wrinkled her forehead and leaned back a little. Crossed her arms. "I haven't said anything about Lise."

"But that she had boyfriends . . . and drank and stuff. Was screwing someone. Sten says you were."

She laid her head back, watching me from under half-closed eyelids. "What sort of shit is that to say?"

I shrugged, not daring to meet her eyes.

I'd heard Laurel was smart. Smarter than all the boys, and even smarter than Professor Anton, who had moved to Aarhus to study physics. Laurel had had the highest average in class when she and Lise had graduated from the ninth grade. She had gotten a job at Carletti, and was apparently happy with it.

"Okay," she said. "I can promise Sten that I won't say anything about any boyfriends. As far as I know, Lise didn't have any. That was one of the reasons why we were hardly ever together in the spring. We were fighting because of something that happened down at the bar."

She got up and poured boiling water from the kettle into a dark-blue mug. She dipped an already-used teabag into the water and reached for a packet of cigarettes on the windowsill. She remained standing with her arms and legs crossed in the not-quite-long-enough T-shirt. Lit her cigarette and continued to click the lighter.

"We were supposed to meet a couple of guys from the agricultural school, Søren and Ladefoged. But it ended up being awkward, because they only talked to me."

"Why?"

She lifted her eyebrows and flashed me an innocent smile, obviously thinking there was no need for further explanation. And there wasn't. Laurel wasn't pretty, but there was something lazy and shameless about her that made you think dirty thoughts. The appraising look from under her fine, thin eyelids and the fact that she was moving around the kitchen so freely, despite her T-shirt being too short and the hair that was still visible under her bikini line.

Lise, forever uptight and with a downward-set mouth, wouldn't have had a leg to stand on in a competition. And maybe it had been. Part of it, at least.

"She got angry, and it wasn't the first time. She had trouble with guys, because . . . well, you know how she was. It was a shame, but it was kind of her own fault, if you ask me, because she was always so angry. Guys don't like that! I told her plenty of times. But at least the police have checked out Søren and Ladefoged, and they had nothing to do with it."

"So no men?"

"She probably wasn't a virgin, if that's what you're wondering. There are men who like ugly girls. Loads. All you could wish for. But it's usually the older ones, isn't it? The ones who are satisfied as long as the flesh is smooth and the tits are stiff. They were the ones who would buy beer for her at the bar. The over-thirty-fives. If you danced with them, they'd just stand up and sway in the polka position while they tried to rub a hard-on between your legs."

I looked down at the floor to hide that everything was hot and wrong in my head. She was shameless. Evil.

"Yeah, sorry," she said, squinting exhaustedly. "Ask me no questions, and I'll tell you no lies."

"What?"

"B.B. King. Blues."

There was something catlike in the way she was looking at me. A hint of lazy irritation.

"I always say no when I get asked by those kind of men, but Lise always said yes. Afterward she was ashamed, but it was better than nothing. I think she screwed a couple of them, but I don't know for sure. And that's what I've said to anyone who's asked me. I'm sorry if it's hurt Sten."

She opened the kitchen window a little and puffed out smoke through the tiny crack. Narrowed her eyes.

"The police have asked me about all this, too. And if there were any girls she was unfriendly with. Big idiots. All men are, of course. They know that someone killed her, but that's all."

"What do you mean?"

"Well, what the hell do I know? I was nearly always drunk when I hung out with Lise. But when it comes to what happened to her, girls don't matter. Do you know why?" The glow from her cigarette circled dangerously close to my eyes, and I shook my head.

"Because what happened to Lise stinks of man. Men kill, not women. Take it from someone who's done a good bit of fieldwork out there in reality. Men can get so completely insane because we have a hole they want to stick their cock in. And if they're not allowed—"

She raised a knowing eyebrow.

"You don't believe me?"

She joined her hands in front of her, pushing her small, pointed breasts up at the same time so her nipples were clearly drawn under the T-shirt. I tried to stop staring as the hint of a triumphant smile spread over her face. Then she grew serious again.

"Would you like to touch them?"

I didn't answer. My ears were ringing, my heart loudly skipping beats.

"Go ahead."

The wind tore at the sparse weeping birch on the lawn, and the sky was packed with drifting gray clouds. The blackbird outside was singing like crazy, and the kettle had boiled dry on the hot stove and was panting, exhausted, under its range hood.

"Yeah."

She came and stood before me while I remained paralyzed in the chair. I pictured her pink panties as I slowly stretched my hand and lifted up her T-shirt a little. Her navel and a pair of sharp white hip bones appeared, and I let my hand slide farther up and grab something at once soft and hot and bumpy, which wasn't comparable to anything I'd ever touched before. The nipple contracted, becoming hard between my fingers, the second before she pushed away my hand, laughing.

"Now, now," she said. "That's enough."

I thought about Ellen. About how real her breast had been under her blouse that night by the fire. And how much I'd wanted to get closer to her. Laurel was making me confused and uncomfortable. As if I'd left my body and was looking at it from somewhere up near the ceiling.

Painting of a boy with a strange woman's breast.

I could no longer remember why I'd come, but I collapsed under my humiliating, defeating horniness. And an anger that I didn't know the source of.

She caught my eye. "So," she said calmly. "Men can get extremely upset when things go wrong. She met some gross dog or other."

Laurel tugged a little at the edge of her T-shirt and was normal again, but I could no longer meet her gaze. Instead, I looked obliquely at her thin white thighs, where fine light-blue veins twisted beneath her skin like a microscopic river estuary on a map.

"You're really very nice, Jacob Errbo. Come back when you've grown up. There's a good boy."

I felt like I'd betrayed Ellen, when I—like an idiot—shook her hand in farewell.

She was sitting at the register, just like she had been the first day I'd returned. The long, bony upper body leaning backward to reach for a bottle of Jägermeister on the lower shelf. She smiled at her customer and counted the change, then shouted something to a crookedly grown teenager down at the refrigerated counter.

"Hi again."

She lifted her eyes and sat silent for a moment, smiling. Her hair was pulled back into a tight thin ponytail, and her earlobes were being pulled down by slightly too heavy dangling creole earrings.

"Laurel?"

She laughed.

"Good God," she said. "When I told you to come back when you'd grown up, I didn't mean you had to wait *so* long. Nobody has that much time."

"Sorry. There were things I had to do in other parts of the country."

"Yeah, well." She got up and patted the red breast pocket of her T-shirt. Cigarettes, pen, and lighter.

"What brings you to these parts, Jacob Errbo?"

I raised my eyebrows. "Someone has a good memory, even though they're past forty. But . . . family. And right now, shopping."

She nodded and waved me over to the candy counter, which she began to fill from a box on the floor. She gave me a hesitant sidelong glance.

"I thought maybe we could talk a little, now that I'm here."

She turned and gave me the same curious look that she had that day.

"About what?"

"About that summer," I said. "I'm looking for one of the girls who lived in the commune."

"Okay." She waved for the teenager at the back of the store and pointed at the door. "I doubt I can help you, but let's go outside. I need a smoke anyway."

"SO, IT'S NOT me you've come back for?" Laurel asked, giving me a strangely serious sidelong look.

We sat on the concrete loading bay in front of the entrance, our legs dangling over the edge like we were children as we looked out at the old station building. Laurel offered me a Kæmpe Eskimo ice cream from the store's freezer before we lit our cigarettes.

"No, I'm fine."

"Okay."

She laughed, coughed a little and nodded to the dad of a young family rushing into Brugsen, dragging a red-eyed four-year-old by the hand. It was twilight between the old trees on the other side of the road. The railway lines and Feed Stuffs were an abandoned no-man's-land, heavily laden with scrap, heavy goods vehicles, used condoms and beer cans.

"You recognized me the other day?"

Laurel shrugged. "You look like yourself. Haven't become too thick or too thin. Thought it might be about time, too."

"What do you mean?"

"Most people start cleaning up their messes when they've hit fifty. And you're from here."

She smiled, scrunched up her ice cream wrapper and threw it, hitting her mark squarely in the trash can against the wall behind us.

"Did you ever visit the commune?"

"In Pinderup? Yes, but not often. There were so many drugs, and Lise and I were too conservative for what they were into. We drank mostly beer and juice with vodka. Extremely prudish when it came down to it. I actually think you were the first one to see my breasts in daylight. I was a little beside myself that day."

I smiled and took a drag of my cigarette.

"I'm sure you say that to all the boys."

"Of course."

She laughed quietly and looked at me.

"So, what's with her? Ellen."

"Like you said, it's a . . . cleanup."

"Your mess or someone else's?"

I hesitated. "Both, I think."

"You shouldn't exert yourself so much." Laurel raised her voice as a passing train thundered by the station on the other side of the road. "The truth can be terribly disturbing."

I nodded down to a bunch of loitering youngsters in skinny jeans who'd set themselves up a little farther along the main street. They stood nonchalantly leaning against the wall of a house with their bikes and a crate of canned beers, waiting for us to leave their street corner.

"I have to get a few things for dinner," I said, heaving myself up to stand. "I'll drop in again." A siren approached, increased in strength and faded away into a low wail somewhere above the fields.

"You know he's still living on the farm, don't you?" she said. "Maybe you should talk to him, too. Now that you're here."

"That's not why I've come," I said.

"No," she said. "Only you can know that."

THE BLUE FLASHES stood out against the evening sky above the farm from a good distance, but until I turned into the yard, I was hoping for a small accident. Somebody breaking the speed limit on the bypass, an unfortunate fall in the bathroom. Everything other than what I knew it was.

Cold, hard light chiseled sharp shadows in the stable and farmhouse. Both the ambulance and the doctor's car were carelessly parked at the angles at which they'd entered the driveway.

The back door of the farmhouse was open. One of Anton's wooden clogs had been kicked to the side, and inside in the hallway, the stretcher was parked up against the old buzzing chest freezer with a rust stain on the lid.

Mumbling men moved around the kitchen, the atmosphere tense under their calm movements. I could see Anders sitting at the kitchen table with a stiff, nervous grin and a cup of coffee in front of him on the oilcloth as he followed the carefully choreographed activity on the floor.

Two men kneeling over Anton. I could only see his legs.

"Family?" A third man placed himself in the entryway, his smile professionally subdued.

"Yes, I'm—"

"If you wouldn't mind remaining where you are," he said, "we're a bit short on space in here."

"How bad is it?"

He looked back and waved a little dismissively. "It looks like a blood clot in his heart, but he managed to call us himself. Pretty well done, actually. It's a big one, so a lot happened quickly. He didn't have a pulse when we got here, but now it's ticking again, so we'll see. And now we have to . . . If you wouldn't mind going outside? That'd be easiest."

I retreated, but I listened as they counted and lifted on three. Shortly after they had Anton on the stretcher, they were taking him the last few feet to the ambulance.

The doctor, a man my age, jotted something down and gave me a tired look, obviously of the opinion that I was a coconspirator to life's general sadness and unavoidable end.

"Listen," he said, tapping his pen on the notepad. "We're going to drive him to Skejby and let the cardiologists take a look at him. Then we just have to hope for the best."

"And I can call you there?"

"Of course. If you give your number to the paramedics, the hospital can also call you."

And he was on his way. Anton had disappeared into the bright opening of the ambulance, and I stood back beside Anders, who sat stooped over the dining table.

HIS WHOLE BODY was still shaking as I warmed our frozen burgers from Brugsen in the oven. Two for each of us. Two plates, two glasses and two beers. It felt absurd, him and me together.

Worse than it had been with Anton.

"Anton," he said.

I nodded. "Would you like a beer, Anders?"

He looked at me without answering, but I popped open a can of beer anyway and poured a full glass for him.

"So you can sleep better," I said. "And when you wake up tomorrow, I'm sure Anton will be fine. Maybe we can even call him."

Something rubbed itself against my leg, and I saw a weedy kitten that must have snuck in while the door was open. A shrill whimper.

"What's the kitten called, Anders?"

I lifted it up onto my lap, where it dug sharp, frayed claws into my pants and walked back and forth with a trembling, upright tail. It was terribly skinny and stank of cat shit, its matchstick-thin ribs and sharp spine serrations clearly visible beneath its coat.

He didn't answer.

I broke off a piece of my burger and offered it to the kitten, who chewed it with violent grimaces, still purring. Anders looked neither at it nor at me.

I should have asked the doctor for something to calm him, I thought irritatedly. Beer would probably help him fall asleep if I could get it into him, but it wasn't ideal. It gave uneasy dreams, and who knew what nightmares were already on their way up to the surface.

"Drink," I said, pushing the glass toward him a little. "If you drink a few beers, you won't think so much."

His eyes were so different from Anton's. A bright blue, like the water of a tropical lagoon. He reached out and took the glass, drank most of it and wiped the corners of his mouth with his thumb and index finger.

I refilled his glass and we drank the next beer together. Smoked a cigarette while trucks on the bypass occasionally caused the house to shake violently. Anders stroked the kitten over its neck with a forefinger; he'd had three beers now, and that was enough. His bright eyes had dulled, and his head sloped heavily to the right when I got up and gently eased him out to the toilet. I let him stand swaying in front of the toilet and waited for something to happen. Then it hit me that it might not be enough.

"Can you do it yourself, Anders? Or should I . . . help?"

He shook his head, but remained motionless.

"I remember you. And your friend," he said. "You were a bad boy."

"Was I, Anders?" I made sure to keep my tone light. Pulled his pants and underpants down, after which he grabbed his flaccid dick and pissed into the toilet to my great relief. Wiped himself slowly and carefully with a single piece of toilet paper. There was soft pink-and-white scar tissue over his backside and thighs, but I pretended not to see it.

"You have to wash your hands, too."

He shook his head and walked past me out into the hall. Opened some cupboards and slammed them shut again with sharp, angry bangs without looking at me. Outside, it was a quiet evening, and the tires of the cars sang in the asphalt as they headed farther away.

"Go to bed, Anders. We'll call Anton tomorrow."

"Ladies," he said. "You were fond of the ladies."

"I still am."

He nodded, and it was as though an image shone briefly in his mind. I imagined blurred memories fluttering through his inelastic brain tissue, slowly through him. A pair of naked ladies he'd seen once on television, maybe. Or Ellen.

"A bad boy," he said, looking at the floor. "You were a very bad boy."

I lay a hand on his shoulder, but he pulled away, holding his hands clenched in front of his face like a boxer on his way into the ring, eyes completely unfocused.

I woke up to Anders moving around in the hallway. Shuffling steps and low mumbling penetrated the thin door, and I knew I'd slept too long. The sun was already falling in through skylight, drawing white stripes on the carpet, and it was wrong that Anders had gotten up himself. Anton normally woke him up and helped him to the toilet.

I went out into the claustrophobic, low-ceilinged hall. Banged my head on the sloping wall and cursed softly.

"Anders?"

He was by the narrow gable window, looking out. His thin hair was still flat on his neck after the night's sleep, but he'd taken off his pajama top and was standing in his bare upper body, his arms crossed. His skin lay in loose, tired folds over his hips, chest and ribs, but you could see that he'd been strong once. His body's ropes of muscle and tendon were still softly marked beneath the white skin of his back. Uneven scars crisscrossed like a long-nailed giant had tried to scratch something out of him.

"What are you doing, Anders?"

He turned around, and now I could see that he was hugging something close to him. A crumpled sheet.

He lifted the lump toward me.

"Do you need a clean sheet?"

He neither nodded nor shook his head. Just looked down at himself like he had to make sure he was still there. His worn, light-blue pajama pants had a big wet spot on the front.

"Ah, hell, Anders. I'm sorry I overslept. I'll find a new one for you. Just go downstairs and take those off. I'll be down now."

I gently eased the sheet from his arms and threw it on the floor, and he shot me a look I couldn't quite decipher before turning around and going into his old room. He opened the built-in closet and started pulling the contents out onto the floor. Towels and underwear and tablecloths.

"Anders. Stop! I'll find what you need."

I lay a hand on his warm, damp shoulder and tried to hold his gaze, but he pulled away, furious.

"It's. My. Room."

"I know that, Anders. But I'll take care of everything."

"Everything?"

"Yes, I'll take care of everything."

He straightened to his full height and swung at me, heavy and uncoordinated. He hit my shoulder with his bony knuckles before turning around and stalking off. Slow, heavy steps down the stairs. Jesus Christ. It was almost ten o'clock, and the fragment of sky I could see through the skylight was the purest cruel blue. Still no sign of rain.

No one answered when I dialed the number I'd gotten from the ambulance driver, but I still let it ring three times before giving up and going downstairs with the wet sheet. I threw it into the washing machine in the hall and put it on a hot water cycle. Then I went into the living room, where Anders was standing on the carpet, still in the soaked underwear that stank like a urinal.

He scowled at me while I helped him out of them, my face turned away. I asked him to go out and wash himself.

It wasn't because he said no. He just didn't do it. Instead, he sat motionless with his bare ass on the edge of his bed, waiting.

"You have to at least splash some water on yourself, Anders. Come on. You'll get tired of the smell of yourself in a while."

Nothing.

His face was sullen and unfathomable. Eventually, I got up,

kneeled in front of him, lifted his feet into clean underwear, pulled them up to his knees, and did the same with his pants afterward.

"Your brother is a saint, do you know that?"

He nodded, a distant expression in his water-blue eyes.

"Where is Anton?"

"He's still in the hospital. I don't know when he'll be back, but I'll try to find out."

"Tomorrow?"

"I haven't spoken to the doctors yet."

That answer seemed to be enough, and he trotted out to the kitchen after me. He sat fiddling with a loose thread on the edge of the oilcloth while I made coffee and toast. I put some instant rye bread porridge into a pot and poured in some raisins to sweeten it, then cooled the porridge with a drop of milk and put the bowl in front of him on the table. He pushed so hard that it toppled over, sending some rye bread porridge flying over the tablecloth. I straightened it up and pushed it back, lifting the spoon toward him as if he were a baby. On the gingham tablecloth in front of us, porridge and milk mixed together in large, greasy splotches, and I saw myself lift the spoon and mimic chewing movements with my mouth as I made small soothing noises. Just like when I'd had small children.

"You have to eat something, Anders."

He stared at me, his moist lower lip protruding.

"Because otherwise you'll get sick, too, and there'll be trouble."

I opened my mouth like an idiot and carried a new spoonful of rye bread porridge to him. I even considered making tractor or airplane noises. And then maybe shooting myself in the head afterward. He hit the spoon in a surprisingly quick motion, and another glob of milk and porridge landed on the tablecloth.

"*Fuck!*"

It just slipped out, but maybe it didn't matter. It didn't seem like Anders was even listening. He clenched his teeth so hard that his

jaw trembled and small bubbles of spit seeped out from the corners of his mouth. Furious again. Just like me. Kirsten had called
me calm in her speech at our silver wedding anniversary. My calm.
My ability to balance my life. The qualities that made me her rock,
her safe haven, and her shelter from the storm, which was what
she loved and couldn't live without.

On the telephone table in the living room was a directory from
1996 and a book with a long list of numbers in curly handwriting
and different pens. Kjeld and Lene. The Sørensens. Hansen, in
Ulsted. Most had been crossed off. Former friends and dead neighbors. The last one added was the doctor on the line under *Home
Help*—written in round, feminine letters and boldly underlined.
There was also a number for Jette, who didn't pick up.

"She's sick, so she won't be going out to her regular clients."

The lady from the home care office sounded friendly but prepared for combat.

"What about a replacement?"

"Jette has noted here that the next of kin is providing care at
the moment. And we are, of course, happy about that. We have
many carers out sick right now due to the summer flu."

I took a deep breath. I wanted to fight with her.

"I haven't made an agreement with anyone."

The lady hesitated.

"But you're at the address now?"

"Yes, because I can't go anywhere."

"And we appreciate that very much." The woman typed something on her computer. "I've noted that you would like a quick
clarification of the situation regarding Anders Svenningsen."

"Do you realize how he smells?"

"I'm a nurse," she said, sounding for the first time like a real
human being. "So yes, I do know, but there's nothing I can do about
it right now. We prioritize the sickest first, and Anders is as strong
as an elephant. Jette's had a few bruises to prove it."

I hung up. Tore off some paper towels from the kitchen roll and removed the biggest blobs of porridge from the tablecloth and my own pants while Anders watched me carefully, suspiciously chewing on nothing. I went over to the kitchen table and started washing up the pot and bowl, then rinsed the cloudy residue into the sink and wiped down the oilcloth. I didn't know what to say.

"Are you bored?" I sat down in front of him and tried to hold his gaze. "We can go for a walk if you'd like."

He averted his eyes, moving his index finger along the lines of the oilcloth. Shook his head.

"Let's go for a walk," I said. "Most places have been harvested, so nothing will happen if we go up to the top of the hill and look around."

He looked out of the window, where the old Volvo drove past again. Slowly, as though it were the only participant in a funeral procession.

"Do you know who that is, Anders?"

There was only a blue nothingness in his eyes. No fear, no sorrow and no wrath, but he lay one shaking hand over the other as if to calm them both.

He hadn't been outside once during the days I'd been here. Not even near the door.

"I have to do something," I said. "I'll be back soon."

The gravel road had been widened to allow for bigger machines, and the grass on the edges had been trimmed in sparse, newly planted and already dying strips. The six-foot-tall linden trees were still taped to their posts, and the earth around their trunks was naked and unprotected in the sun. Someone should have watered them, but someone also should have watered the dry cornfields on both sides that rattled in the light wind. Impeded growth and pale yellow.

On one side were straight, unbroken rows of corn, and on the other, more corn and a little patch of fir trees at hip height. The pond on the south side of the farmhouse, where Sten's mom had once kept a pair of fat ducks, had been drained and turned into an uneven, mossy lawn surrounded by a closely clipped hedge, and the yard was covered with dazzling white gravel and had been carefully sprayed free of weeds.

My shirt was already stuck to my back, and I had to regularly wipe sweat from my forehead and eyebrows, but there was something calming in the physical exertion of moving forward.

Anamorphosis.

Despite standing in the same place that you've stood decades years ago, you can see only a distortion of the old reality. You can't swim in the same river twice, et cetera. I was sure Janne could have explained it better, but my memory of her had already started to comfortably fade into pale sepia.

The older Volvo I'd seen a few times now was parked on the shaded side of the stable with the keys in the ignition. Everything met my expectations so nauseatingly precisely that I had to stand for a while, convincing myself of the necessity of it.

The door to the barn was open, and a man trampled over to a muddy forklift without deigning to look at me. An employee, I assumed. Too young, at least, to be someone I knew. I raised an arm and waved, but he didn't see me. Just started the forklift and let it stand, coughing in the heat for a moment before putting it in gear and driving over to the other side of the barn, diesel engine and hydraulics screeching bad-temperedly.

The barn buildings were discouraging, their doors closed and their windows opaque with a thick layer of dirt. The industrial hall diagonally behind the left barn wing was still standing, but it looked as though it had been a while since it had last been used. The plates were rusty, and the weeds in front of the door to the small room where the overalls hung were knee-high. But a new and bigger hall had sprouted up beside it—slaughter pigs. I knew them from the smell and the circus-like slurry tank a little farther out in the field.

I walked up to the front door and let the knocker fall a few times. Heat radiated from the stone staircase, which had been covered with black tiles since I'd last been there. New plastic windows and a freshly painted black plinth that was sweating sticky black drops of tar down into the white gravel.

Nobody opened the door, but there were sounds. Fragments of a melody seeping out through an open kitchen window. The curtains waved behind it. I knocked again, harder this time, and a chair scratched across the floor, followed by footsteps behind the door.

"WHAT THE HELL?"

Sten was still Sten. He'd grown older and a good deal broader, and he'd adopted the exact same hairstyle as his father—a layer of curly comb-over that barely covered his sun-spotted crown. His beard stubble was light brown and gray, mostly gray, but his eyes were the same, as were his far-too-big teeth and his slightly too-quick blink with his right eye. I raised my hand halfway, but he didn't see it. He was too busy staring at me.

"Do you remember me, Sten?"

"Yes . . . hell, of course I do, Jacob. But I also heard you were visiting."

"Or maybe you saw me? When you drove past?"

He didn't look as much as blink, and I let my hand drop. I nodded and tried to smile, but couldn't meet his eyes.

"Yeah, the two of us have gotten old," I said.

Sten waved his hand dismissively.

"Come in and have a cup of coffee. You probably need it."

He surveyed me again with narrow eyes, letting his gaze remain on the massive sweat patches on my shirt. Under my arms, and even on my stomach and chest.

"Or maybe a beer? You look like you ran all the way here."

"You need a bit of exercise at our age."

"Yeah, that's what the smart ones say."

I followed him through the hallway into the kitchen, where he poured water and beans into the coffee machine next to the fridge. Two single invoices were pinned onto the fridge with black magnets. No postcards or pictures. Things had changed a lot. The wall separating the kitchen from the old dining room had been knocked down, and reddish quarry tiles had been laid everywhere. The kitchen cabinets were now in a subdued white plastic laminate. There was a dining table and a sideboard and two grotesque, large-flowered bloated armchairs with matching footstools in the far corners. Although it was neat and tidy, the room was naked and impersonal in the way that bachelor pads often ended up. There were no pictures on the walls, no books or candles on the shelves. The furniture had been bought and set up, undoubtedly just as it had been on display on a field near Herning, but nobody cared for it, or was even using it for that matter.

Sten put two beers on the table. They could fill the wait until the coffee had run through, he said. He made a sweeping gesture with his hand and sat down. A puff of old alcohol hit me when his body moved the air.

"So, how have you been passing the time?"

"I'm an architect. Live in Copenhagen. Wife and two children."

Sten opened his beer with a movement that seemed a bit too routine. His forearms were slender and sinewy with large and small pink-and-white scars. Farmers were marred in the same way as their heavy machinery—shredded and cut and crushed by animals and ropes and V-belts.

"Well, nothing much has happened up here. The old parents moved to Tostrup, but that was a few years ago. And I've rebuilt things. Modernized it a little."

He closed his lips over the protruding front teeth in an awkward schoolboy smile.

"Yes, it's nice."

I didn't ask about a wife or girlfriend. He'd been in love with the same girl throughout our time in elementary school: Hanne, a girl who, at an early age, dressed in delicate colors and had procured an army of worshippers who hung on her every word. Sten's love had been as imaginative as it was hopeless, because even when Hanne got a boyfriend who was three years older, drove a moped and was an apprentice carpenter, he kept up his ritual. Standing by the bicycle shed every morning, picking his frayed nail beds while he stared with a half-open mouth after her on his way to class.

"But, Sten," I said, opening a beer for myself, "I've really come to hear what you . . . What are you looking for at the brothers'?"

He shrugged, looking away. He sat there, letting the silence between us grow dense and suffocating. Again, the screwed-up eyes that I couldn't fully decipher. Was he angry with me? How could he be?

"I'd also like to know if you ever saw Ellen again. The woman who lived on the farm with the brothers one summer."

"No, should I have?"

He took a sip again without taking his eyes off mine, and I became even surer of the alcohol. Sten's father had been lean and pale, but in spite of everything, he looked like what he was: a man who worked outdoors and used his body. Sten's color, on the other hand, was a flourishing, inflamed red on his cheeks and nose.

"I'm trying to find her."

The thin kitchen chair creaked as he leaned back with his arms folded over his chest.

"Where did you say she lived?"

"With the brothers that summer."

He shrugged again. "Well then, sorry. I can't remember that far back, Jacob. There's a lot I don't remember from back then."

Sten stroked the thin hair into place over his crown. Then he stood up and got a few more beers, which he set on the table without looking at me. His hands shook a little when he opened them. Parkinson's, nerve damage after toiling with the earth or maybe alcohol. At its worst with my father, he'd had a hard time holding a pen or a cup of coffee if his blood alcohol level dropped too low.

"And what about you?" I tried to catch his eye, wishing I'd rung instead and gotten it quickly over with.

"What do you mean?"

He looked straight at me now, eyes shiny with emotion or some other runny fluid. Beer number two, which stood in front of him, was already half-empty. He looked like an alcoholic, and he drank like one, too. I pulled back a little on the chair to try to escape the smell of his skin and breath.

"Your father . . ." He laughed, played with his beer, and then, as if in thought, relaxed. "Your dad was really in the shit back then. Is he still alive?"

"Alive and kicking."

"Yeah." He blinked quickly. "It was nice of you to come, at least."

I could tell he wanted me to leave. He was already looking at the next beer on the table, but just like my father back then, he preferred to drink alone after the preliminary rounds. It wasn't the first two beers on a hot afternoon that revealed the alcoholic. It was numbers three, four, five and six.

"Yeah, I'll be here for a few more days."

There was a light knock on the door, and a young guy in dirty work clothes and a T-shirt came in with a shopping bag from Brugsen. He nodded to me. No smile, just a statement of my presence. Light eyes and hair that had been trimmed so he was nearly bald. He rounded his hand around the butt of a filterless glowing cigarette as he took milk, beer and a packet of minced beef from the bag and put it all in the fridge.

Sten mumbled something unintelligible, seeming annoyed; the time for further talk had passed. Even though the young man had retreated again without saying anything to either of us.

"Yes, come and have a beer again. The Poles can mind the pigs meanwhile." He laughed. "In fact, they're supposed to *work* for me . . . That's what's in their papers, but they're as lazy as the damn pigs."

He had a drunkard's cruel streak in his eye now, the same scornful curl of mouth as my father.

"Yes, well," I said. "He seemed pretty quiet."

"Yeah, yeah. What the hell would I know about it?" said Sten, opening the door for me. There was a drop of petty mockery in his eyes. "I'm not the one who went to Copenhagen and became an architect. I'm not the one who walked away from everything."

I turned around in the doorway and looked over at the rusty industrial halls. The solidified tractor tracks in the driveway, and the heat that waved over the desert of snow-white pebbles and gravel, making the yard look like an empty aquarium.

"Maybe you should have done that, too, Sten."

"Fuck you, Jacob." He stared at me with his hanging lower lip and a smile that didn't seem so convincing. "Fuck you."

1978

The residential neighborhood seemed faded and lifeless as I cycled my Raleigh Grand Prix over the potholed roads.

It was late in the afternoon, so nobody was in the gardens, the sandboxes were covered with boards and wire netting and the garden tools had been put away in empty garages, but our own house was alive in the midst of all the death. It pulsed and growled weakly in the silence between birch and fruit trees. All the windows were open, as though my father was trying to air out evil spirits. The long branches of the weeping birch whispered over the ground in the cool wind.

I'd hoped he wouldn't be home, but where else would he be? I just had to bank on him being so deaf and blind from drink that I could sneak in unnoticed and get what I needed. But something made me hesitate.

I remained standing on the sidewalk, wavering indecisively in my rubber boots before finally getting it together. I took a deep breath and exhaled between my teeth, like we'd learned to do in soccer before a game. I carefully took hold of the door handle, which wasn't locked. The hallway was painted a warm chocolate brown, and mom's Bjørn Wiinblad poster, which had been relegated from the living room because Dad hated "the colored border," was still on the wall. All the familiar smells, mixed with something wild and strange. Turpentine and spirits, and under all that, a presence of compost and rot. Someone had hauled a wide track of muddy boots over the new, light-gray carpet.

"Dad?"

I didn't know why I'd called him, or why I'd whispered. The kitchen table was covered in unwashed dishes of dried leftover food. Half potatoes, brown and hard. Congealed sauce. Stewed strawberries in a solid border of dark-yellow milk. Pots with gray, cloudy water stacked in the sink. Through the closed door to the living room, I could hear a stream of curses. "Damn" and "hell" and "the hell I will." Like a badly tuned radio broadcast from a dark, sad place. The scratch of glass over the coffee table's red tiles.

I tiptoed to the bottom of the stairs. I had some extra equipment for my bike in my room, new brake pads. And there were other things I might need. Socks, and underpants and an extra pair of long pants. It had grown cooler, and I'd put it off for far too long. I put my foot on the first step at the exact same time the living room door opened and a heavy man came out into the hallway.

"Are you not coming in to say hello to your father?"

I knew this man well. The hot temper, the blotchy red cheeks and the eyes almost hidden under swollen eyelids that made him look like he'd just been crying. I'd seen him a number of times before. Mathisen. When the weather was good, he sat at the entrance to the Hansen's Drugstore warehouse, drinking beer. Sometimes alone, sometimes with others in a similar state.

"No." I hesitated but continued past Mathisen.

"You could go to the drugstore, too," he said, rummaging in his back pocket. The worn velvet trousers were needfully attached to his waist with a tight belt. A heavy, formless paunch hung out over his pants like a strange body part that didn't fit the thin arms and legs.

I pretended not to see his outstretched hand with a curly fifty-kroner note. My dad had woken up in the living room, was rummaging with something.

"Jacob!"

I inhaled deeply and looked inside. The long, orange curtains were drawn, and the air was foggy with smoke, and sweat and beer, plus something stronger—whiskey maybe, or schnapps. My father's indistinct form sat on the modular sofa. When he saw me, he straightened up so suddenly that he almost overbalanced off the sofa and sat there for a moment, swaying. He had a half-smoked cigarette resting between his middle and forefinger, the ash almost as long as the remaining butt.

"It's so good that you came, Jacob," he said. "I have guests, and we're running out of . . ."

He gestured toward the many empty bottles on the coffee table. White ash from his cigarette sprinkled like snow through the dense smoke.

"I'm not staying," I said. "But I can see you're coping well."

He grinned and shrugged.

"Things are fine, Jacob. As you can see. I'm in good company."

Mathisen, who had sunk down into an armchair, was glaring at me with glassy, gray-shadowed eyes. Lost to the outside world. I stepped backward, crunched glass under my sneakers and heard my dad mumble something, then reach out for the radio on the windowsill, where he turned the dial. He landed on a crackly, static version of "Mandalay," the slow one with Mogens Wieth. He liked that song, always had, but loathed the Four Jacks' vulgar rendition of its melancholic sound, a subject on which he always lectured me. A crime against art.

"I'm going," I said.

He nodded without looking at me, lost in the song and the smoke still coiling from his cigarette up to the ceiling.

"Go, just like your mother," he said, smiling venomously. "I'll just say, it's good to have my friends. They don't leave me. Otherwise I'd have been finished when you left, Jacob. People can actually die from it, you know."

His brand-new friend Mathisen exposed his yellow teeth in a broad smile, nodding facetiously.

"But one thing before you go."

I remained standing in the doorway. When he was in this mood, he never said anything nice. It was always so-called truth about either me or my mom. And it always hurt. But I couldn't tear myself away and leave.

"Ask Anton why he locked Anders in all those years." Dad lifted his eyebrows lightly, dropping ash beside the ashtray on the coffee table, and smiled at the sofa's armrest. I turned and left.

"Remember to ask him, now!" he shouted. "Not everyone benefits from living as free as a bird."

I LATER FOUND Anders behind the chickens with Ellen, shoveling crushed beach shells into the feeders. He threw a shovelful over the back of the aggressive gobbler, then mimicked its alcohol-red wattle.

Ellen had bound a red scarf around her head, almost like a turban, and her lips glistened in the same color. Her clothes were new, too, less hippie: a soft white shirt and light-blue elephant pants. She'd been gone all day, as far as I knew, and must've taken the train to Aarhus early that morning. She laughed.

"Where have you been?" I asked.

She sniffed and gave me a quick look.

"Where have *you* been, Utzon? You smell like a bar. Your friend has asked for you. More than once. But he didn't want to wait inside. He's over there."

She nodded toward the hedge out by the road, and I could see Sten's figure flickering among the leaves.

He was watching us. Ellen, Anders and me. His legs and the rest of his body seemed strangely stiff. His face was backlit, his eyes nothing but shadows under the short hair. It was impossible to say how long he'd been in that spot, but I had a sudden, troubling feeling that he'd seen everything and for some reason he didn't like it. Any of it. I didn't want to talk to him.

I breathed in her spicy scent of chamomile and Lux hand soap, and something stronger underneath that I had the wild, irrational urge to taste.

"I saw him early this morning, too," she said.

I nodded and waved to Sten, who bent over and picked up his bike from the ditch, characteristically nodding his head, which signaled for me to follow.

WE WALKED SLOWLY, side by side along the narrow dirt track down toward Bønbækken. Green corn plants towered on both sides, unripe husks with silky soft brown hair that was lifted by the wind. Cornfields were rare and adventure-like. You could hide between the rows of stiff, whispering plants and play tag. Last year, Sten, Flemming and I had chased each other with homemade bows made out of too-thin and flexible branches. The arrows were crooked bamboo sticks chopped from the bushes in Flemming's mom's backyard, sharpened with my scout's dagger. The only bull's-eye shot was when Flemming fell and I put my foot on his back so I could fire an arrow into his ass. But that was a long time ago. Today, everything seemed gray and sallow in the pale sun.

"What is it?"

Sten's throat, hands and forearms were red and scaly from a rash I hadn't noticed before. There were sores on his knees that he picked at while looking around at everything but me.

"This is because I can't sleep at night. Not a wink." He gave me a sidelong glance, as though he was afraid I'd laugh at him.

"What do you mean?"

Another look of uncertainty. "Well, I close my eyes like I usually do. But it's like they're still working in there. I can see my own eyelids and everything. And the darkness. I don't fall asleep any-more. I'm completely . . ."

He held his head with his torn red hands, and there were tears now. He cried with a hoarse, whining sound while he rocked his hands and head. For the first time, I wondered if people could die of sadness. Or confusion, whatever it was Sten had been attacked by. It seemed like he was going crazy, and I had no idea what to do.

"What about your mom?" I said carefully. "Or your dad? Can they help somehow? Maybe you can get some sleeping pills or something."

He shook his head, sniffed loudly and tried to pull himself together.

"Why did she do that?" he said. "Why did she have to go out like that? In that skirt. Why do I have to cope with everything alone now?"

"Sten, that . . . No one is saying you have to."

He looked at me, ugly, his eyes swimming.

"Yeah," he said briefly, wiping his nose on the back of his hand. "I have to do it myself."

"What?"

There was a drizzle on the wind now, and nowhere we could really take shelter. I settled for digging my hands into my pockets and letting the rain come.

"You know what I think, Sten?"

He shook his head. Looked like a thin baby bird with his damp hair in sticky tufts on his forehead.

"I think we need to have some fun."

I walked, furious and sweaty, back through the cornfield on the other side of the chicken farm, stepped over the tracks at a tractor crossing and continued on to the old marl pit. The water at the bottom of the pit was low and brown and overgrown. Only out in the middle was there still a spot of shiny water that mirrored the trees and sky.

I recognized a few of the big trees, even the big beech branch stretched out over the water that I'd cast my line from when I'd hunted Anders's mythological pike. But there were also new things down there. A soaked roll of toilet paper and a pair of empty chip bags with brown water at the bottom, and a well-tarred wheel hoe lying like a decrepit dinosaur in the muddy pool.

From the field above the slope, a combine harvester changed gears hot-temperedly and drove up in circles. Its low-pitched thunder drowned out all the other sounds in the world.

My phone vibrated in my pocket, but it was only when it rang for the third time that I answered it. I shouted through the infernal noise, holding my other ear.

"It's home care."

"Yes?"

"You called earlier about Anders Svenningsen. You were having some problems?"

I nodded, trying to concentrate on the weak metallic noise on the line.

"I'm calling because one of the neighbors just phoned. She knows the brothers a little, says she sometimes does the shopping for Anton, and she saw an elderly man walking over the fields from there half an hour ago. It might be Anders—that surprised her, because he doesn't usually go out."

I stood up laboriously and began to climb the slope.

"I've just spoken to him," I said.

The combine harvester had finally disappeared over the hill, chewing its way through the straw-shortened grain with a pulsing energy that sent husks and dust up into the blue sky.

"Today? Right now?" She didn't wait for an answer. "Oh, well then, everything's all right. That's good to hear. I thought it was unlikely for him to go off like that. He never goes anywhere."

"No, everything is fine."

I'd reached the top of the slope and was squinting against the sun. I tried to calculate how long I'd been gone. An hour at most, I determined. It wasn't noon yet. The brothers' farm lay bathed in the hard sun from the fields, but beyond the whispering, rattling sea of plants, there was no life to be seen.

Still sweating, I strode back along the fence, picking up speed along the way without knowing why. It was a sudden, unnerving feeling of everything going awry and slanting at unnatural angles. Like in Tivoli's Fun House, or the nightmares in which the backdrops around you are replaced while you're still onstage.

The low front door was open, although I clearly remembered shutting it because of the heat. The kitten was on the steps, leaning against an upturned wooden clog. Its wide-open blue eyes looked at me, wild and tin-plated in the bright light, while its tail whipped playfully. I stepped over it and noticed the drops of liquid running through the hallway and on to a small puddle in the middle of the brown linoleum floor in the kitchen, where it stank of an old man's urine and sweat. But there was no Anders—neither inside the house nor in the barn buildings outside. I didn't even need to search the outbuildings to know it. The sense of abandonment was as penetrating as the smell of piss. He was gone.

I hesitated for the split second it took me to go through the possibilities. That I could find him myself. That he wasn't gone at all. That I could take the first train to Aarhus and back to the world.

And then I dialed 112.

THE POLICE CAME straightaway with the dogs and let them run with waving tails over the hot-flickering stubble fields.

I couldn't get in touch with Anton. The nurses assured me he was in good hands, but he was only half-conscious and couldn't get out of bed on his own, much less talk on the phone. Maybe later, in the afternoon.

I felt caught in a tightly bound ribbon of time when I began to walk through the outhouses. The barn. The tractor shed. The old chicken house, where the bedding from the last hens had been left to rot under the nesting boxes. The cowshed and milking parlor, covered in white dust; the pigpen full of empty, cleaned stalls. An old chest of drawers; open sacks of crumbling, moldy compound feed; torn rubber boots; cardboard boxes; and piles of rope filled the feeding room.

I walked along the feeding passage through the massive pillars of dust rising in the sunlight, despite knowing he wasn't in there. Then farther down to the calf boxes, where I opened and closed the creaking doors, eliminating every blind angle. Just to be sure. And there, in the very last box, was my Raleigh Grand Prix. It was dusty and resting on its wheel rims, but undeniably my old Raleigh, with the rolled R on its front wheel fork, its thin tires, and its dark-red varnish with the little glints. It still had its stickers on it.

An unexpected ripple of pure happiness ran through me as I rubbed the dust off the crossbar and recognized every little scratch.

"Beautiful bike."

A man in his late fifties with a barrel-shaped upper body appeared behind me. He offered me his hand.

"Bjarke Nielsen. Neighbor. It was my wife who called home care. She regrets not running out after him immediately now, but that's how it is sometimes."

I nodded. Wishing he would leave.

"He doesn't usually go out," he said. "We've never seen him outside the house. He's a bit special. I've heard his brother has difficulty controlling him."

Maybe he thought his opinion would comfort me, but I was already feeling cold and paralyzed. Like ice had been breathed onto my bones. "What else have you heard?"

"Argh . . ." He drew it out. "There's so much talk. You must know some of the stories yourself, if you came here as a child."

"Tell me anyway."

"Well, nothing other than he's always been difficult to control, right? Even as a young man. It was a relief for the neighbors when he was kept indoors. That's what I've heard. But the brother is a good man. I talk to him once in a while. But, well—the wife said I should ask if I could help with anything? And if you need something to eat?"

"Thanks, that's nice of her."

"Yes, that's the way she is. We live in number fifty-two. But you'll see—he won't have made it that far. He's an old man."

I nodded, although I wasn't sure he was right. I'd seen the sinewy muscles that still existed in Anders' upper arms and shoulders, and felt the physical resistance when I'd tried to help him up onto his legs. Those muscles were condensed, rock-hard remnants of a life of physical work. If he'd moved at even a somewhat regular pace, the search team would have to cover an enormous area.

Anders didn't know the land. He had no water. And old people could dehydrate if they were left sitting fifteen minutes too long in the living room of a nursing home.

The man looked like he was about to lay a hand on my shoulder, but stopped himself.

"Try to relax as much as you can, given the circumstances. They say Anton is in the hospital. Has he been told?"

I shook my head. Relaxing in this situation was perhaps impossible. I hadn't relaxed in four months.

"How well would you say you know the brothers?" The man turned in the stable doorway.

"They're my father's uncles."

I lifted my bike and turned the pedals with one foot. It was sluggish, but the gear clicked dry.

"My wife has a friend who knows his home carer. She says Anders must have had an accident. Lots of huge scars."

I turned to the man.

"I don't know anything about that."

My phone buzzed. A text from Kirsten, brief and poisonous.

Talked to the girl. She looks like the one you knew in Hvidovre.

Anton looked worse than I'd feared.

The skin on his face was tight, and his teeth were exposed as if his skeleton were trying to work its way out of his body. His breath was fast, never reaching his chest despite him being hooked up to an oxygen machine beside the bed.

An IV shunt in his wrist.

A port on his sternum.

Bags with urine and discharge.

I'd seen it all before with my mother and aunt. A colleague with bowel cancer, a friend with a blood clot in the brain. You learned how to react to it over time. The aging, waxy yellow skin, a brave smile, the smell of chemicals and body.

"Anton."

I laid a hand over his; he opened his eyes and looked at me, but didn't answer.

"How are you feeling? Are you in pain?"

Anton shifted, grimaced, and shook his head, but I was far from sure the movement had anything to do with me.

I placed the far-too-nicely packed box of chocolates cautiously on the bedside table. The cellophane crackled under the flow of news from the television on the wall. More refugees somewhere in the world. A snake of people moving forward, heads bowed. The sun was shining outside through the half-rolled-up blinds, and a fly buzzed against the window. Anton's brow shone with sweat.

"I have to tell you, Anton—Anders is gone," I said carefully. "He's been missing for a few hours now, but the police are looking for him, and they'll probably find him soon."

I couldn't tell if he could hear or understand me. His eyelids were half-closed, and he seemed at once transparent and illuminated, like paper held up to a naked light bulb. The fine blood vessels pulsed slightly under his thin skin, and the little electronic heart on the screen next to the bed beat faster.

"Anders can't . . . be outside." Even though his pulse had risen, his hands lay calm and heavy on the comforter; his eyes reflected the sunlight streaming in through the window as he turned his head and looked over the tops of drought-yellow birch trees.

He didn't say anything else. Turned away, sighing heavily.

I looked around the room, trying to avoid eye contact with the two patients lying closest to the door. Dying people are brutal company. Their heads are in twilight country, and there's no place for small talk. My mom's last important messages were almost screamed back across the River Styx with a megaphone.

"Make sure your father doesn't drink too much," and "Promise me you'll stop smoking."

A young nurse with a light ponytail and quick, efficient steps slipped between us for a moment. She smiled as she pulled the blind all the way down.

"You won't get much out of him," she said. "He's very confused. Can't really figure out what's happening. We had to give him something to calm him down because he was struggling all night. Are you family?"

Anton suddenly sat up in bed, swung his legs over the edge and put his feet on the floor. The electronics shook and beeped, and both the nurse and I grabbed him, but there was still so much power in his body that he succeeded on his first attempt to wriggle free and continue toward the door. Half caught in the comforter, the catheter and oxygen tube dangled like loose tethers.

I grabbed him again as he tried to open the door to the hallway. Held on to his shoulders as the sweet smell of old man and fever hit me. His face burned hot against my neck.

"I have to go home now," he said.

The nurse lay the back of her hand against his neck and shook her head.

"Fever. Anton, you have to get back into bed and lie down now."

His body gave in to the pressure, the explosion of energy that had gotten him up on his legs finally leaving him. And maybe he'd also come to a little. He allowed us to guide him by the elbow back to bed, where he sat down so I could lift his feet up. His eyes were closed, and his breathing heavy.

"I shouldn't have called you," he said, and for a moment his dark eyes, the same shade as mine, rested heavily on me. It was like seeing my own reflection in troubled water.

The nurse looked as though she felt personally responsible for our unfortunate turn in conversation. "It's not often fever develops after the procedure he's had," she said apologetically. "But he is ninety-three. He probably had a little infection we should have looked at. If you like, I can call you when the fever has passed and he's more himself."

"Yes, please." I looked back at Anton. He was lying with his eyes closed, breathing quickly and shallowly like a dog in the summer heat.

"Anton?"

He didn't respond.

"Anton, where did Anders go?"

He shifted slightly. "The girls," he said. "Anders visits the girls."

"What girls?"

He didn't answer, having dozed off. I glanced at the blank display on my cell phone and thought of the huge agricultural machines trawling the crackled clay around the farm right at that moment. Tractors and combine harvesters. And Anders, walking around somewhere out there between rotating blades, shards of glass in his pockets, looking for Ellen and the other girls.

1 9 7 8

We faced a strong headwind as we cycled down to the commune, so much in several places that we almost came to a stop on the hill. Sten's face was hard and obstinate in the wet wind. I didn't know what he was thinking, but I imagined he was relieved. Like a man with a broken leg on his way to the hospital. Or maybe it was just me who felt that way.

I had a few beers that I'd pocketed from the brothers' pantry in my backpack. And Sten had his newest LP, Gasolin's *Stakkels Jim*, in two plastic bags clamped to the bike's luggage carrier.

"What did you say to your mom?"

"Nothing."

Sten threw his bike down onto the disheveled lot in front of the house. There were grass, thistles and a pasture circle with dried horse droppings, plus an overturned water tank, which Sten kicked on the way in. The blue Volkswagen T2 was in its usual spot in the driveway. The light was pale and gray; the houses looked dead from the road, but down by the black-scorched, soaked bonfire, the two little boys had managed to get a fire going and were pushing a black cast-iron pot into it. The flames were pale, almost invisible in the gray daylight, and the boys' thin arms were covered in soot almost all the way up. They glared at us through the hot air over the fire as it sent light flakes of ashes up into the sky.

I walked over to the boys and nodded toward the pot.

"What are you making?"

"Soup."

The older of the two looked at me defiantly, like he expected me to laugh at him. A blazing red burn was fresh on the back of one dirty hand.

"What kind of soup?"

He shrugged, then stuck a black-burned stick into the handle and gently pulled the steaming pot out through the ash. Tipped off its lid. Water and boiled dark-green dandelion leaves. Yellow flowers, curly stalks, and a pale, boiled frog lying with its blue-white stomach in the air.

"We're natives," he said seriously. "We live on nature."

Karsten had come around the corner, smiling, a home-rolled cigarette clasped between his lips and a hammer in one hand.

"Boys. You're just in time for coffee."

Sten sent me a questioning look. I nodded, then followed Karsten to the open kitchen door with Sten on my heels. Karsten was already inside, standing with his back to us as he fumbled with the kettle at the freestanding stove.

"Tea or coffee?"

I cleared my throat and said tea, so as not to be impolite. "Sten doesn't feel so good," I said. "So we thought we might stay here for a little bit."

Karsten, who still stood with his back to us, nodded with sweeping head motions. He found some bread in a bag on the homemade kitchen table and cut a few thick chunks, then spread some butter on them.

"I'm minding the boys this afternoon, but you can take a seat and get a consultation with Doctor Cannabis, of course."

Sten's upper lip curled upward into something that resembled disgust as he let his gaze glide around the kitchen. The broken floorboards, the dirt in the corners and along the brown panels. But he followed willingly into the living room and accepted the clumsily rolled joint that Karsten offered him. Plopped onto the worn-out sofa, we covered ourselves with cold, stiff blankets. There was a switched-off television on the shelves in front of us, and the floor was littered with the two boys' collection of scratched toy cars, mostly cheap plastic ones and a few made out of metal whose paint was completely worn off. We each sat with our joints in our hands for a few moments before Sten fished out his lighter and lit them for us. He took a greedy drag, as if he hadn't been able to get air for several weeks.

"Yes, little man. That's good for you." Karsten picked up Sten's LP from the beer box he'd thrown it on, took it out of its cover and placed it carefully on the record player. The needle crackled and the music started, and Sten finally leaned back and closed his eyes. *Stakkels Jim.*

My own joint disappeared at a calmer pace. I gave myself time, with long, deep drags, and concentrated on drawing patterns with the smoke as I watched the boys by the fire through the moisture-beaded living room window. They both sat by the pot, prodding the soup with their sticks.

"Where are the others?"

Karsten cleared his throat and picked a piece of tobacco off his tongue.

"In Randers, looking at an apartment. The girls won't live here as long as there's no . . ." He nodded toward Sten, who was still sitting with his eyes closed. "If they don't find the guy who did it soon. There's not much inside the house, but they don't want to go out alone. That kind of thing."

Sten turned his head and watched me through a narrow slit under thin, white eyelids. Smiled as though he could see what I was thinking. Serious and calm and deep, like a well of clear water. The music had been nice, velvety-red and dark-green pennants.

"The old men. The retard," continued Karsten. "How off is he?"

Even in my slightly veiled world, I knew I had to be careful here. So I laughed.

"He's nice enough."

"But you . . ." He scooched forward on the sofa and tapped ash onto a plate on the floor with dried circles of red tomato sauce in it. "You've considered the possibility. Haven't you?"

Sten had opened his eyes and was staring at me with something between infinite understanding and predatory instinct.

"Not at all," I said. "Anders has never done anything to anyone."

Karsten shook his head.

"Maybe not," he said. "But someone needs to talk to him. To be sure."

Outside, the boys disappeared in the gray blanket of rain, their flames finally extinguished in black, wet ashes.

IT WAS LATE evening, almost nighttime, when Anton came to get us.

He drove the dove-gray car up to the front of the house, turned off the engine, and honked once. I'd had no idea how he'd figured out where we were—maybe he'd caught sight of our bikes. Or maybe one of the women from the commune had called him. They had come home earlier that evening; I didn't know when, but they were inside the house, just like the little boys, who were now sleeping heavily. I'd seen them lying in a tangled pile on a bed as I'd wandered through the rooms in search of something to eat. A bunch of red cheeks and warm, heavy breathing in half darkness.

I didn't know what time it was, but at one point Sten had sat alone on the sofa, crying with all the windows open into the dark-blue summer sky. I'd sat beside him, stroking his sweaty hair until he laid his head in my lap, sniffling, sighing and gasping.

I knew I was drunk, but it didn't matter. It all felt very comfortable, at least until Karsten came back and put on a new record without turning on the light. The bass vibrated through my chest and diaphragm, causing the spit to run too fast in my mouth. I managed to make it to the yard before throwing up in the sandbox in long, corrosive belches, which was when Anton came.

THE LADIES BROUGHT us out to the car. One of them put Sten's arm over her shoulder and lifted him up from the sofa. On the way out, he dangled dumbly from her, giggling, a Tuborg still clenched in one hand.

I could feel my senses wavering, and my arms and hands wouldn't obey when I followed them with my shirt in my hand, but I wasn't out of it in the same way as Sten. I felt rough and alert, like a razor was being held against my throat.

The driver's-side window of the dove-gray car was rolled down, so I immediately saw Anton's motionless profile with its flat cap and cigar stump in its mouth. It was well past his usual bedtime, but he didn't look as though he'd been sleeping. The doors to the rear and passenger seats were already open, and a wind ran through in the wet, waving tree branches; yellow birch leaves sailed through the air, and I felt it all. The earwig crawling over my hand, the cold, and the mosquitoes' microscopic feet on my neck.

The lady helped me into the passenger seat and Sten, who still had a beer in hand, into the back.

Anton put his arm on the back of my headrest, looked back, and started to reverse. Left his arm there as he turned and trundled down the narrow road.

I didn't say anything, just rolled down the window and stretched my arm out as far as I could.

"Stop that." Anton's voice was sharp as a whip. "You'll hit a telephone pole, and then I'll have to go out and find your arm."

We were a good distance from the telephone poles.

"I can't—"

"Just stop."

I pulled my arm in, feeling strangely betrayed. Anton never played the adult with me like this. We had a kind of tacit agreement that he spoke to me like I was an adult in return for me behaving somewhat like one. It was how it had always been, even when I was younger. In fact, I didn't even think Anton knew how to be an adult in the way that parents did.

"You should've told me where you were."

"It was just—"

His blow to the steering wheel was as hard as it was surprising. A flat smack and no more. Both hands back on the steering wheel.

I could feel my heart pounding in my throat. I couldn't say anything. Just sat there like an idiot beside him, staring out of the window, blood rushing in my ears. I was afraid I might start crying if I looked at him.

There was no sound from the back seat, where Sten sat picking the label of the almost-empty beer with a distant smile. I could see him in the rearview mirror, head leaned back and legs spread. A man without a worry in the world.

PART II

It was as though the house had shrunk while I was gone. The decay became clearer without the two old men; the marks on the wall from the old picture frames, the Amager shelf in the living room, the empty shelves. Anton's bed, freshly made under the only surviving wall decoration in Great-Grandmother's room—a small, clumsy crucifix, the kind sold in flea markets. Not even Jette had been able to cope with the greasy layer of dust congealed in pudding form on the wall over the kitchen table. The brown linoleum on the kitchen floor was worn down to the raw splintered floorboards in some places. I let the water run a little in the steel sink before filling my glass and feeling the warmth throb in my temples after the drive.

The mangy kitten was nowhere to be seen.

I'd called the leader of the search team on my way home, but he didn't think it was realistic to ask the farmers to stop their combine harvesters.

"This is farming country, and those who know have said the heat wave will end with a bang tomorrow night. Torrential rain and rain all day every day for the week. Anders and his brother will understand that the machines can't be stopped now. But we've called everyone who is harvesting in the area and asked them to be extra careful. And they will be. Believe me, nobody wants to end up with a man wrapped up in their hay bale."

"All right," I said.

"Yes, you understand."

The wind hit the microphone, and I could hear him saying something to someone above the noise. Then he was back. "Does

Anders know anyone in the area? Old friends. Someone he may have wanted to visit. We've already talked to the home carer, but she didn't really know anything."

"Anders is—he's afraid of other people."

"Hmm. Yes, we're almost at seven hours now. So it's beginning to get a bit harder. But keep yourself busy. We'll call if something happens."

A new text from Kirsten, who had called twice, too.

If you want to talk about it.

I stared for a long time at the unfinished sentence. If I wanted to talk about it, then what, Kirsten? It seemed like the kind of outstretched hand that people felt obliged to offer the acutely suicidal.

The night she'd found my letters to Janne on the computer, she'd become physically ill with fever and vomiting. I came home to a house with all the windows wide open and found her in bed, covered only with a crumpled, soaked sheet. She'd printed out the letters from my laptop and put them in a circle around her so she could effortlessly reach out for a random read, then put it back again. It didn't help that the letters had never been sent. Nor did it help that I slammed doors, threatened to walk out and later pleaded for her forgiveness. Nothing helped. And she rejected my care. Sat stubborn and restless in bed, reached out for a glass of water and the tray with toast and a banana cut into slices and locked the door whenever she dragged herself to the toilet to vomit with a deep, hoarse gurgle.

If we were together, I'd have you wear only thin stockings that go up to the middle of your thin thighs. So any time and anywhere I wanted, I could put a hand under your dress and caress your stomach, and your ass, and your shiny wet pussy.

"Who is she?" she asked.

But I couldn't even begin to explain.

"What the hell were you doing on my computer? They're not letters for anyone. I'm writing a novel."

Later, when she was up and about, I tried to talk to her, suggesting we should be honest with each other. She looked at me as if I were a half-dead toad that had dragged itself in over the kitchen floor. Words that I'd never heard her say before came out of her mouth. Asshole. Lecher. Pussy.

"You haven't been so easy to be married to, either," I said, causing her to expel a low, snorting laugh before turning away and crying into a pot of pasta.

"Guess we'll just have to hope your young girlfriend can live with your little cock," she said. "I hope you're really happy together."

I could no longer remember if I tried to deny again that the letters were letters, or if my guilt was fully established.

"It's not my job to stabilize your fragile ego anymore. Your cock is like your morality—a bit below the waist. I say that in keeping with the new honesty between us."

And then she left. Left me alone on the kitchen floor with my below-average manhood.

I EMPTIED THE washing machine and hung the clean white sheet on the line in the small patch of garden out by the road. It sagged heavy and dead in the still heat, and it was hard to cope with the mosquitoes and rainbow-colored flies swarming around my wet neck.

In the darkness of Great-Grandmother's room, I opened the wardrobe and tried to get an overview of its contents. Seventies-style shirts and pants, some newer and softer in dark fleece, and woolen underwear from Bilka. I thought I recognized Jette's practical taste and her synthetic flower-perfumed fabric softener. To the right, a beautifully folded stack of sheets and plastic covers for the mattress. Old age was frighteningly concrete when you stood holding that kind of thing. I went back to the living room and smoothed the light, white sheet over Anders's hospital bed.

It was stiflingly warm under the hot roof tiles up on the second floor. The floor of Anders's old room was still covered in stuffed plastic bags, holed linen, tablecloths with crocheted edging and my great-grandmother's initials embroidered in the corners.

I opened the window and lit cigarette number thirteen of the day. The statistics didn't lie when they said that divorced men smoke and drink too much and die like flies. I was reducing the number of active years with a present high quality of life. Men without women were fragile creatures, except maybe for those who'd never been married.

Where had Anders gone?

By now, he could have reached Auning or Grenå or wherever the hell it suited him to disappear to. There were bogs, streams, ditches and plantations where an old man could lay down to rest and never wake again.

I didn't care for the way nature consumed human beings—that you could end up lying in the woods for foxes and ants and wind and forgetfulness. There was nothing as cruel and universally meaningless as a death without spectators. But that was the very nature of nature, of Satan.

I picked up some folded tablecloths and put them on a shelf in the closet. Grabbed a full, old-fashioned plastic bag, got a glimpse of its contents and stopped.

The first thing I noticed when I poured everything from the bag out onto the floor was that I needed to take a piss. Badly.

I got up on creaking knees and tramped down to the bathroom, where I pulled down my zipper and released my pathetically warm pee. It hurt, and I stood there for a long time like a storm-damaged tree, leaning over the toilet with my dick in my hand.

Then I washed my hands and walked slowly up the stairs again. Sat on the floor and spread Anders's treasures out in front of me. All his stones, his glass, his pearls and, in the middle of it all, a single white mussel shell on a dark leather cord.

1978

Something had been trapped in the atmosphere.

After days of cold rain and wind, the heat had returned and settled heavily over the fields. The sun shone white, stinging against bare skin.

When I went down to the field in the afternoon to bring in the cows for milking, the animals and I were attacked by horseflies and black mosquitoes. A whirring, devilish cloud that went after my sweaty neck and the cows' tense udders and big wet eyes. The heavy animals moved uneasily, kicking out and rearing at the slightest touch.

"Kipkipkip!"

I had a bruise on my thigh after being caught between a panicked cow and a watering trough the day before, and burn marks on both hands from the rope she'd dragged away with her. It still hurt, but I didn't want to sit there staring and doing nothing. It was better to get the work done and think as little as possible.

I ran a few steps in front of the cows and opened the wire fence at its two springy plastic handles. Pushed the hot, strong-smelling bodies as they pushed past me, rushing directly toward the open barn door.

Behind the yard, Soffi was yapping, hot-tempered and persistent.

"Do you need any help?"

Sten had suddenly appeared behind me. He strode up next to me, hands in his pockets. He'd put his dagger in his belt, just like he used to when we were younger. Kept picking nervously at its shaft.

I prodded a bony cow's ass with the stick. For some reason, I couldn't look at him, even though he seemed more okay than he had in a long time.

"You can help with the milking cups," I said.

He nodded and hammered a flat hand hard on one of the cows' asses to prove his perseverance. The animal jumped forward in an uneven run, so I had to chase it down, make soothing noises and click my tongue to calm it.

"Good thing you're not a bull," I said.

Sten pointed to one of the reddish cows that had begun to take a shit. Dung ran down over its flaps and legs.

"Ugh, dammit."

There was something hard in his voice, as though he'd come to pick a fight. I didn't say anything, just walked into the stable after the animals and locked iron rings around the necks of those already in their boxes. I scratched their wide, greasy foreheads, grabbed their sharp horns and rubbed their thin skin at the root so they shook their heads impatiently. Then I went into the milking parlor and picked up the three buckets, lids and suction cups.

Sten didn't move.

He was still standing there with his hands buried in his pockets, shaking a little in the cool of the cowshed. His shoulder blades were sharp wing stumps under his T-shirt. The shed smelled of ammonia and cow and fermented straw. The chains rattled, and a little farther down the hall, a cow spread its stiff legs, letting piss splash down into the waste channel.

"You can take water and cloths into the milking parlor," I said.

He did as I said, and we walked down our respective sides of the hallway, bending and washing the teats of the greenish cakes of dried shit, dust and urine that clung to them. Rubbed the cows down on their hot flanks.

"Thanks for the other day."

I was happy I was standing with my back to him. Didn't want to reveal anything natural or vulnerable to this version of Sten.

"Yeah. It was good, wasn't it?"

I connected the suction cups and milking machines to the vacuum in the ceiling, and Sten put the cups on the first cow. The machine's rhythmic thump and champing suck mixed with the noises of the cows in the connectors. I started the next machine and went over to a cow whose teats were reddish and fever-warm, and whose udder was hard as stone in my hands. I'd seen what Anton did with these kinds of udder infections before. Started gently with the cow udder cream as I clicked my tongue and gently massaged from the top and down until the first trick-les of blood-streaked milk ran into the dung channel. The cow stomped in pain during the first touches, but I continued to milk until the udder was as soft as dough.

"There's something I've been thinking about," said Sten. "Or we. Me and Karsten." He'd been standing there, watching me and the cow with shiny large eyes in the dusk.

"Yeah?"

"Anders walks a lot by himself, down to the forest and such."

"Yeah?"

He smiled, but you could see too much of his teeth. It wasn't genuine.

"We talked about the fact that he doesn't know anyone down that way. So that's a bit strange."

"He just walks. That's what adults do."

I knew where he was going with this. He was unable to think of anything other than Lise lately, and I couldn't halt the idea that was hatching in his boiling brain.

"Adults, yes. *Adults.*" He glared at me with a significant look.

"But Anders isn't a real adult, is he? What do you think he does out there?"

"I don't know, Sten," I said. "That's up to him."

The first bucket was full, so I carried it into the milking parlor and emptied it in the tank. Wiped my forehead with my forearm. The gray striped cat that had snuck in through the open stable door meowed ingratiatingly in the thick reek of warm milk. Sten followed me.

"Haven't you noticed something strange about him? The way he follows Ellen so closely. It's disgusting to watch."

I stiffened. "They just talk," I said. "He's not doing anything." I tried to avoid eye contact with him as I spoke.

"Well, not yet. But we'd like to talk to him without his brother being there."

He took out a cigarette and lit it without looking at me.

"He's a peeping Tom, Jacob. A creep who sneaks all over the place, staring at ladies and doing all sorts of perverted things. Tons of people are saying it. Someone saw him hanging around at Damgården."

"And what—"

"There're three girls at Damgården. You know that, too."

"Just shut up, Sten. You don't know him at all."

I put the bucket down and grabbed him. I was about to give him a pinch or squeeze his neck. Hard. Why'd he have to be an idiot and start all this now? I could feel his bone as I bore my fingers into his upper arm.

"Ow, hell." He wrestled himself free, waving the lit cigarette in front of my face, but was still astonishingly calm. As if I were a three-year-old he was trying to calm down. "Are you stupid in the head or what? You've seen him yourself, drooling over her. And the police aren't doing shit anymore. They're finished. It's over. They've packed up their stuff and have gone back to Randers or Aarhus or wherever the hell they came from."

I stopped. He was right in a way about Ellen, and the way Anders looked at her. But we all looked at girls all the time. All types.

"You've peeped on the girls' locker room yourself," I said. "Plenty of times."

He shook his head.

"You know there's a difference. He's old and crazy. Try to imagine it. A whole life without sex. That drives a man insane, and then suddenly . . ." He clicked his fingers. "People can have all sorts of peculiar thoughts in their heads, just like animals. And most people can control it. But not Anders. He's crazy, and if it is him, who's . . ."

Sten stopped, wiping his eyes with the back of his hand. They were still enormous and shiny.

"Come on," I said, hearing the pleading tone in my own voice. "You're not thinking straight, Sten. The way you are."

"I can see. And you know very well what I'm talking about. Karsten is worried about Ellen, and maybe you should be, too."

His eyes burned, and his cheeks flushed a hot red under his sharp cheekbones. Something I recognized as a sure sign he was about to start crying. I turned away to save us both the humiliation.

"You don't have to do anything but call me the next time Anton goes somewhere. We can easily figure out the rest. We're just going to talk to him, find out."

"I don't know, Sten."

It was strange, because I usually thought Sten was . . . an idiot. He was a friend, of course, but he was the kind of friend it was easy to talk into things. Because he had no one other than me and Jørgen and them. And because he was a little dense. Read like someone in the fifth grade. Stammered with his big Adam's apple hopping nervously up and down. It was usually me who told him what to do. Not the other way around. Now it was as though what had happened to Lise made it completely impossible to argue with him. Not because I felt sorry for him, but because he seemed older and harder, like he knew what had to be done.

"Maybe."

He let out a short, unhappy laugh. Raised one hand and made a peace sign while the other fumbled for his cigarettes in his back pocket.

"Thanks, Jacob."

He sounded like an adult who had just persuaded an unreasonable toddler to hand over the knife he'd been playing with. "You're still the best. You and him, Karsten. I've started sleeping at night again."

He looked like himself for a moment. The big, stupid boy he should still have been.

"That's good, Sten."

He smiled pallidly.

"Yeah, I know what to do now," he said. "You're a good friend, Jacob. You always have been."

1 9 7 8

There was larvae in the cabbage again. Fat, spotted, hairy larvae that rasped the outermost cabbage leaves and in toward the hard, white core. Tiny little black-glittering heads moving forward in eager jerks, their bodies leaving long, wet stripes of shit that were dark-green and resembled bile.

Damned creepy crawlies.

I'd been confirmed last year; a relatively peaceful affair, if you forgot about Dad getting drunk on the wine that had been bought for the occasion the week before, and Mom having to run to Hansen's Drugstore that day and butter him up for twenty bottles on credit. The story of God punishing the Egyptians for their wicked conduct was one of the few that had stuck. Water to blood. Mosquitoes, swarms of blowflies, pests, boils, darkness and death. Frogs, which I'd personally wondered about—they couldn't really have been a plague—and then the locusts, who ate everything, leaving the ground empty and barren.

The cabbage larvae were probably not on the same level as the ten plagues, but they seemed like a kind of heavenly punishment for my compulsive masturbating to my own drawings of Ellen. At any rate, Anton had sent me out in the rain with a bowl to pick the cabbages clean, then feed the gross creatures and their excrement to the chickens.

The cherries hung swollen and ruined in the brothers' orchard, their dark fruit bursting out through cracked skin; the apples had scabies, and the carrots were small and worm-eaten, but the worst was of course the corn that had blown off in the damp wind, causing Anton to scowl markedly at the sky. Every afternoon, he walked restlessly along the edge of the field with wet ears of corn crushed in his large hand.

"Jacob."

I looked up and saw Anders. He was standing a few feet behind me, his hands hanging relaxed by his sides.

"Yeah?"

I'd been kneeling by the cabbage so long that my legs were stiff and had pins and needles. Anders's gaze flickered from my wooden clogs and to a place on my stomach.

"Jacob . . . it's Soffi."

"What?"

I reached out and grabbed two more soft larvae, which I dropped into my bowl. Didn't even look up at him.

"I don't know," he said hesitantly. "She's lying down on the dung heap."

"Is she sick?"

I looked at him properly now, because there was something wrong with his face. It seemed rigid, the wet corners of his mouth pulled down tight. I realized he didn't actually look okay. Despite it not being too warm, his brow was glossy with sweat. His eyes were wide and shiny under his cap.

"No, not sick."

I got up and stretched my sore legs, then looked down the rows of cabbage and up to the sky, which was white along the horizon. The sun was invisible behind the clouds.

"Would you like me to go down to check on her with you?"

He nodded and quickly turned around. Took long steps in the clumsy clogs and kept turning his head back to make sure I was still behind him. I wished Anton was here. Or Ellen. But I knew

Ellen was out buying groceries, and Anton was God knew where. I'd have to deal with whatever this was alone.

"Oh no, oh no, oh no," Anders chanted to himself when we reached the whitewashed half wall fencing it in.

Now I could see Soffi, who was lying outstretched on the sticky cakes of straw, and I immediately knew she was dead. No dog would lie as still as that, not even asleep, and once I got a little closer I could see the wound in her throat, which had bled fresh, red blood into the straw.

"You'd better stand over there, Anders."

I found a place for him on the other side of the half wall, and he stayed there willingly, the big, bony man moving his hands restlessly over his face. He didn't say anything else.

I gently stroked the dog over the neck and pulled her head back a little so I could better see the gaping wound in her throat. A fight with another dog maybe, but it looked more like a straight cut, and there was also something strange about her tail. A stick, no thicker than two fingers, was sticking out strangely from her hindquarters, but it was only when I grabbed it and felt the resistance that I understood why. Someone had shoved the stick into her. I pulled it out and threw it hard, then lifted Soffi up and carried her out to the grass.

I'd never seen Anders like that before—petrified. He didn't even want to go over to the dog, keeping a few yards away with his side to us. A hand still over his face. He must have known she was dead when he came to get me. Anders had seen plenty of dead animals in his life, so how could he have been in any doubt?

"Anders . . ." I looked for Anton in vain again. "Soffi is dead. She . . ."

I didn't know if I should say anything about her throat. That somebody had killed her. He'd seen himself how she'd lain there.

He shook his head, scratched his forehead and then set off without looking back.

ANDERS WOULDN'T TALK to anyone afterward. He sat with his head hung over the kitchen table while rain washed Soffi's blood into the grass and made her stiff and cold.

"We'll have to bury her at some point," Anton said, but only after dinner. Ellen bent over Anders's shoulder and whispered something in his ear. He got up and went out into the pouring rain with her, and a little while later we heard the engine of the blue Taunus in the yard. We sat in the darkness like on a typical winter evening when the light from headlights swept in through the kitchen windows and across the remains of pork patties and stewed beans.

"What's happening, Jacob?"

Anton caught my gaze, but quickly looked away again, as if he already regretted his question.

I shrugged gently. "What do you mean?"

"Stop playing the idiot."

He refocused his eyes on me with a jerk; the dark, narrow slits in the unsmiling face made me jump. His transformation was so total that for a split second, I didn't believe it was him.

"I don't know," I said. "It could've been anyone."

He uttered something barely resembling a short laugh. "Anyone?"

I didn't know what to say, so I started moving the dishes to the sink and scraping the remains into the bucket for the chickens. His eyes were still on me, angry. Uneasy. Reproachful? Either he was breathing heavier than he usually did, or the silence in the kitchen was denser than it had ever been before.

"I'm going to the stable," he said.

"Yeah."

I stood with my back half to him and waited until the light from the stable windows cut through the rain and the darkness. Only then did I look at my hands, shaking under the cold water from the faucet.

They were the kind of pretty things that glistened and sparkled and cost nothing. A bronze brooch with green glass, polished like a diamond. A crumpled fabric rose you could slip into a band in your hair. Marbles and a red velvet band, a single yellow ankle sock in size six or smaller. A picture of Lily Broberg in a bra that made her breasts look rock-hard, pointed and unnatural on her soft body. All his shards of glass, mostly green, but also in blue and red and white and yellow. Clear and edged between soft, hazy fragments.

Ellen's necklace had been added to the top of the bag like a last grave gift before the sealing of a burial chamber. Farther in, in the closet, was a folder with Ellen's name on it, written with a sporadically failing pen. The script was edged, masculine and made sloppy to suit a half-student communist with great plans for his art. The glossy pictures big and beautifully shot. Fifteen variations of the same motif. A laughing Ellen standing sideways, both hands shaped like bowls around her little breasts. Ellen sitting on a chair with her back and head leaning back so the tendons and muscles stood out on her bare neck, and her long hair almost touching the floor. I pictured Anders standing by Ellen's bed, arms hanging heavily at his sides.

His crime seemed at once greater and lesser than it really was. He might have been in her room and gone through her things, but she could have forgotten them or simply left them there when she disappeared. In any case, I understood his impulse to keep them and call them his own.

The pictures in themselves were so infinitely beautiful, almost innocent—at least by modern standards—that it was difficult to be offended. Some of them completely without breasts and pussy. But you could see the birthmarks on Ellen's thighs, the pale skin from her knees and shoulders and neck, the excited darkness in her dilated pupils. Small, pert breasts, the vertical, soft markings between ribs and hip, the spread legs, and the dark crack revealed to the photographer. It was clear she'd been in love when the pictures had been taken. Not because she was flirting with the camera, but because she wasn't. Her look was serious, curious and focused directly on the eye behind the lens.

I was a man who had plowed my way through mountains of dicks and shaved pussies in cyberspace, and before that through greasy editions of the *Ugens Report* and *Playboy*. My relationship to naked women was just as obsessive as most other men's. If there were breasts, I had to look at them and fantasize about their taste, weight, and firmness. The same was true for all the spread legs I'd encountered through time. For those who are unclean, everything remains unclean.

IT WAS LIKE the heat had sucked all the color out of the world below. The trees were gray, and the air thick both inside and outside the dark hall. I'd left the door ajar and watched with bizarre relief as the ravenous kitten came tumbling across the yard and up the stairs when it spotted me. I stroked its back and felt the fast, wheezy breath in its little body.

I gave it a bowl of water and a lump of liver pâté out in the hall and stood there awhile, observing the creature as it ate. I lit a cigarette and tried to find my Zen before heading into the kitchen and spreading the pictures of Ellen over the small dining table. I placed the little stack of black-and-white snapshots that had been in the bottom of a brown envelope beside them. Happy days in the commune. Around the fire, and a completion ceremony for a playhouse. Lambs being bottle-fed in a snow-covered field. A pair of snot-nosed pale and curly-haired boys in a sandbox; a cat in the windowsill. The whole flock grinning widely in the kitchen garden, nonchalantly leaning on pitchforks and hoes. The men with impressive full beards and the women with loose, tangled hair. Ellen with a beer and one arm around the neck of a blonde girl by the campfire in Pinderup. And the same pair immersed in a single book. The images were blurred by dusk and covered with a milky-gray film due to poor focus. The girls' eyes weren't much more than shining dots in the dark.

My phone grunted in my back pocket, and I reluctantly got up. An unfamiliar number.

"We have a question."

I recognized the Randers drawl of the on-site commander at once.

"Yes?"

"The dogs haven't really picked up anything, and it's starting to take a little longer than we'd like." He sounded irritated. As if he just needed to think out loud with someone who wouldn't answer back.

"We got out quick."

"Yeah?"

Silence. Then he coughed, and cursed at something in the background. "We don't believe he's in the bog," he said. "There's not much water left out there, and the first few feet are so shallow that we couldn't *not* see him if he was lying there. If he drowned, it wasn't an accident. But that's something I have to ask you about, too."

"What?"

"Whether, in your opinion, he was suicidal. Sometimes it can be hard to tell with the old ones. They just do it all of a sudden. And then there's what's happened with his brother."

I thought of Anders and his lowered eyes. Was there any room for such complicated feelings in the cramped space his soul had been confined to?

"I really don't think he's capable of that," I said.

"No, no . . ." I could hear the on-site commander chewing on that. "Okay, I'll tell you what we're going to do now. We'll send a missing person's report to the press, television, and online media, what have you. And we'll continue to search until dark. If we don't find him, we will, of course, resume the search tomorrow, but that's when it starts to get very difficult. He has no water with him, and there isn't really any out there."

"I know."

A new hesitation and this time his voice a bit softer, more cautious. "Are you dealing with this on your own?"

"Yes."

"These things can be a strain if they take a long time. I understand you're not very close, but still."

"But it's not—we're not close in that way."

"No? Okay." He cleared his throat. "But you'll hear from us if there's any news, and you can just call. You have my number."

I sat in the kitchen for a while with the pictures scattered in front of me. Thought about Ellen. You look differently at old pictures than you do new ones. So much can happen to a smile and eyes in nearly forty years. Life has a way of wearing away all the shine. For that very same reason, there weren't a lot of pictures of myself from my childhood and youth. I'd thrown most of them out. Didn't care for that boy's sincere gaze and unblemished personality. It also seemed inappropriate for me to have smiled so brightly and optimistically at the camera when my story turned out so infinitely trivial.

A text from a number I hadn't seen before.

Dear Jacob, I've found the registered deeds for the property from 1976 and have two names for you. Nikolaj Ballin and Karsten Villadsen. Hope you're lucky enough to find the woman you're looking for. Best regards, Sara

1978

We drove the hay in. Ellen, Anton, Anders and me.

Early in the morning, it was me who drove the tractor to the hay trailer, where Anders worked on splitting it, his huge body stooped over the coupling while Anton directed me with a raised hand.

Ellen was already sitting on the trailer with her legs dangling off, grimacing at the sharp sun and pitchfork next to her. She was in rubber boots and a pair of old overalls that were far too big. Under that, a T-shirt and bare, freckled arms.

I'd found her at the chicken run while Anton was doing the morning milking. She sat smoking under the whispering trees. She used to take her little breaks there. She liked watching the chickens, she said, because they looked so happy. She loved the two big gobbling tom turkeys, too, when they puffed themselves up and the loose, bobbing skin on their throats flared bright red over their dusty feather suits.

"Utzon." She looked up at me and smiled, her eyes still screwed up against the bright sky. A loosely rolled cigarette was clasped between her lips. "Come, sit down."

I nodded and sat carefully beside her. Couldn't help looking at her arms and thinking how little she looked like Laurel, or any other girl, for that matter.

"I've been thinking about this place." She stubbed her cigarette out in the grass and intertwined her slender fingers. "That it might not be the right place for me. What with everything going on . . ."

My stomach twisted in the same way it had when I was little and had been sent to the basement for beer. As though I had to shit or run or both to survive.

"Because of what happened to Soffi?"

"No." She was quiet for a moment. "Or yes, maybe. Because of what happened to Soffi, and because of Lise, and because of Karsten. I shouldn't have stayed here. But it's magical out here, isn't it? Time moves both too slow and too fast. It's like in a fairy tale, when the young hero rests his head on Elves' Hill for a moment, and when he goes down again he's a hundred years old."

I nodded, pretending that made sense.

"Do you know who did it to Soffi?"

I shook my head, despite that obviously being a lie. It was Sten and the dagger in his belt, but was that really why she was leaving? She'd let me touch her breast and laid her head against my shoulder, and now she wanted to leave?

I got up suddenly, but it didn't look like she noticed. She was somewhere else. The dew on the grass had soaked the knees of my trousers, giving me goose bumps, but we'd quickly work ourselves warm again out in the field. And Anton and Anders were waiting for the tractor. We were ready.

I'D DRIVEN THE tractor before, but mostly on flat ground. Now we were trundling over the dirt road, then farther down the paved road to reach the far corner of the field on the other side of the track. The noise was deafening, and the cab, which consisted of only a windshield, roof and two door holes, smelled of greasy, hot diesel from the stamping engine and heavily vibrating transmission. Through the scratches on the Plexiglas window, I could see the blue sky, and farther along at the edge of the forest was the day's work laid out on the stubble field. Hay bales distributed unevenly by a heavy, pounding bale processor rented from the machine station.

Anton shouted incomprehensible orders through the rhythmic hack of the tractor, directing me with big arm movements so the tractor and trailer stayed on the right path. Then Ellen straightened up, grabbed the heavy steering wheel with both hands and put the tractor into first gear as I climbed onto the loading bay to receive and stack.

The first few bales he lifted up to me with the fork were heavy and pressed too hard. Grass, weeds and thistles from the moist, low-lying green area in the shadow of the trees. The hay wasn't good right here in general. Instead of shining butter yellow, it was dark and gray, and after lifting the bales with the fork, Anton left most of them there and moved on to the next row.

I got quickly into the rhythm from last year. Lifted the strings, pressed my knees against them and slid them into place one by one while Anton and Anders strode next to the open side of the trailer, tossing the bales up to me in turn in smooth, hard shoves.

Everything scratched and poked.

Under my shirt, on my ankles above my blue tennis shoes and on my wrists, where the skin swelled up in stinging, skin-flaying scratches. First layer at the bottom; second layer on the other side with a hole on the trailer side so they didn't need to throw so high. Third layer to be laid across, which demanded I lift the bale and crawl over the load, making it slower. Ellen had to stop the tractor once in a while so I could keep up. Sometimes Anders jumped up on the trailer to help me; other times, he trudged across the field after the closest bales, which he gathered in a pile beside me. A steady pace without breaks.

I'd never seen Anton without a shirt, but if you'd ever seen him work, you knew how strong he was. Just as strong as Anders. And not only in body. He had what my father lacked: a kind of savage toughness, which on days like today could drive him to work until he dropped without showing any signs of pain along the way.

The bales were passed to me as high as Anton's arms and the fork could stretch, and I took them and set them in the right pattern. Pulled two of the heavy, defiant, prickly bastards up against each other, kicking them into place so that they sat wedged, and the load grew layer by layer until Anton jumped up into the tractor cab and began trundling the hay trailer back over the fields. The rest of us were still atop the rocking load. Ellen and I lay side by side at one end, staring up at the blue sky. The sweat was steamed off me by the wind, and though my nails were flayed and ripped to bleeding, my hands white and red from scratched skin, nothing hurt.

"I didn't know it could be like this, Utzon."

Ellen turned her head and looked at me with glittering eyes.

I would have liked to ask her what she meant, but everything inside me throbbed dull and painful when I looked at her. I couldn't take her hand like I wanted to. I couldn't even smile without tears welling up in my eyes. So I just lay there, watching her and torturing myself with the idea of a final farewell as she raised her arms over her head and grabbed beech and lime leaves, pulled all the green off and left them stripped down to skinny skeletons.

The same work awaited us inside the barn, just in reverse order. Ellen stood on the trailer, throwing hay bales down to Anton, who again stuck the pitchfork in them and heaved them up onto the conveyor belt to the open barn hatch. I stood in the loft with Anders, flipping them into place in the dusty darkness. One painstaking hay bale at a time. First lengthways, and then across, and then lengthways again. We'd been in the kitchen half an hour earlier to butter some rye bread with lard and liver pâté, as well as have pickled beetroot, and later we drank a cup of coffee with our burning hands folded around the thin porcelain. About half past eight, we ate some more before driving out for the last load.

The light had become soft, freshening up from the slowly fading sky in the west, but you could smell the rain on the wind over the newly harvested fields. Everything was slower now. The tractor stood still more often so Anton and Anders or I could catch up on the backlog, but somehow it still turned out all right. We'd done most of what we needed to, and we still had the evening ahead of us. The landscape dissolved into shadows with blurred edges around the tractor's jumping headlights.

And finally, a trailer that was only half-full. Anton drove home over the stubble fields with the insects whirling through the white glow from the headlights, and Anders and I sat on the half load, which we didn't need to drag up to the loft before the weekend, as long as it was under the lean-to. Ellen walked like a silent, black shadow beside the trailer.

"Wait here," said Anton, smiling in the dark. Soon afterward, he returned with four cold beers, which he opened by tapping the caps against the edge of the trailer. He handed us a bottle each before climbing up and sitting down on the hay.

"Cheers, and thanks for all your help," he said.

I let the beer bottle cool my burning palms. I looked up to meet Ellen's eyes, but she didn't notice me. Anders had moved closer to her, but that didn't seem to bother her. On the contrary, she rested her forehead against Anders's shoulder for a moment and closed her eyes.

It was so dark in there that I could only imagine his profile against the brighter sky outside.

We drank our beer in silence, and Anton took his pipe and a bag of tobacco out from a pants pocket, stuffing the bowl with a shaking hand.

"Light?"

I found my lighter and held the flame over the pipe. Saw him suck it down until it completely disappeared and the tobacco started to glow.

He was relaxed. Maybe happy? There was something almost unrestrained about the way Anton was sitting. Leaning back with a hand beneath his neck and his feet thrown youthfully up over another bale. I'd never seen that before. He didn't even allow himself to put his feet up on the sofa—he only sat up straight, drinking his coffee. The harvest was a relief, even though there were green sprouts at the bottom of the straw and money had to be used to get the corn dried. It was in now, and everything would coast to a different rhythm. The wet hay in the field would have to be burned off at some point, graphite-gray plumes of smoke in the cool September wind. Black earth and glossy wet clay that the plow would leave in silky smooth furrows. It would be time to sleep and stay in, and walk down along the rows of cows in the stalls, watching the hot breath steam from their wet muzzles on the first frosty mornings. The sour, vomit-like smell of silage and peas.

If only she would stay.

I tried to catch her gaze again, a little more overtly this time, but she picked silently at her beer label and still didn't see me as she let Anders's troubled hands stroke her leg and then her shoulder without saying anything.

"Maybe you should go in with Jacob, Ellen. Anders and I will lock up the animals."

She smiled. "Later," she said, pointing to the sky. "I just want to see the last bit."

Violent gusts grabbed the trees, and I felt cold splash against my forehead and lips as I walked in alone.

IN THE BATHROOM, I poured lukewarm water into the washbasin, pulled my T-shirt off and dipped both hands and forearms in until the scratches and wounds stopped burning. Afterward, I washed my face and cleaned my ears and nose of stiffened flakes of black dust. My face and neck were warm and sunburned, and my muscles so tired that my hands shook, but I could sleep all day tomorrow if I wanted.

The door out in the hall creaked. Light steps in the hallway, then farther into the kitchen, where someone brushed their teeth with the water drumming in the kitchen sink. Then it was quiet again.

"Ellen?"

The light was turned off in both the kitchen and the living room, but I could see her shadow dancing in the narrow strip of light from the half-open door to Great-Grandmother's room. Her little breath when the heavy overalls fell to the floor and she pulled her blouse over her head. Her bare feet back and forth. And then, from the corner of my eye, I saw movement outside the living room window. An indistinct black brush stroke behind the pouring creek of rain.

The rain was ice cold against my bare upper body when I ran out into the yard. The darkness was complete without moon or stars, and the water ran down into my eyebrows and eyelashes, making it difficult to see where I was going. I hadn't put shoes on, and I regretted it as soon as I turned the corner of the house and felt the sludgy mud under my feet and the sharp stones that I couldn't avoid. Nevertheless, I jogged the last piece until I had a view of the south side of the house and Ellen's illuminated window.

The figure that stood peeping a few steps from the window wasn't doing much to hide. He'd only retreated a little, letting darkness do the work. But I could see him, weakly lit up as he was, and I recognized the heavy body, imperturbably leaning forward, and the hands buried deep in pockets filled with jingling shards of glass.

I stood frozen to the spot as I saw the light turn off in Ellen's room, and Anders slowly turn around and disappear into the darkness like an animal from the forest.

The road to Egå was a wide river of asphalt through lighting, carpet and kitchen stores, fast-food joints and warehouses. Cars that stopped bumper to bumper at red lights.

The sunlight was sharp as it entered the windshield of the dove-gray car, my personal time warp, which lacked both air-conditioning and horsepower. The car wasn't built for an ever-warming planet of asphalt, shining like water, and neither was I. I was pouring sweat. Hadn't had anything to drink other than coffee when I'd gone in to refuel and check the address again.

Nikolaj Ballin. Owner of a pest control company at the same address where he lived. The only Nikolaj Ballin in Denmark.

I turned onto a residential street with newer houses, dense green hedges, parched lawns and kettle grills in the garages. The heat sailed over light-gray sidewalks. A white-haired girl around five years old in a yellow summer dress was crouched, painting big pink and green circles on the cement with a bag of colored chalk in her hand. She waved to me as I slowed down and finally came to a complete stop.

"What are you doing, mister?"

She tilted her small head a little, giving me the inquisitive look of the female sex. Pouting, with laid-back skepticism.

"Going to talk to the folks who live in the house."

"That's Nikolaj and Karin. It smells."

I nodded and smiled, then walked to the door, the little girl's gaze on my back.

THE MAN WHO opened the door was stocky, almost fat, and dressed in a summer uniform of bare feet, knee-length shorts and a red T-shirt with a company name—SOS PESTS—written in large white letters across his sizable stomach. SPECIALISTS IN CREEPING, CRAWLING AND FLYING INSECTS. His eyes were narrow crevices in his bloated red face, and he resembled someone not doing well with either the heat or the seventy-plus years he had to be.

"Yes?"

"Nikolaj Ballin?"

He nodded and pushed a pair of shoes a little farther in toward the wall with the tip of a bluish big toenail, his feet and calves inflamed with liquid in the heat.

"I'm looking for someone who knows Ellen Høgh and perhaps where to find her."

"Ellen?" Nikolaj Ballin considered me with renewed interest. "Of course. I went to high school with her. May I ask why you're looking for her?"

"It's a long story. From Tostrup."

"Yes, that was a few years ago now." He wiped his hand over his neck and threw a quick look over his shoulder into the hall. "Well, you'd better come inside. Sorry about the mess. It's been . . ."

I followed him into the long, dark hall, where he panted between an old chest of drawers and two shelves with boxes stacked from floor to ceiling. It smelled stuffy and moldy.

"It's the wife," he said apologetically. "She collects things."

I didn't answer.

The living room, despite the light let in by its south-facing windows, was packed tight with old furniture. Small coffee tables, chairs, sofas with vases, decorative tablecloths with ruffles and porcelain dolls with long party frocks positioned in neat seating arrangements like at a life-sized tea party.

"She's sleeping now. Shall we sit out on the terrace?"

He opened the door, leaving it ajar so the draft made the porcelain dolls' party dresses move a little. He looked up at the merciless blue sky.

"Like in the hot countries," he said. "Isn't it wonderful?"

I forced a smile. I wanted vodka and negative temperatures that froze my breath to snow. There was something nostalgic about the cold nowadays. A forgotten echo of crisp ice on puddles that could be crushed under boots. This summer heat would make me lose my mind, if I hadn't already. Nikolaj blinked cheerfully, reaching for the coffeepot that was already on the table.

"Can I get a cup for you?"

"No, thank you."

"You come from Tostrup?"

A garden sprinkler swirled lazily in the perennial bed, and it smelled of sunshine and camping under the awning that was stretched over the corner of the garden that had the table. The grass on the lawn had gone to seed and was pushing up between the cracked patio tiles.

"Originally, yes," I said. "We've actually met each other a couple of times. You were at the chicken farm, too, when they found the girl. Lise."

He blinked at me once, pulling a meaty hand through the thin hair on his crown.

"Yes, that's one of the very few things I remember from that time. Lise. That was her name, yes. But it's Ellen you're looking for? Can't help you much there. She went to Berlin for a few years, I know, then came home . . . got married to someone with a common name. Jensen? Petersen? Something like that. That's all I got from her boyfriend back then. Karsten."

It was strange to hear she'd married. In my mind, she'd never grown older than when I'd last seen her, and despite all these years, she must have remained in my consciousness as a prospect, waiting for me once I'd finished with Kirsten. When the children had grown up. When I became young again. Now she was married, tamed, held down like everyone else.

"I don't know if you already know about her family?" Nikolaj Ballin wiped his forehead with a handkerchief, breathing heavily.

I hesitated.

"I don't know anything. In fact, I only knew Ellen quite briefly." I found my cigarettes and sent him a questioning look for good measure. He nodded.

"Beautiful girl," he said. "Sweet, but"—he waved a hand—"chaotic, right? Even in high school. A little crazy. But she also had some problems to deal with at home."

"Like?"

"Her father was a devil. High school teacher and wannabe artist in his spare time. A sculptor. In other words, all right, but not if you want to be blunt about it. It wasn't art, but craftsmanship. No imagination. Not bad, but certainly not art."

"And what about Ellen?"

"Yes, what about her?" He shrugged. "She had what he didn't. I actually have a drawing she gave me as a graduation gift. It's quite exceptional. Hold on."

He went into the living room and came back a moment later with a framed drawing. It was of a beach. Shadows in the sand, stone, seaweed spread sparingly over the white paper. A pair of pitch-black, broken pound net posts were placed at the top of an almost invisible transition to the water, which had the same color as the solid ground. White on white. In the bottom right corner was an edged ELLEN.

Nikolaj Ballin held it out with raised eyebrows.

"Fantastic. It strikes me every time I look at it. Not everyone can get so much out of so little. There were only two problems."

"Yes?"

"One problem was she didn't want to pursue it in the traditional sense. And the other was that she eclipsed her father. She had the kind of inherent talent you can practice all your life without having. But with that came rebellion."

"What kind?"

Nikolaj Ballin shot me a subtle smile.

"She smoked hash. Took other drugs, too. She was the one who introduced me and Karsten to them in time. She was able to control it. We weren't, but that's a completely different story. One night when she was stoned, high and flying, she took a hammer and chisel and went down to her father's studio. Hacked the noses and ears off all the busts and ran away. That was that. The old man refused her in absentia. We found an apartment and started a commune. First in the town, then in the country."

I tapped ash onto the tile.

"Are you still in contact with Karsten Villadsen?"

"Our friendship didn't last in the commune," he said, leaning back in the garden chair. "Too many drugs and quarrels about dishes and money in the end. And then there was Lise . . . and Karsten."

He met my eyes and sat at ease in his chair for the first time, the sweat running down over his forehead. His SOS PESTS T-shirt had begun to darken over his chest and stomach.

"It's so many years ago now," he said. "But it gnaws away some-where in me. That miserable doubt."

"About?"

"Ellen and Karsten were like cat and dog near the end, and in the middle of it all, Ellen went to Berlin for a few months. In the spring. While she was there, I saw Lise and Karsten together. Just once in early May, but still. They screwed in the woods. Not lying down or anything; it was so unromantic and practical, right? Her hands on a tree trunk while he took her from behind. I didn't say anything to him or anyone else back then."

I pulled the plastic chair out from the table and stood up on stiff legs. "But why didn't you tell the police?"

Nikolaj lowered his eyes and rubbed his sweaty forehead with his hand.

"We had our own little business, Karsten and I. Hash, mostly. Innocent really, but anyway. If I'd thought it was him who killed Lise, I would've told them. But when you're young, you always think the best of people. And we weren't exactly fans of law enforcement back then."

Karsten and Lise. The young man with the beautiful lips and fantasies of a socialist paradise and Lise, the ordinary office worker from a chicken farm. There was no plausible universe where that romance existed. Certainly not happily.

"Karsten wasn't picky." Nikolaj Ballin sniggered. "He found loving other girls easy, from time to time. But he loved Ellen most."

"Where do you think she is now?"

He shook his head.

"Far away. Otherwise, you would have come across her drawings again."

"Maybe she just dropped art," I said. "That kind of thing happens. Actors get stage fright, and painters get scared of empty canvases. Or they get their fill and find something else to do. Something useful."

"Maybe." Nikolaj Ballin shrugged, laid a hand on the picture. Touched a mussel shell that was almost obliterated by the sand.

"But like I said before: what she had was God-given. Could you ever stop if you were able to do this? I think you'd die first."

Night fell as I drove toward Risskov.

The asphalt shone like oil in the setting sun. The weather fore-casters had given the farmers until evening to get the harvest in, the bit there was, but there was already something hostile in the shaky wind and dark sky. Bale processors, tractors, hay trailers and trailers of dull, gray corn tops filled the small roads, heavy and stinking of diesel, long tails of glittering dust trailing behind them.

The radio hoarsely came and went on a channel where the host and guest were discussing life on other planets. Wormholes and the Einstein-Rosen Bridge. We were all time travelers, moving forward in time at the same speed. Onward and onward, with no known way back.

My phone was silent when I turned onto the road with the many splendid villas and parked a distance from the overgrown drive-way. No news about Anders, and nothing from the hospital. I sat smoking for a little while, windows rolled down, as I tried to pre-pare for what was about to happen. Laughter and muted music reached me from the beach, and I could see yachts between the trees, rocking with slacked sails on the mercury-glazed water.

"HE'S NOT HOME."

It was hard to tell whether Karsten's son recognized me. He seemed completely indifferent. The phone was still stuck to his right hand; he wore canvas shorts and flip-flops. There was also a half smile—the kind rich kids were raised to share with servants and ordinary people.

"Do you know when he'll be home?"

He shrugged and waved at a couple of other teenagers trudging through the hall, and farther on into the kitchen behind him.

"I don't know, he's at work. Or in Copenhagen or something. I haven't seen him today," he said.

"Do you think your mom knows?"

"No, she's on a shopping trip in London. I think. But I can give you Dad's cell number if you don't already have it."

"Thank you, that'd be great."

I handed him my phone so he could enter it in with his firm young fingers. Someone called him from the kitchen, and he gave it back to me with an impatient jerk of his head. Eyed me up and down with a cold teenage appraisal, and I could tell all too clearly what he saw. An old man with a potbelly hanging out over a pair of slightly too youthful designer jeans.

"Well—"

"The bathroom," I said. "Perhaps I could use your bathroom for a moment?"

He glared at me, the corners of his mouth turned discreetly downward. Probably an unwelcome snapshot of me on the john. Teenagers were delicate souls. But he nodded and let me come in, pointing to a hall on the left.

"Second door on the right," he said, smiling cautiously. He had apparently already forgotten about me as I plodded down the hall and found the beautiful guest bathroom. Cream-colored tiles, freshly polished brass faucets, and one of those completely flat hand-washing basins that couldn't hold water. Karsten's wife must have gotten her clutches on one of the more puffed-up interior designers. I squeezed out a few drops, waited a few minutes before wiping myself and washing my hands, and pulled out my phone again. Called the number the boy had entered for me.

It went directly to voice mail. No rings.

I cursed softly, walked into the living room and turned off the light, sitting down on the voluptuously padded eight-seater sofa.

The French doors to the garden and water were wide open, so the wind ran through the now-almost-empty house, and I might have slept a little. I probably did. Time had, at any rate, disintegrated somewhere after ten o'clock; it was now dazzling one-thirty in white digital numbers as I straightened up to listen to the darkness.

Someone put their shoes away in the hall and moved in stocking feet across the creaking parquet floor, perhaps already on their way up the stairs to disappear into the huge house.

Disoriented, I got up and groped toward the door in the darkness, hitting my shinbone on a low table that gave off the unmistakable aura of being an expensive art piece. Something crashed to the floor, and I stumbled and fell, knocking teeth and nose on the hard arm of the sofa. I felt a snow-white pain when the bridge of my nose gave with a wet crunch. The steps in the hall came to a stop, replaced first by silence, and then by a shining light as the door opened.

"What the hell? What's going on?"

Karsten Villadsen looked relatively calm, standing there in his office attire.

I struggled to get up, knocked over something behind me and almost stumbled again. Something had happened to my shoulder in the fall, and when I breathed, my mouth filled with warm, velvety blood.

"I had a couple more questions for you."

He looked mildly surprised.

"Wait a moment." He dug into his breast pocket and, with a gentlemanly flourish, conjured a handkerchief, which he handed to me. "You're bleeding all over my antique carpet. Whiskey?"

He went over to a cupboard and retrieved a bottle and two glasses. Walked past me into the living room and turned on a table lamp that I hadn't yet knocked to the floor. He sat down, rubbing his face with a bony hand.

"I'm too old for nighttime meetings," he said. "Actually, I'm probably too old for most things now. If there's something you're aching to get off your chest, then do it fast. I'm so fucking tired."

"Ellen. Where is she?"

He stared at me, disoriented. He did look genuinely tired and not the least bit guarded.

"I've already told you, I don't know. I have literally no idea. Look, everything that happened back then—I've tried to move on, just like you obviously did. I looked you up online. An architect with your own company, a wife and children. What the hell more do you want? Jesus Christ, I was about to get my gun and shoot your head off just a minute ago."

"You were an adult back then. You could have stopped it."

"Hey." He threw both hands in the air, then got up and went over to close the door to the garden. "You're going on my confession alone here. I was an idiot. I was chronically stoned on something or other during those years. But I have no idea where Ellen is, and now I really need to sleep."

He brushed past me. His body radiated cognac and cologne and an arrogance that made me furious. I came up on my legs and pushed him with a flat hand toward the built-in shelves. Clinton's smiling face on the back of his biography was right at eye level. I weighed at least forty pounds more than Karsten, and it wasn't all just fat. I could feel him shove against me with all his might, but I was in control now.

"Give it a rest! Stop." He was slightly out of breath now. "What the hell is wrong with you?"

"Did you do something to her?"

He panted angrily against my shoulder in short jerks that slowly ebbed. His breath was tropically warm on my neck. The intimacy was nauseating, just like the blood still flowing into my throat.

I let him go, taking a step back, and he stood staring at me, his lips curled in as he breathed quickly through his nose.

"Of course I didn't do anything to Ellen!" he said. "I was fucked up, but not *that* bad. Believe it or not, Ellen and I loved each other. I stopped drinking after that. Stopped the drugs, cleaned up my shit. It *is* actually possible to become a decent person over time." He grinned and gave half a laugh as he wiped his forehead. "Fuck it," he said. "I did. Get on with your life and let me sleep. I'm an old man."

I drained my glass.

"And Lise? I spoke to Nikolaj. He saw you two together."

He lifted his eyebrows.

"Ballin? He never mentioned that to me. But okay. Lise and I screwed for a pretty short time, but we kept it a secret. Ellen was in Berlin, and I was unhappy and wanted her back, so I made Lise promise not to tell anyone. Which wasn't particularly nice; I think she was in love with me. But otherwise, I was nice to her. Always walked her home and waited until she'd turned on the light in her room. The night she disappeared, too."

Something cold swam at the back of my consciousness. Something I'd refused to think about all these years.

"You saw her go up to her room?"

He nodded.

"Maybe she went out again later. Maybe she was seeing someone else. It wasn't me, at least."

I took out the picture I had in my back pocket. One of the torn little snapshots from the commune. Ellen side by side with a light-haired girl I was almost sure I knew. I could feel the sweat run in drops down over my chest and stomach when I leaned forward.

"Who's that girl there?"

Karsten accepted the picture that I handed him and looked at it in the light of the table lamp.

"I remember her," he said. "Lise's friend, right? Funny girl. Tall.

Ellen was mad about her. She also made sure Ellen got some shifts at some factory every so often, but we didn't see her that much. She couldn't stand our toilet out in the stable."

"And you know nothing about what happened to Ellen?"

He looked at me with tired indulgence over the edge of his whiskey glass.

"Hell no. That's what I keep saying. And I could just as easily ask you. As far as I remember, you weren't exactly an angel yourself."

1978

"You're only going to talk to him, right?"

Sten nodded. "Yes, just talk to him. Nothing else."

Anders and I were alone on the farm. Anton had driven to Randers to buy a calf, and Ellen had taken the train to Aarhus. The rain had paused as we stood there on the edge between our property and the neighbor's. It was Sten's idea to meet here so the pair could cross the fields, instead of the road where everyone could see them. For some reason, he was wearing a far-too-big dark-green jacket and had a pair of binoculars hanging around his neck. He looked more like a spaz than usual, while Karsten looked like himself. Jeans and shirt with sleeves rolled up over the sinewy tanned arms.

He stank of beer. They both did.

"Are you coming?" Sten narrowed his clear, gray-blue eyes at me. He'd already asked on the phone—"The more, the better . . . Are you with us or against us?"—but I didn't give a shit. There was absolutely nothing that would get me down to the farm with them. The thought alone made me feel nauseous.

"I think it's best if I stay out here," I said, hoping I didn't sound like a coward. "I know him."

Sten shrugged, pulled something that looked like a nylon stocking out of the giant jacket and handed it to me.

"What's this?"

"For your head, dammit. So he won't recognize you. Lise had a whole drawer of them."

He pulled his own stocking impatiently down over his head, so his face turned into a pale lump of a turnip with the shadows of his mouth and eyes as the only human indicators. He quickly pulled it off again and straightened his damp bangs with misplaced vanity. Like he was getting ready for a party.

"You can borrow it." His voice tensed at a slightly higher pitch than normal. "I don't care if he sees me. What the hell's he going to do about it?"

Was he serious? A stocking? Like it would really mask our identities.

"No, thanks."

"Okay."

He nodded to Karsten, who stood with his fingers wrapped around a cigarette, breathing smoke into the wind, and they started walking. An inharmonious duo: a starved boy and his fully grown second, both ignited and engulfed by a sacred flame. And as if they were parodying a soldier's life, they'd begun to walk in step.

My nausea rose and sank with their rhythmic marching, and I didn't feel okay. My thoughts were like pedals on a bike when the chain had fallen off. Moving too quickly without catching hold, and had been that way since last night.

I hadn't slept. I almost couldn't breathe when I thought of Anders' monstrous strength. The expression in his eyes when the enormous boar lay over the gilt. The wood-like hands that constantly grazed Ellen's shoulders, chest and back, that could kill her with a single well-placed blow. The thick forehead that I'd thought stored nothing but that in reality was a confused stream of drives, just like a boar's.

Sten and Karsten disappeared around the corner of the pigpen. I wasn't wearing a watch. If the sun had been shining, I could have banged a stick into the ground and watched the shadow wander patiently from A to B. We'd done it in physics. But the light was gray and diffuse, and it would be confusing under slowly pulsating clouds in any case. The sun was only visible as a chlorine-bleached spot among them.

I pulled a tuft of couch grass up from the earth and pulled it apart. Then poked a black molehill with a stick, occasionally looking down at the stable, hoping they'd appear. But nothing happened and I was pretty sure a while had passed. At least half an hour, maybe even an hour. How long did this kind of thing take? I had no idea, and suddenly, it struck me that they might not walk back over the fields. Maybe they'd already gone home the normal way without saying anything to me.

I got up and peered down at the farm with an unease that for the first time in several days had nothing to do with Ellen. Too much time had passed. It could be afternoon already, and I was still picturing Sten's formless face in the pale nylon stocking.

After a couple of steps in every direction, I decided to at least go down to the corner of the stable and take a look at the yard. When I finally got moving, my head felt like a soap bubble, and my body wrong somehow. My pants were wet and dirty after sitting in the grass for so long.

There was nobody to be seen. No one out on the road or at the farm or on the hill. Only the wet, freshly cut fields dressed in shitty yellow and brown with large fluttering flocks of crows and jackdaws and storm gulls in search of crushed mice and partridges.

I continued around the stable, struggling to breathe.

THE YARD WAS deserted. Doors and windows closed and off-putting in the gray noon light.

I stood for a long moment, collecting myself before gently opening the back door and listening down the narrow hallway.

First silence.

Then more silence.

And then a dumb bray—a deep, breathless breath, as though huge animals were moving around in the building.

Someone or something moved or was being moved around in explosive jerks, causing things to fall and shatter on the floor.

A wild roar.

"Arggghhhh!"

I snuck into the kitchen, not because I dared to, but because I didn't dare not to. The door to the living room stood open, and the first thing I noticed was Sten, standing with his back to me, his ridiculous nylon stocking hat half-torn and his arms out to the sides. Like a soccer goalie ready for his penalty kick. A meat tenderizer that was usually in one of the kitchen drawers in one hand.

Karsten was on his knees in front of him, looking like someone about to propose, his long hair hanging over his eyes and all his weight on the back of a lifeless—or almost lifeless—body. The muscles on Karsten's arms were tensed all the way up to the pulsating veins on his throat and neck, the sweat running off him like he was still out in the rain.

Anders's arm, which was twisted behind his back, moved a little. His head was squashed sideways down on the carpet, and there was a cake of blood on his bald crown. Fortunately, I couldn't see his face.

"You have to hold him tighter!"

Sten's eyes were wild, and his voice broke into a half laugh, as if from a place between panic and uncontrollable glee. His nose was bleeding, and he was awkwardly holding one of his own arms, lifting it gently in toward his body.

Karsten swore loudly.

And then Sten spotted me; he pulled his lips back crookedly over his huge teeth, so his smile resembled a sneer.

"He went berserk, Jacob," he said. "When he saw me wearing

the stocking. He just went crazy. We couldn't—but now he admits it himself. He did it. Bad boy. Bad *boy*!"

The exclamation sounded both tired and elated. He threw out a stiff arm before fixing his gaze on Anders again.

"He did it. The pig."

And then, like a sudden flash, he planted four fast kicks into Anders's heavy body, each followed by a deep, painful grunt. Then Sten opened his clasped hand and pressed something sharp into my palm. A butterfly hair clip.

"He had it in his pocket," he said. "Give me your belt."

I stared at him.

"Come on, quickly."

I looked over at Karsten, who was the adult, but his eyes were as tin-plated as that night by the fire. Drunk or worse. Why hadn't I seen it when they crossed the field?

"I thought you just wanted to talk to him."

"Well, we can't exactly do that now, can we? We'll do it ourselves. A retard like him would never be put in prison."

Sten might have been on the edge of crying. It seemed that way, but it was probably something else. Lunacy, fury. His movements were spasmodic and quick, as though he were dancing out the same anger as a boxer in the ring.

"Jacob! Come on, dammit."

Now he screamed. Took a step toward me and pushed me in the chest. Not once, but twice, and with such frightening strength that I lost my balance for a moment and banged my head on the door frame. Ellen and Anton. They'd be home soon, and it hit me that everything would be over quicker and better if I did something.

I pulled my belt from its loops and handed it to Sten.

"Pull up his shirt."

I stepped forward. Anders's unmoving body steamed with heat, and there was a stench of urine and blood and something else,

more stringent, which oozed out of all three of them and myself.
A fearful sweat. Anders's shirt was clammy and hard to pull up
over his back, but I eventually managed to roll it up to his shoulders, where it lay like a wet sausage over his pale skin.

"And his pants."

"Dammit, Sten—"

"Hell!"

Karsten had stood up. Pushed the long, sweaty hair back behind
his ears, breathing in and out through clenched teeth. Then he
grabbed the back pockets on Anders's pants and pulled them down
over his buttocks in hard, abrupt jerks. There was shit everywhere.
On his butt cheeks, on his pants, and on the carpet, but Sten didn't
even blink. His first blow with the belt hit before Karsten had
moved completely out of the way, leaving a wide, red line over
Anders' white lower back. The next split the skin with a crisp
sound like biting into an apple, making blood trickle out of the
gash.

"Isn't that enough?"

I kept looking from Anders to the door to the kitchen and back.
Strangely enough, I still wondered how late it was, whether Anton
was on his way home from the auction in Randers. And Ellen. She'd
left an infinity ago and would, of course, come home again. My
sense of time was long gone, and I thought of the expressions in
their eyes when they caught us in the living room in the middle of
this horrific catastrophe. Ellen would be furious with me. And
Anton. I also wondered how I would ever get the shit out of the
carpet.

"Your turn."

Sten handed me the belt while he wiped his open mouth with
the back of his hand. And I accepted it. Hit twice, just like him, but
not hard enough for it to bleed. Only new, flaming red marks.

"Harder," said Sten angrily. "Otherwise, we'll never be done. Do
it like this."

He took the belt out of my hand and struck again, leaving four new gashes. Skin and flesh quivered a little, but Anders was still quiet. I tried to get myself fired up. To feel the rage I'd felt last night. The belief that Anders was dangerous and would kill Ellen. But it was no longer in me.

All of it was gone, leaving behind powerless muscles and even stronger nausea.

"Last time, okay? Then we're done."

I was still looking desperately for a clock in the living room, but had to settle for the heavy ticking outside in the kitchen. The light outside was unquestionably gray, so who knew what time it was.

I struck once. Hard. And then, like he'd been hit by an electric shock, Anders moved. He was up on his knees with a jolt, fumbling for something to hold with his eyes closed, and grabbed the edge of the coffee table. Tried to stand completely, but stumbled on the first attempt on the pants that were still around his knees.

I felt a shot of panic at the sight of his tormented face. Sounds bubbled out of his mouth, mixed with blood and chipped fragments of teeth. I wished he'd be quiet again and stop the broken, complaining moans before my head exploded.

Karsten had thrown both hands in the air and had taken a step back toward the door, but Anders was standing now, eyes narrowed in bloody cracks. He struck out, struggling to keep his balance on his bound legs.

"Ah, hell!"

Karsten spit on the floor. His face was still crimson after the effort of taking down Anders, and there was clearly no fight left in him. With his hands raised in defense against the shadow boxer, he went into the kitchen, leaving Sten and me there, petrified.

"Hit him in the head," whispered Sten. "Knock him out."

Anders fell again, put out his arms, but still landed heavy and hard on the coffee table, where he wrestled and turned, leaving wide, bloody tracks on the tiles. Got up again.

"Do it yourself!"

"You're bigger than me! Or . . ."

Sten was as freaked out as me now, his voice thin.

"And where am I supposed to go afterward?"

I wanted to hit Sten. Grab his small, poultry-thin neck and squeeze, but I didn't get to. Instead, I was hit so hard on the side of the head that it was as though the light had been turned up and down for nauseatingly long moments. I'd fallen without really noticing, but got back up on my legs again just in time to see the blind giant tumble over me and crush me against the wall. Blood and salt on my tongue. His hands and naked abdomen and body odor, and something that hurt my elbow, maybe from the fall. I tried to push him away, his shoulders sticky and wet with blood. His eyes turned up toward the ceiling.

I heard the smacks from the belt when Sten began to whip it manically against Anders's back and felt his jerky trembles under the blows, but he didn't back away. He stood heavy, stooping over me. A mountain of flesh and bones that could squeeze the air out of me with its weight alone.

Time was stretched thin and transparent, and there were continuous intermittent, cracking strokes that penetrated me despite my being buried in body and sweat.

The next thing that hit me was a woman screaming, and it was as though Anders teetered back at the sound alone. He stood, swaying indecisively, blood still running down into his eyes.

I pushed him as hard as I could, for Ellen . . . because it was Ellen standing in the living room with wild eyes, screaming in a voice I didn't recognize.

"What are you doing? What the *hell* are you doing?"

Anders whirled around clumsily, his legs tangled in his shit-covered pants, reached out for her and fell face-first onto the soiled floor.

The scream that followed didn't resemble anything I'd ever

heard. It went on and on, both a roar and a cry, interrupted only by inhalations, deep and gurgling, like someone drowning. He curled around himself. His back was blood; his thighs and buttocks and testicles were blood.

"Call a doctor, Jacob."

"But—"

Ellen's face was unrecognizable. Blanched through the suntan, her mouth and eyes narrow cracks in a stiff mask.

"Call one-one-two, Jacob."

I went to the phone and lifted the receiver while looking at Sten and Karsten, who were standing in the door out to the kitchen. There was something eerily calm and silent about everything surrounding Anders. Every movement was slow and heavy, like walking in knee-deep water at Følle Strand. Only Anders's shaking body moved in the present.

112.

The voice on the phone was clear and metallic, and I spoke to someone who answered me and asked about something. Our address. My name. But I didn't answer. Just stood there, winding the gray spiral cord around my bloodstained fingers.

THE NEXT THING I knew, I was standing outside in the yard, watching Sten and Karsten disappear behind the stable and Ellen come out. Anders had stopped screaming inside, and Ellen seemed calm now. Pale, but calm. She'd taken out a cigarette, which she lit with shaking hands.

"Will you tell me what happened, Jacob?"

I could tell I was close to throwing up, but I just stood there, unable to think.

"It was Anders who killed Lise. He was watching you, too. I saw him. I was trying to protect you."

"Me?"

She sent me a look that was hard to endure. Like we didn't know each other at all. No laughter, no friendliness, no kindness. Only even, cold interest.

"How . . ." The hand with the cigarette gestured toward the door behind us. "How the hell do you think what happened in there is about me?"

"He killed Lise," I protested.

Ellen laughed, but it was a hard laugh that made her lips curl in a new way. She'd cried in there at Anders; her face was wet and broken and ugly.

"God, you're an idiot, Utzon. What do you know about that? What do you really know about anything? You're fifteen years old. Do you even have hair on your dick? Do you? Who do you really think you are? Anders wouldn't dare approach women. Hasn't ever even touched one that way. I *know*. I know him."

And then, as if at the wave of a magic wand, the anger hit me in a scorching, corrosive shower.

Had I not tried to protect her? To save her? Was I not the only man she'd met who loved her like this? And had I not just done the most abhorrent thing for her sake? I didn't deserve her contempt.

I lay a hand on her shoulder and turned her around so we were standing face-to-face. I was a head taller than her, at least. It wasn't difficult to hold her tight once I'd grabbed her thin wrist. I could easily reach around them with my hands, and I didn't need to use a lot of effort to pull her closer.

She was looking directly into my eyes now, surprised. She was afraid of me, and that made me even angrier, because it was so unreasonable. So ridiculous when I'd spent every waking hour wondering how to make her happy.

She tried to free herself again, and I pulled her even closer, feeling myself harden on the edge of her soft, beautiful hip.

"Let go of me."

She tried to hit my face with the hand she'd freed, but she didn't have room for a proper swing, and the attempt ended with a dead slap just above my left cheekbone.

I ignored it.

Thought of Sussi when she pushed the tip of her tongue out between her front teeth. And of Laurel when she laughed at me. Of how unfair Ellen was. How unreasonable she'd always been, and how little she deserved all my thoughts and everything that I'd given her.

I grasped her chest, which was shaking uneasily in her attempt to free herself. And I squeezed and saw how my fingers left red marks on her soft skin.

"He did it," I said. "And you were going to be next. He's been in your room, and he stares in through your window. I saw it, dammit."

She was still staring at me, her teeth exposed in a silent snarl that I'd never seen on a person before. The beauty was gone, and Utzon was gone, as was the moment she'd held my hand, hovering over the sketch pad in the woods, never to come back.

"Believe me," I said.

And I could see that some of the hardness had crumbled away, leaving her with blank and open eyes. She understood.

Somewhere outside of my consciousness, I heard the sound of Anton's Taunus, and even farther away, the complaining sirens of an ambulance.

Then I ran out over the fields.

I COULDN'T GO back for my bike, but walked along the train tracks most of the way toward the town. The fields shone like pale gold under the heavy dark-blue sky; I could feel there was more rain on the way. I was far away from the farm now, and it was windy, but when I got to the top of the hill, I could still see the flashing lights of the ambulance in the yard.

I'd vomited several times already, trying to turn myself inside out, but no heart or entrails came up. Only a cool, dark-yellow liquid that burned my throat and nose. On the desolate residential street, autumn-yellow birch leaves drifted over the asphalt, despite it only being August. The trees had drowned, I thought, just like the corn and the downy baby moles that had been washed out of their tunnels after the torrential rains.

Mom was standing at the front door, rattling her keys. She looked tired, her hair gathered up in its usual ponytail, suitcase at her feet. She turned when she heard my footsteps in the gravel and lit up in a smile.

"There you are," she said, leaving the suitcase where it was and almost running down the steps to put her arms around me. "I've missed you so much, my little boy. But . . ."

She took a step back and wrinkled her nose, and it was as though I was still shaking from my core. Like a tuning fork that caused blood, nerves, and bones to vibrate.

"I was mucking out the pigs," I said. "I'll go in and take a shower."

"Yes, do that," she said, stroking my sweaty hair.

"Mom?"

She had entered the hall. Shoes lay higgledy-piggledy, and there was a trail of dirt from Dad's boots into the kitchen. Her shoulders sank.

"Mom, I won't go back there again."

My stomach and chest felt so heavy, just there where her hand had been. Like when Sten and Flemming had once dug a hole in the sand on Følle Strand the size of a coffin, and I'd lain down in it and let them fill the grave with damp sand until the weight prevented me from lifting my arms, breathing and noticing nothing other than my heavy, muted heartbeat.

"Of course not, Jacob." She turned to me with an absent smile. "You can just stay with me."

A gray, hot, humid morning. A window was opened onto the main street.

Dansevise. Jørgen and Grethe Ingmann in a dark, melancholy duet about the terrible farewell waved out through the open window, but nobody answered when I rang. The low house was located on the town's lifeless main street, windows at hip height, and right out onto the broken sidewalk tiles. Dusty plastic blinds blocked out both light and wandering eyes. A few potted plants with thick waxy leaves sweated on the windowsill.

I opened the door, which gave without resistance, and called out into the narrow hallway.

"Hello?"

No response, but from where I stood, I could see into a tidy but uninventive kitchen. The tabletop in gray laminate, plank flooring and white kitchen elements. Some pictures on the fridge and yellowed pine chairs around a small dining table.

I called again, and this time there were steps on the upper floor, a creak from a staircase in the living room somewhere. The radio was switched to Anne Linnet—I still had time to change my mind. Suddenly, I didn't even know why the hell I was standing here, beyond the obvious. That I had to find an answer to it all.

"God, you don't look so good."

She appeared in the door of the living room, looking at me with quiet seriousness. Then she took a bag of ice out of the freezer and laid it against my hot, thumping jaw. It hurt after last night's meeting with the floor of Karsten's house. When I moved my tongue, two of my molars wobbled with a squelching sound, leaking a taste of iron and salt. She half smiled, crossed the floor and turned off the radio with a grimace that could be out of irritation.

"I heard about your uncle. You could probably use a drink?"

I nodded. Today was a good day to drink myself into a little stupor. That was why I'd come. That, and the company.

"A whiskey, if you have it."

"Of course."

She shut the door to the living room behind her and threw out her long hands. Found whiskey and a glass in the fridge and poured a couple of fingers for each of us.

"Thanks." I stopped and pulled out a chair so she could sit, even though she was the host.

She took her glass and drank like a man, with neither grace nor vanity. Sitting in her wet T-shirt and loose, gray pants over her wide, bony hips. Her hair was damp from sweat and pulled back into a tight ponytail, and despite her holding her arms close to her body, the large, dark patches were clearly visible on the T-shirt. She ran a hand over her hair and smiled, looking strangely uncomfortable.

"Sorry for looking like this," she said. "I haven't had a shower yet, and it's been a hot night. Menopause and this summer is a bitch. Personally, I'd have preferred a little ice age if you absolutely had to mess around with climate zones."

She poured a new glass and sent me an expectant look. "Why are you here?"

"You knew Ellen?"

She nodded slowly and leaned back in the chair, her glass resting on one hot cheek.

"We all knew each other back then. It's a small town."

"But you never said anything."

"She doesn't want to be found, Jacob. Not by you or anyone else from that time."

"I'd like to talk to her."

Laurel wrinkled her forehead.

"It's been years since I spoke to her. I don't even know if she's still alive."

I took a deep breath and thought it was time for me to go back to Copenhagen. Perhaps I should never have come. I could have gotten drunk under much more comfortable conditions in Nørrebro. There was no forgiveness for sins here, no cleansing fire. I wasn't sure why I'd tried to tell myself anything different.

"What happened after . . . the accident? Can you tell me that, at least?"

"That day?"

I nodded, eyes down.

"Anton arrived at the same time as the ambulance, and Ellen stayed until they'd driven Anton and Anders off. It all happened fast, because he was bleeding so much. There were injuries to everything, because he was naked, you know? Or half-naked. So Ellen watched them drive off. Afterward, she came to visit the commune, then left town."

"I'd like to talk to her. It's important to me. And to Anton. He thinks she's dead. And then there's Anders. I think she might know where he is."

Laurel leaned back, looking at me thoughtfully over the edge of her whiskey glass.

"Have you ever thought Anton might not only be interested in Ellen, but also in you? That he'd like to know why it happened, why you all did it? He was good to you; never went to the police, didn't say anything to the neighbors. What I know, I know from Ellen."

"He knows damn well why, and so do you. Lise. Anders was the one who did it, and Anton knew it. If he's saying otherwise, it's because he's lying to himself. He knew Anders couldn't stay away from the girls. It was dangerous."

Laurel emptied her whiskey glass, watching me curiously. My own glass sat on the table, untouched.

"You think she knows where Anders is?"

"It's possible. She was closer to him than anyone, and I think he was in love with her. He told her things he didn't tell us."

She nodded and got up. Disappeared into the living room and closed the door again. I could hear her talking for a while in a hushed voice.

Ellen.

Her voice reached me like a weak, but clear song through time and space. My imagination, of course. Like re-creating the guitar solo from "Stairway to Heaven" by way of just closing your eyes and remembering. The feeling of dying and being healed in the same fire.

"HERE?"

"This was Ellen's best guess," said Laurel.

I parked the car and looked at the farm on the other side of the road. It had three wings. A farmhouse in red brick with dusty, double-paneled windows from the '70s. Red-and-white FOR SALE signs were stuck to the two facing the road. Pared of soil, machinery and other vital internal organs left behind to the flocks of crows and jackdaws.

Part of me wanted to just stay in the car with Laurel. Smoke a ridiculous number of cigarettes and laugh about that time I'd touched her nice young breast. Amazingly, the thought still made me blush. The teenager and his delicate nerve endings hadn't been completely scratched from my bones yet.

I laid my head back and closed my eyes. Tried to curb the shakes with long, deep breaths. I missed Kirsten's calm, warm breath, her cool fingers on my temples and down over my eyelids when I had a headache like I did now. I'd become too old to drink beer every day and get away with it.

Laurel opened the car door and smiled in relief when the wind caught her hair.

"Too hot," she said. "It's always too hot, isn't it? That's just how it is now."

I looked at the purple-black sky above the forest. The rain that was on its way would drown the meadows, viaducts and freestanding houses. It would thrash the dusty soil, rinsing a piece of the world into the ocean. With childish euphoria, I looked forward to the first tap on the car window.

But first, there were things that had to be done; I stepped out onto the dry grass that crunched under my feet and walked up the overgrown driveway with Laurel a few steps behind me. The glass in the front door was dark yellow sun spirals in green panels. I pressed down the handle, and the door opened with a weak protest from its hinges.

The hall was solar-heated and bare. There were nude, darkly varnished floorboards and veneered doors to the kitchen, and the large, empty living room farther on in. The original wall-to-wall carpet still covered the full length of the room, light green with something that had once been thickly woven flower petals and crowns. The wallpaper in green-and-gold stripes down from the low ceiling. Faded oak beams and cracked windowsills; the house was trying to work itself out of its own form. Here, just like at the brothers', people had been sung out for the last time, and life would never really return.

I stood in a sunbeam, looking out at the lawn where an enormous copper beech spread its branches in all directions. And there he was. A collapsed figure, half leaning up against the tree trunk, eyes closed and palms facing the sky.

Laurel reacted faster than me. She pushed open the door to the porch, ran across the lawn and was already kneeling beside him with her bottle of water by the time I reached them. His eyes were closed, and at some point he'd taken off his shirt. Leaves and small flies were crawling over his white chest and soft stomach.

"Anders?"

He opened his eyes and looked at us calmly. Drank willingly from the water bottle that Laurel put to his lips. His forehead was dry under my hand.

"I couldn't find my way home," he said. "You were all gone."

A heavy drop landed behind us, the introduction to a quickly accelerating drum on the roof of the house and grass and bloodred leaves above us, making it hard to hear what I was saying on the phone when I called 112.

When I finally disconnected, Laurel had turned her face toward the rain and loosened her ponytail. She sat next to Anders, who'd closed his eyes again. For the first time in a long time, she looked like someone comfortable in her own skin. The fields steamed, and the world smelled of wet hay and soil and dried thistles, and the black sky thundered, low and distant. It had grown dark, like on a late autumn night.

I sat down on the other side of Anders and let him rest his head on my shoulder.

He'd been waiting for me. Or I suspected he had.

The Polish workers were nowhere to be seen, and the yard was empty of cars. Out in the stable, the pigs were screaming in hunger when I slammed the car door behind me and walked up to the main staircase.

I knocked on the door and walked in, sensing a slowly pulsing heartbeat from the redbrick house. The kitchen door was open, and even inside the hall I could smell the rotten minced meat on the kitchen table. Fat bluebottles buzzed lazily on the ceiling.

"Sten?"

I walked up the stairs to the second floor, music flowing from somewhere above me. "Rabalderstræde" by Gasolin. The landing was full of old furniture, but you could still move along a narrow path over the dusty green carpet to what had once been Sten's room. I gently pushed open the door. The curtains to the gable window were drawn, and it smelled like alcohol and smoke and anxiety. I'd recognize that smell anywhere.

Sten's bony figure sat on a small sofa he'd set up beside his old pine bed, his hand hanging over the armrest, an empty bottle of schnapps on the floor. His eyes half-closed.

"Sten?"

He smiled weakly. Sat up so suddenly that he almost fell off the sofa. He swayed with squinting eyes. He had a half-smoked cigarette resting between his index and middle fingers.

"I fired the two monkeys," he said. "It's better that way."

I sat down carefully on the bed with the yellow, discolored mattress. His soccer posters still hung on the wall. The wallpaper was the same gray blue that he himself had decorated the room with when he was fourteen. Sherman tanks on the bookless shelves of the bookcase.

"And what about the pigs? Do you have them under control?"

He shrugged and smiled a strange, hiccupping grin, and I stood up to turn off the radio. Kim Larsen & Kjukken in an infantile choir with sounds of the '80s.

"They'll manage," he said, directing his swimming eyes. "It's all fine. But it's good you came anyway, Jacob. Because I think I'm dying from what's inside me. It's grown up through my throat. I can't go anywhere, because everyone else can see it."

I leaned back carefully in the silence and looked at him. The boy with the protruding teeth and shining eyes.

"Would you like to tell me what happened to you and Lise that night?"

He smiled, the corners of his mouth tight, but didn't answer. Threw out a hand at the many empty bottles. White ash from the cigarette sprinkled through the dense smoke over the coffee table.

"What do *you* know about that evening, Jacob? Not a damn thing."

"I know there was a man who followed Lise home and saw her turn on the light in her room. Did she go back out again?"

Sten slowly shook his head.

"She was tired. And freezing. Wanted to go straight to bed, but she couldn't, you know? Because I was there."

"And then what happened?"

He curled his mouth up in a snarl.

"I'd found condoms around the place. Down at the bus stop. And behind the stable. I didn't know who she was with, but I knew she was with someone, and I wanted to . . . scare her. I'd collected the condoms in a bag and said I'd show them to Mom the next day, so she chased me. Without shoes on, and all the way across the yard. She was afraid of those chickens, and the way she freaked out was so ridiculous. Cry-your-eyes-out-laughing funny."

"And she followed you?"

He nodded briefly. "I kept teasing her with those condoms. Whacked the bag on her head. It was fun. It *was* fun. Until she fell. I don't know if I pushed her. Maybe I did a little, but she was so drunk. Her head hit the boards on the way down. I could hear it crack."

"I wish you'd told me back then," I said, and he nodded without looking at me, having lost himself in the smoke still wafting from his cigarette and up to the ceiling.

"It wasn't that I lied to you," he said. "I myself believed it was Anders that summer. In fact, I almost kept believing it until I saw you out here again. Not quite, but almost. It was better that way. For Mom and Dad, too."

I thought of Sten that spring. All his stupid jokes.

How do you make your wife cry during sex? You call her!

Dear, if I'd known you were a virgin, I would have taken more time.—Dear, if I'd known you could take more time, I'd have removed my tights.

Why do guys always give girls their jackets? Because nobody wants to get a blow job from a girl with chattering teeth.

"Sten?" I looked at his hands, shaking on his thighs. "What do you want to happen now?"

There was something both old and young in his smile.

"First, I think I'd like to talk to a priest," he said. "And afterward, I'd like to try to sleep without dreaming about her. Do you think I can?"

When my mother had died, it was as though she'd invaded my consciousness. I was a grown man when it happened, the father of two young children and busy at work, but for the first six months, I dreamed about her every single night. Heard her voice, smelled her heavy perfume, saw her walk thoughtfully through my and Kirsten's living room as she ran a finger over lampshades and windowsills. She haunted me until I finally found the place where we lay our dead.

"I hope you can, Sten," I said.

PART III

"I can't stay much longer."

I put the flowers in a vase on the table next to Anton. He was himself again; the fever was gone, his eyes were clear and it was raining outside for the fourth day in a row. A heavy rain that would take what hadn't been saved of the farmers' harvest, leaving it rotten on the fields in dark brown and gray and stinging green.

"Do you have to work?"

I shook my head.

"Just have to go home. To get my life in order."

"And Anders?"

"He's been released. Jette is taking care of him until you come home."

He nodded and closed his eyes.

"Of course, we can't keep going, Anders and I," he said. "No one can. But it doesn't matter. Not now. I'm glad you came."

I leaned back, observing him. I could see he still looked like my father, and therefore me. But Anton had hung on to things. The farm, Anders. The backbreaking work, all by himself, with Anders sitting inside by the window.

"I knew it was you back then," he said. His eyes still closed. "You and Sten Poulsen. And maybe Ellen . . . I knew it when none of you came back."

"It was an accident."

His hands that had carried out all the hard work were, for once, resting quietly on the comforter.

"If you had come back sooner, I could have told you I wasn't

angry. You were just big boys. Hopeless. I couldn't do anything for
Sten Poulsen. But I'd always hoped you'd come back one day. You
just disappeared. Like her."

I SAT ON a bench at the bus stop until I saw her come, walking
through the rain.

A woman her age looked so much more incredibly alive than
men who were just as old. There was that smile, still hidden in
there in the blue eyes. The almost-dancing steps between
puddles in the parking lot. Still light on her feet, because women
died more slowly than men, and could move like dancers long
into old age.

I looked down. I had all my stuff packed into two plastic bags
and a backpack I'd found under my great-grandmother's bed when
I'd vacuumed. My old T-shirt and underpants, neatly washed and
folded. The book about Eigtved and my old sketch pad. Pencils
and eraser in my red leather pencil case. A piece of paper stuck
among all my blurred and yellowed naked ladies.

She'd called the day before, and her voice was just like it had
been then. Edged and hoarse.

"How about you?" I'd asked her.

"I stopped drawing," she said. "Got married and divorced. No
children. I thought of you all sometimes. Utzon and Anton and
Anders, and how you all were, but not as much as I probably should
have. Are you married?"

"Kind of."

She laughed.

"That doesn't sound good, but maybe not too bad. And all mar-
riages of more than twenty years are worth working on. There's
usually something salvageable in the cinders. Did you like my gift?"

"What gift?"

"I put something small in your backpack for you, so you wouldn't be so unhappy. I really liked you, Utzon. After that, too. Believe it or not."

She walked past me, her long, bottle-green coat fluttering in the wind. It was already soaked in hot rain, flowers in her arms and the hint of a smile as she glided through the slowly circulating swing doors of the hospital, and a picture came back to me from that time on the farm. Anton and Ellen side by side on their way over the fields to find the hidden lark nests. Her laughter in the wind and him, standing straighter and happier and more alive than I'd ever seen him before.

It had been them all along, but it wasn't something a fifteen-year-old boy could see—or understand, for that matter.

I opened my old backpack and pulled out the paper again. I held it gently under the bus stop shelter and unfolded it. A drawing of a boy—me—that she must have sneakily done while I'd been occupied with something else.

The profile was drawn in an almost-invisible line, the lips soft and slightly parted, like they are with children and young people who are lost to the outside world. Only the upward-turned eyes were drawn in dark, clearly marked lines. The light in the pupils was almost supernaturally brilliant, and every eyelash calligraphically accurate. You could tell I was fifteen years old, almost sixteen, but it was still a child that she'd drawn. A boy. In the right corner a soft, sweeping dedication: TO MY FRIEND UTZON. ALL IS WELL! ELLEN.

THERE WERE SEVEN unread messages from Kirsten on my phone. A picture of the living room, all the furniture gone, only bare walls and green trees in pots.

A selfie where she sat under a tree, looking down into the camera over the edge of her blue reading glasses, a book in her hand. Pouting. *Divorce—the difficult choice.*

A picture of her arm covered in water droplets.

Her again, wearing a yellow southwestern coat, looking distrustfully at the dark gray sky.

And finally, words. Scoured of "dear" and hearts and smileys, which she otherwise abused at every opportunity.

Ready to start again.

Kirsten